the NATURE OF SMOKE

the NATURE OF SMOKE

ANNE HARRIS

A Tom Doherty Associates Book New York

This is a work of fiction. All the characters and events portrayed in this book are either fictitious or are used fictitiously.

THE NATURE OF SMOKE

This book is printed on acid-free paper.

Edited by James Frenkel

A Tor Book
Published by Tom Doherty Associates, Inc.
175 Fifth Avenue
New York, NY 10010

Tor Books on the World Wide Web:
http://www.tor.com

Library of Congress Cataloging-in-Publication Data

Harris, Anne L., date
The nature of smoke / by Anne Harris.
p. cm.
"A Tom Doherty Associates book."
ISBN 0-312-85286-X
1. Women—New York (N.Y.)—Fiction. I. Title.
PS3558.A64257N38 1996
813'.54—dc20 95-53143

First edition: June 1996

Printed in the United States of America

0 9 8 7 6 5 4 3 2 1

To Mike, who did the time

acknowledgments

I am deeply grateful to all the people who have encouraged me during the writing of this book. My thanks to Steve Ainsworth, Mike Harris, Deborah Crow, Dorene Steel, and the Thursday Night Traveller and General Weirdness Society, all of whom contributed far more to this book than they probably know.

My thanks to Ru Emerson for her input on an early draft and her unflagging enthusiasm for the book since that time, and to Christian Klaver and Ron Warren for their sound advice. I'd also like to thank Gene Wolfe for his support and friendship over the past few years.

My heartfelt thanks to Nevenah Smith, who midwifed this book into the world, and to my editor, James Frenkel, whose insight has been indispensable. I also want to thank my agent, Virginia Kidd, for her tireless efforts on my behalf.

And I would like to thank Mom, Dad, Betsy, Rick, Juney, Harriet, and Annie for a childhood filled with stories.

—A.H.

the NATURE OF SMOKE

PROLOGUE—THE QUEEN OF TV

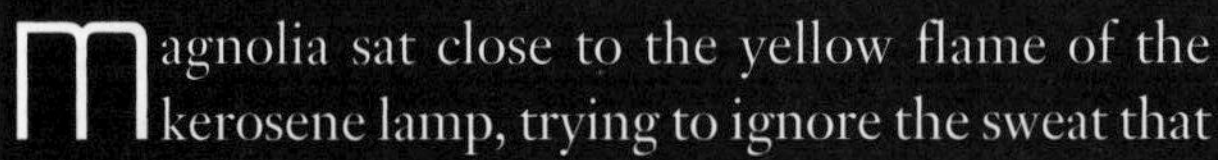

Magnolia sat close to the yellow flame of the kerosene lamp, trying to ignore the sweat that trickled down the side of her face as she rewired a circuit breaker. It was a hot night, and the broken-out windows of the squat were welcome damage. She raised her head to catch a breeze coming through the open front door. Her father, Drew, sat on the front steps, cleaning a Colt Police with meditative ease. In a dusty corner near the stove her mother, Semolina, nursed Magnolia's youngest brother.

Except for the sloshing of dishwater and the suckling of the infant, the squat was silent. Albert was up on the roof, smoking marijuana. Cherry and Manus played outside among half-demolished buildings like the one they were squatting in now; the legacy of the Detroit Tax Partitions.

Magnolia glanced at her older sister. Doralee stood at a makeshift plywood table, washing dishes in a rubber tub and frowning. Frowning because she knew what Magnolia knew and what Semolina ignored. Daddy was going looting tonight.

Magnolia got up and walked slowly towards her father, showing him the finished circuit breaker. His tan, boyish face wrinkled into a scowl. "Give me that, girl," he said, making a grab for her hand. She was too fast for him. She danced away across the squat, stopping behind and just to the left of the rickety table where Doralee did the dishes.

Magnolia licked her lips and started her spiel. "You can have it if you take me with you tonight. . . . It'd be a good idea, see this clamp?" She held the circuit breaker up. "It'll cut through the wire housing and take out the alarm system." Carefully she took another step backwards and delivered the hook. "Want it?" she said, smiling coyly.

For a split second Drew stood frozen in the doorway, his lean body silhouetted in the fading light. Then he was charging across the room, fast, silent, and furious. When he was almost upon her, Magnolia stepped behind Doralee. Drew snarled and swerved to grab her, but he overcorrected and went careening into the table instead. Its plywood legs wobbled valiantly before collapsing and sending the washtub crashing to the floor. Water and broken plastic splattered everywhere.

"Damn it!" Doralee screamed. "Get the hell out of here! Both of you!"

Drew had caught Magnolia by the wrists, and she was kicking him violently in the shins. "You little bitch!" he roared.

Semolina looked up, and the baby began to cry. Her voice was barely audible over the din. "Take her with you, Drew."

The rest of Magnolia's siblings were crowded at the door, along with a few neighbors who'd turned out for the show. Drew released her, but Magnolia didn't rub her sore wrists, not now. She looked past Drew to her brother Albert, a year younger than she was, but the oldest boy, and she smiled.

Later Magnolia leaned against the rusting framework of a swing set, listening to the night noises and waiting. The summer evening air was warm and gentle against her skin. The screen door of the broken-down, one-story house they were squatting in swung open and snapped shut, and her sister Cherry shuffled reluctantly towards her in the dusk. Her eyes were downcast, and she scrupulously kept her distance from Magnolia. "Albert says Daddy won't take you," she said, nudging a pebble with a dirty toe.

Magnolia's face flushed with anger. "Albert's full of shit," she said, baring her teeth in the gloom. "He saw what happened." She leaned closer to her sister, who flinched. "I won the bet. Tell him I'm waiting. He knows what we agreed on."

Cherry glanced dubiously at her from the corner of her eye and went back into the house. A few minutes later she returned with Albert's Molly Zee T-shirt. Albert had won it from Ritchie Coops, and now Magnolia had won it from Albert. She took it from Cherry and pulled it on over her dirty tank top. Molly Zee's mirrored eyes sparkled in the moonlight, one each where someday Magnolia would have tits. Then Drew came out of the house and headed north, and she ran after him.

They hit an appliance repair shop in Ferndale. Drew used Magnolia's breaker to get past the alarm. The front of this place had a big tensile glass window. No shutters, no bars, no screen. They kept to the back of the shop, filling a mailbag with two coffeemakers with multiprocessor brains, an automatic injection cooker, a box of microchips, and a robotic lint picker.

Apparently they weren't the only ones interested in after-hours discounts. From the front of the store came the sound of shattering glass as the tensile window dissolved under a sonic transmitter. Drew ran for the back door with the bulging sack. Magnolia ducked behind the counter and found herself staring at a portable TV with directional tuning and a self-contained generator. Somebody stepped through the broken window, a heavy foot crunching the glass beneath it. Magnolia grabbed the set and ran.

She was fast, and she didn't have a whole bag of loot weighing her down. She got back to the squat well before Drew did. A TV like this would be valuable for its generator alone, but Magnolia didn't want to sell it, or scrap it; she wanted to watch it.

At the back of the squat, next to the stove, there was a set of steel shelves bolted to the wall. With the TV under one arm and her brothers and sisters trailing behind her, Magnolia climbed on top of the shelves.

Albert made a grab for her leg, and she deftly kicked his hand away. "What is it?" he asked, nursing his wrist.

Magnolia swept a pile of transistors and solenoids off the shelf, put the set down, and turned it on.

A skinny man with narrow eyes and a wide-brimmed hat was riding a—a horse. His face was deadpan. Another man rode up on another horse, and the first man shot him. Magnolia and the rest sat enrapt in the images unfolding before them. It turned out that the skinny man was defending a settlement from a band of men who wanted to rape all the women there. There wasn't any electricity, and nobody drank the water, and the men all carried guns. It was a lot like the partition.

"What are we watching, Maggie?" asked Cherry, fumbling with a burnt-out transistor.

Magnolia looked back at the screen. The skinny man was walking away from a woman in some crazy-ass dress. The land around them was empty, just a few bushes and rocks. Nothing like here, where the weeds grew thick and tall in every abandoned field. Old Mr. Kenicki, who'd died the winter before last, told her once about a place his people came from a long time ago. "Things are different over here," he'd said.

"I think it's Europe," said Magnolia.

That summer she was the Queen of TV. Every day she took the set out into the ruins and held forth with it. All the kids came, and some of the old folks too. She let anyone watch, but she controlled the stations.

She liked movies the best, particularly the ones with guns and cops, or monsters and crazies, and it got so that the guns and the monsters and the crazies and the cops were indistinguishable from one another. But once in a while there was a woman, someone like Weaver or Sarandon, a real kick-ass bitch, and those movies were the best of all, because they seemed more like real life.

When they weren't watching the TV, the children of the River Rouge Partition acted out the scenes they saw there, and Magnolia was always the hero. With a steely glint in her eye she blew away her enemies, or danced with an elegant grace the patterns that left them reeling. At night she slept on top of the steel shelves, her body curled around the TV, its generator warming her.

One day she slept late. When she awoke, sunlight was streaming into the squat, and her head felt thick. 'Ludes, she thought, only she hadn't taken any 'ludes. Groggily she sat up and reached for the power switch on the TV. Her hand glided through the space where smooth plastic should have greeted it. Gradually her vision focused on the shelf around her, empty except for a tattered pink blanket and a few discarded wires.

There was no one in the squat except for her and Manus, who sat in a corner chattering busily to an array of empty beer cans. He eyed her sheepishly as she jumped off the shelf and walked towards him.

Magnolia's hands clenched the thin fabric of his T-shirt, and she lifted him up. With her face no more than an inch away from his she snarled, "Who?" but Manus only whimpered and began to cry. In disgust Magnolia deposited him on top of the beer cans and left the squat.

She didn't have to ask anyone, really. It was obvious. The day before, Drew had found a radio, intact and working. With the money he bought food, and they all ate together. That had to be when Albert slipped her the 'ludes. Albert had some Birmingham connections. The next day, when Drew showed up at the squat with new boots, the picture was complete.

That winter they were in another squat. A big, rambling place with a leaky roof and no heat. It snowed all the time. Doralee and Semolina dragged a steel plate into the living room and built a fire on it, which made the place smoky and damp, instead of cold and wet. The baby caught a cold. It went into his chest, and he died.

The next spring Augustina was born, and the year after that, Moriarty. When Moriarty was a year old, Manus stepped on a nail and didn't tell anyone about it. The infection got halfway up his leg before Doralee noticed him limping.

Magnolia was hanging around the doorway of the house, smoking a cigarette, when Corinne Washington came up the steps with a fold of clean white cloth and a pot of boiling water. Inside, Manus lay on the kitchen table, out cold from five of Albert's 'ludes.

Corinne examined the infected leg with an expert eye. Nodding to herself, she placed the cloth on the table beside him and unfolded it to reveal the saw. She rolled up her sleeves and washed her hands in the sterilized water. "I want everyone out of here," she declared as she tied a length of rubber tubing tightly around his upper thigh. "This is going to be a real mess."

In silence Semolina sat on the front porch, surrounded by her three eldest children: Doralee, Magnolia, and Albert. Drew had been gone for over a week now, which was not unusual. He hated being around the squat these days, with all the kids, the dirt, the noise. Cherry had Moriarty and Augustina with her out by the old lumberyard, looking for scrap wood. A couple of dogs, thin and pitiful, slunk around the porch steps in desperate anticipation. Albert chucked stones at them, and they retreated to the temporary safety of an abandoned pickup truck.

Magnolia lit another cigarette and peered through the window into the kitchen. "Get away from the window, Maggie," her mother said crossly. She ignored her, forcing herself to watch as Mrs. Washington sawed off her brother's leg.

Manus came through the amputation all right. His leg healed, and there was no more infection, only the 'ludes had been too much for him, and he was stupid after that.

Over the next two years Roswell and Corona were born. Semolina started staying in the squat all the time, drinking. Doralee kept after the kids as best she could, but she got no help from Magnolia, who ran in the ruins all day and most of the night.

Doralee started going out with a boy called Joe Joey. Joe Joey knew some people from Southfield. He was selling them everything he could scavenge from the rubble or steal from the suburbs. Magnolia never knew the whole story behind it, but somehow Joe Joey pissed those Southfield boys off.

She was with a boy of her own when she heard the shots. Benny groaned in disappointment as she pushed him off and reached for her T-shirt. "We can come back later," she told him. "I want to find out what that was."

"Somebody got shot," he declared petulantly. "Big deal."

"Yeah, but who?" She stood up, her words suddenly sounding like more than idle curiosity.

They were in an unoccupied house. Sunshine shafted through broken windows, setting alight the dust that swirled in the air. In silence she watched Benny gathering his scattered clothing, cursing under his breath. "See you later," she mumbled lamely, and left, slipping through a hole in the boarded-up back door and scrambling down a pile of rubble that had once been steps.

She had no trouble locating the scene. A crowd had gathered in a vacant lot about a block from the old garage. There hadn't been any cars there since before Magnolia was born, but it was still a favorite hangout of the better scavengers.

As she wove her way through the gawkers she overhead Mule Pritchard talking to Granny Daisy. "Southfield come gunning for Joe Joey, but they missed." By then she was close enough to see Joe Joey, just standing there looking stupid and staring at the bloody smudge that was Doralee's head.

Over to the side Magnolia caught sight of her mother. Semolina crept around the edge of the thinning crowd like a ghost, her eyes wide, her bony hands tugging fretfully at the sleeves of her faded housecoat.

Magnolia heard shouting behind her. Augustina, Moriarty, Roswell, and Corona charged towards her from across the street. Trailing behind by a good ten yards was Manus, struggling to keep up with them on his crutch. Magnolia glanced at Semolina, but she hadn't noticed them. Her eyes looked everywhere not to see her children, alive, dead, and damaged.

Doralee had raised them for the most part, anyway. Now they'd be Magnolia's. That would be her life, she knew, raising first these brats and then her own until she was either killed or her soul died.

She waited for them, in the last moments of her free life. The blue sky overhead pushed down on her, and the ground beneath rose up to crush her. In her ears the shouting of the kids echoed like the screaming of the birds circling above. She couldn't breathe. Augustina reached her hands out towards her, and something inside Magnolia gave in to the pressure all around her.

Something she hadn't even known was there just folded in upon itself and snapped. She ran. Magnolia ran faster and farther than she ever had in her life, and when she stopped, she was in New York City.

Beautiful Monster

Bright sunlight fell through shifting lattices of tropical foliage, dappling the surface of the pond with glittering light. Tumcari drifted in the silken embrace of the water, watching patches of sun and shade slide across his arms and chest. A few small birds, their numbers ever dwindling, darted and chirped in the canopy above him. He'd miss the birds when they were gone. Besides the plant life which teemed around him, they were his only constant companions.

Here in the Arctic, where nothing much grew on its own, glass and copper were fashioned centuries ago to foster life. More recently, the powers of science had been collected in the greenhouse of this ancient mansion to work still greater perversions upon the world.

The familiar click and swoosh of the greenhouse doors brought to him the faintest draft of cold air. A mild reminder of his geographical location. It would be Cid, judging by the angle of the sun. She came here almost every day around this time, always under the pretext of garnering some sample or other from him.

Tumcari just made out the top of her golden head, bobbing above a clump of sansevieria, and then she took a turn in the path and came into clear view. She was a small woman, not much more than five feet tall, with delicate little hands and feet. Her blond hair was shoulder length, with a tendency to hang in her blue, wide-set eyes. Her nose was small and upturned, its bridge dusted with a few faded freckles. She carried a small aluminum suitcase, her lab kit, in which she kept various instruments and containers.

Like many of the people he had known, Cid was a molecular biologist. Officially she worked for Dr. Rahul, and like everyone else here, part of her job was to keep an eye on him, but she was a curious sort, and Tumcari had encouraged her to expand on the good doctor's research. Today, as an affectation, no doubt, she wore a pair of horn-rimmed spectacles and a white lab coat, complete with a pocket protector bristling with pencils. Beneath it her legs were bare, and she wore green, plastic sandals on her feet. "Hey Tumcari, how's it floatin'?"

"Ah Cidiera my dear, how are you today?"

She dumped her lab kit on the gravel and sat down at the edge of the pool. "Eh, so-so"—she wrinkled her nose—"the isolation out here is getting to me. Has gotten to me, I should say." As her eyes widened with irony their blue was the blue of the sky, which Tumcari sometimes saw in snatches through the leaves and glass above. "I actually tried to engage Spider in intelligent conversation last night. Big mistake." She opened her lab kit and took out a scalpel and a Plexiglas culture dish. "Come here." She beckoned to him impatiently.

"What will it be this time," he asked her, "eye of newt or tongue of frog?"

She shook her head, her mouth widening into a smile like the long curve of a swallow's wing. "Just a skin sample."

Tumcari moved to the edge of the pond and settled his shoulders between her knees. With her scalpel she scratched lightly at a spot on the base of his neck, a mild, momentary pain which brought with it memories of a time when he was the object of numerous scrutinies such as this one. How he had hated those attentions at the time, and how happy he'd be to be their focus once more.

"Okay, that's it." Cid slapped him gently on the shoulder and pushed him away with her knees. As he turned around she carefully deposited her sample in the culture dish and snapped the lid over it. The scalpel and sample disappeared into her lab kit, and she took off her horn-rims, laying them carefully on the gravel beside it.

"And how goes the research?" he asked her.

Her smile broadened into a grin. "I may be onto something there." She unbuttoned her lab coat and shrugged out of it, revealing the black one-piece bathing suit she wore underneath. "I've been comparing your cellular biology to Ms. Wujcik's and mine, and I'm finding some interesting things." In a fluid motion she slid into the water and swam freestyle to the opposite side.

Cid was not afraid of being in the water with him. This willingness to put herself at his mercy was one of the things Tumcari liked best about her. Certainly, in his uncooperative days he had sent many a hapless lab tech to the hospital, bloody with lacerations from head to toe. Of course, he'd mellowed considerably since then, boredom being an excellent socializing force. But it wasn't that Cid thought him harmless; she was too bright not to comprehend the damage he could do. Rather, she felt she had no reason to fear him, and as far as he could tell, she was right.

She moved through the water with grace, and it accommodated her with ripples of light, sparkling across her golden skin and hair.

There was something very much of the sun in Cid, an incandescence kindled by her thoughts, perhaps. Floating on her back, she gazed up into the brilliance of her twin as she continued to brief Tumcari. "Something's going on with the electron transport chain in your mitochondria that I've never seen before." At her sides her arms waved slowly, like exotic and articulate water lilies. "It almost seems as if they're, well, synchronized with each other, but in a nonperiodic fashion. I can't explain it; I'm not even sure what it means myself, but it's definitely aberrant." She righted herself, leaned against the side of the pond, and looked at him. "They act as if each one of them knows what the others are doing, even if they are residing in cells that aren't adjacent to each other. I get the impression that somehow, they're communicating."

Tumcari raised his eyebrows in skepticism. "So you're saying my mitochondria, these tiny creatures that live inside my cells, are telepathic?"

"In a way. You ever hear of Bell's theorem?"

Tumcari shook his head. "No, I've had a great deal of science done upon me, but very little actually explained."

Cid nodded. "It states that two quantum particles that have been in contact with each other continue to influence each other even after they have been separated for some time. Somehow, perhaps because of the way quantum reality is structured, they are able to communicate with each other."

"But you're talking about mitochondria—"

"Which are many magnitudes larger and more complex than quantum particles, I know. But if such things are possible at the most basic level of matter, why not at higher ones? 'As above, so below," as the old wiccan saying goes. I'm going to try something, to see if the patterns I've noticed with your mitochondria are caused by some sort of bioquantum communication. If your mito know what's going on with each other, then it's also possible that other aspects of your cellular biology could be . . . mutually aware. I've been keeping that skin cell sample that I took from you last week in culture, and I'm going to inoculate this one with some melanoma virus I've got lying around."

"Why?"

"To see what happens." She shrugged, her eyes whirling with sunlight reflected off the turbulent surface of the water.

After she had gone, Tumcari floated listlessly, waiting for Ms. Wujcik to arrive with the evening news. Each night she came to him, obedient creature that she was, and related to him the comings and goings of Wotroya House and the rest of the world. He looked forward to her visit for the information she would impart, but not for her company. Past the basics of reporting, Ms. Wujcik was an uninspired conversationalist, and he would much prefer the more spontaneous company of Cid or Kelira.

Not since the days of the International Bureau of Research, when his project had been active, had Tumcari been overwhelmed by human attention. At that time, when he was new and knew even less than he did now, he had loathed people; their otherness, their independence, their infuriating mobility.

The humans had studied him, poking and prodding, taking samples, until he marveled that there was anything left to him at all. But for all their fascination with *what* he was, they didn't give a single skin cell for *who* he was. Only his creator, Dr. Remus Rahul, had an interest in him beyond his physiological processes.

"You are the great success of my career," Rahul told him once, on a quiet afternoon when the facility was all but vacant due to the winter holidays. "Others dispute it, and call attention to the development of those highly reproducible automatons, which already overshadow you. But they are nothing more than my unsuccessful attempts to get back to the results I produced with you. Their minds are like sponges, able only to absorb the desires of those around them. But they are useful and profitable, and their study and development will receive funding."

The implications of this were lost on Tumcari, whose entire short life had been one unending R and D circus. He could no more imagine that state of affairs ending than he could picture the world beyond his greenhouse. In the years following that conversation he had berated himself a million times over for his voiceless innocence.

"I wanted to create artificial intelligence," Rahul had said, "and I did, once. Now, I'm afraid, I will make my fortune and my name on the latest incarnation of the toaster oven."

The Evening Carnage

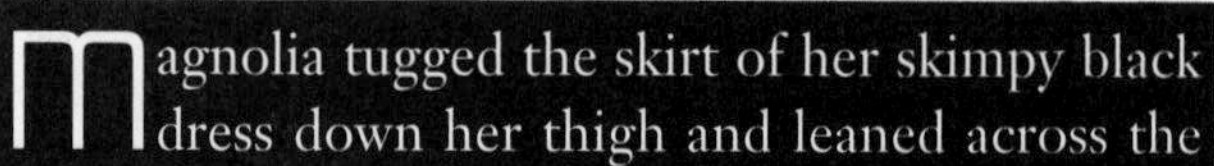

Magnolia tugged the skirt of her skimpy black dress down her thigh and leaned across the bar. "Vodka and tonic—Smirnoff," she said, handing the taciturn bartender a worn ten-dollar Mylar bill. She'd just scored an ounce of pure Bolivian cocaine, and she felt flush. This was an uptown bar, all done in chrome and mirrors. If you had anything in your head at all—and Magnolia had done three lines in the subway on the way over—you couldn't tell where you were. Infinite Maggies drank vodka and tonics from the rest rooms to the piano bar when a guy in a silk suit walked in and sat down beside her.

He had sandy brown hair and light blue eyes. The boxy lines of his suit hung gracefully on his compact, muscular body. "Can I get you a refill?" he asked, glancing at her empty glass.

"Sure." She leaned towards him and spoke in a low, soft voice, "I'll have a vodka and tonic." This close she could see the faint sheen of his whisker stubble, and her nose detected the crisp odor of his cologne. He smelled like money.

He passed a credit card to the bartender. Magnolia tried to catch what it was out of the corner of her eye, but the transaction was too swift for her. "A vodka and tonic, and a gimlet martini, please." He turned to face her again. "What's your name?"

She sighed. "Magnolia."

He raised his eyebrows, protesting her dismay. "That's a pretty name."

She smiled sourly. "Not if you come from poor white trash out of the Midwest."

"Oh, well." He shrugged. "I'm Dano"—he offered his hand—"and it's a pleasure to meet you, Magnolia, wherever you come from."

She shook his hand, which was warm and dry, and their drinks arrived. Dano sipped his martini, watching her thoughtfully over the rim of his glass. "How old are you, Magnolia?"

She opened her mouth to answer him and then caught herself. Looking away, she lied, "I'm eighteen."

He laughed softly, and she looked back at him. His eyes were shining, looking at her with sharp, predatory delight. "I thought so. You haven't been in the city long, have you?"

"Only about three months."

"Yeah." He nodded, still watching her. His eyes were like the flap of a jacket concealing a loaded gun. "I don't spend too much time here, myself. Usually I operate out of Tunis, but I'm in town on business." He smiled suddenly, an incongruous flash of yellowed teeth. "It's really something, isn't it?"

She smiled back at him. "It sure is," she said faintly, doubting it for the first time.

Dano sighed in contentment and raised his glass. "To the big time," he announced, and drained it.

"To the big time," Magnolia echoed, gulping down her drink. She giggled breathlessly, looking at him with liquor-bright eyes.

"Let's dance," he said.

They danced three tunes, close. Wrapped in Dano's arms, Magnolia felt as if she were being transported, her body carried off to an unknown land, leaving her mind behind to follow as best it could. They returned to the bar, and he bought her another vodka and tonic. She slipped away to the bathroom to put in her sponge, and when she returned, she offered to sell him a gram of coke.

Dano smiled broadly. "I'd like that, Magnolia, if you'd share it with me."

She laughed and slipped a quick hand down his front pants pocket. "Let's go to your place," she said.

Dano lived in a tower with two glass walls overlooking lower Manhattan. One wall of the living room was dominated by a huge TV screen. The kitchen was automated, and the bathroom had a Jacuzzi.

They sat on a vat-grown leather couch, drinking espresso and snorting coke. "This is a nice place you've got here," she said, suppressing a giggle.

He nodded and glanced at her slyly, the beginnings of a wicked grin twisting his lips. "It suits my purposes." He leaned towards her, his breath warm at her neck. "You're very beautiful, Magnolia." She closed her eyes as he kissed her mouth, her neck, her breasts.

He sat back, loosening his collar, and Magnolia stood up. "Oh God!" she exclaimed, walking towards the enormous windows, "I feel like I could fly!" Outside, the lights of the city blazed in earthly constellations. The whole apartment vibrated around her. She leaned against the glass wall, feeling it shiver beneath her skin. She imagined herself falling through the air, flying through the air, and then Dano was upon her, his body warm in contrast to the cool glass at her back. His big, hard hands grasped the fabric of her black knit dress and tore it open. She was naked underneath, trembling in the sudden cold.

"Fuck me," she whispered, her hands seeking the warm strength of his chest, his belly. "Fuck me for the world to see."

Dano bit her savagely, his teeth sinking into the soft flesh at the base of her neck. His hands were on her breasts, crushing them. Magnolia unbuttoned his grey dress pants with trembling fingers. His cock sprang out, smooth and hard, plunging towards release. Dano gripped her ass, raising her upwards and slamming her back against the glass as he penetrated her.

Magnolia cried out and clenched herself around him, making him ride her tight. His thrusts quickened and became more violent, until the window shook with every stroke. Pinned between Dano and the glass, Magnolia's ecstasy was heightened by panic. She wrapped her legs around his hips and clasped him to her. Maybe she would fly, maybe she would fall; either way, she figured, she was taking him with her. As Dano roared in inarticulate climax Magnolia ground herself against him and came in an adrenaline rush.

He stepped back, and she nearly fell. Blindly she reached a hand out, steadying herself against his shoulder as she struggled to catch her breath. He lifted her up in his arms and carried her into a bedroom festooned with white gauze.

In the center of the room a white vat-leather slab lay shrouded. Dano parted the curtains and lowered her onto the bed. Magnolia luxuriated on the soft, synthetic hide and closed her eyes. She was tired now, in the wake of orgasm.

Dano went into the bathroom. She heard him pissing, then washing his hands. She sighed and opened her eyes, gazing upwards, straight into the eye of a camera lens nestled among the bunched white fabric like a black and enigmatic sun. Something cold and slimy closed itself about her wrist.

Jerking her arm back, Magnolia found it held fast to one corner of the bed by a black rubber manacle. "Shit!" she gasped as she shot her free hand up into the air and drew her feet under her. There were four of them altogether, snaking towards her from each corner of the bed. She pulled down a hank of gauze and stuffed it into the manacle that was clattering for her other hand, staring in horror as the ring secreted hard foam from its inner surface until it fit tightly around the gauze.

Adrenaline was crashing through her body again, and this time it was for real. She heard Dano's footsteps clearly as he came into the room. Through the gauze she could just make out the glitter of a stainless-steel knife as he began cutting his way through the veils.

The sound of tearing cloth was nearly drowned by the blood pounding in her ears as Magnolia crouched on the far corner of the bed. She rolled onto her back and brought her legs up to her chest. Staring from between her knees, she caught every detail as Dano rent the last layer of gauze and plunged towards her, the knife in his hand held high.

She saw the expression on his face, at first a horrible glee, change to something like surprise as she rocked backwards and kicked forward with both legs. Her feet connected with his breastbone, which gave with a muffled snap. Dano fell forward, grunting with pain, and before she could think, Magnolia had taken the knife from his lax hand and stabbed him twice through the back.

The room was silent except for the soft hiss of the manacles at the foot of the bed as they attached themselves to

Dano's ankles. She yanked savagely at the one around her left hand, but it refused to give.

Shakily, still clutching the blood-smeared knife in her free hand, she crawled off the bed and began searching for a release mechanism. She could probably cut through the rubber chain with the knife, but that would take a long time. At the head of the bed, flush with the surface of the platform on which the mattress rested, there was a button. Anyone manacled to the bed by both hands and feet would be unable to reach it, of course. Magnolia pressed the smooth plastic surface, and the hard foam which had sealed around her wrist dissolved, leaving behind a fine, gritty, black dust.

Presumably the same thing happened to the manacles that held Dano's feet, but he still didn't stir. Blood soaked quietly into the gauze that lay around him like a halo.

She'd need some clothes. Magnolia stepped to the closet and flung open the door. There were only a few things to choose from. Quickly she pulled on a pair of black jeans and grabbed a silk shirt. Dano hadn't been a very big guy; these fit her pretty well. She headed out of the bedroom, but something on the bookshelf near the door caught her eye.

A video monitor provided her with a grainy, black-and-white view of the evening's carnage. Shit, that's right, she thought, remembering the camera lens she'd seen an instant before the attack. Beside the monitor a squat black video recorder gazed cynically at her with a single red light indicating that it was still recording.

She ejected the cassette and pulled the tape out, ripping it from the spools. Then for good measure she yanked out the cable at the back of the monitor. That was when she noticed the other cable disappearing into the wall. The motherfucker was sending the signal out. There was probably a satellite link on the roof.

Dano had been running a little porn station here, and now

his viewers, whoever they were, knew she'd killed him. Magnolia had no idea who he'd been transmitting to, but she knew they'd have money, lots of it. More than enough to come after her.

Dano's pants still lay in a heap by the window. Magnolia fumbled through them frantically until she found his wallet. No cash. Of course not.

The panoramic view of the city wobbled dangerously as Magnolia looked around her. Adrenaline, coke, and caffeine coursed through her body like a hot current. She went back to the bedroom and pulled out each of Dano's dresser drawers in turn, but most of them were empty, and none held what she was looking for. She sprinted into the kitchen and opened the cabinets. They too were vacant for the most part.

On the top shelf above the stove stood a large metal canister. She overturned it. Flour came out in a white cloud, and along with it there was a thump. Bingo. Encased in a Ziploc baggie, on the floor, lay a roll of bills and a handgun.

Magnolia counted the money and slipped it into the front pocket of her jeans. Five hundred would probably get her an airline ticket, but not much else. She took the handgun, an expensive Walther-Kodak, brushed the flour off her clothes, and made for the door.

INSTANT REPLAY

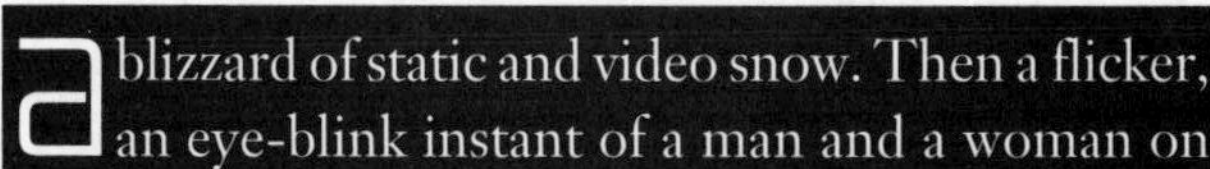

A blizzard of static and video snow. Then a flicker, an eye-blink instant of a man and a woman on a couch, dissolving again into signal noise. Kelira adjusted the tuning on his secondhand Star-Catcher. The image bounced back again, long enough for him to see what they were doing—snorting coke. Diagonal interference lines cut across the screen of his monitor, distorting and then obliterating the picture. This channel was scrambled hard, coded at both the signal point and the satellite relay. Kelira switched on his porta-comp and started scanning through his collection of code breakers.

Rahul lay sprawled on his back on the bed in his hotel room. The ceiling held nothing of any particular interest to him but was no less entertaining than the textured mauve walls. It was a nice room—a far cry from the opulence of his house in

Tunis, but then he wasn't paying for it. He was here at the behest of one Richard Ygrasil, the shadowy head of a shadowy company called VisuAll, some sort of subscriber-only satellite channel.

Rahul had originally been contacted through their Mediterranean office in Tunis, by a man named Edgerton. Between them they had worked out most of the details of the sale, but this Ygrasil character had wanted to see a demonstration and hadn't wanted to leave New York. Since Ygrasil was perfectly willing to pay for the airfare and hotel, Rahul had been willing to oblige him.

He reached over to the nightstand and fished through his open briefcase. Pursing his lips, he gazed once more at the prepared contract. Eight robots at a quarter mil, U.S. currency, each, to be delivered to VisuAll over a period of six months. He smiled as the numbers multiplied themselves in his head. Tomorrow he'd close the deal and be two million dollars richer. Being the world's only supplier of sophisticated human simulacra had its advantages.

As he tossed the contract back into his briefcase his fingers grazed the matte surface of a micro-CD-ROM. The disc was a gift from Ygrasil. It contained the program for descrambling VisuAll satellite transmissions.

Rahul got up and inserted the disc into the slot at the base of the tawdry, twenty-four-inch-screen hotel television. He switched the set on.

The static and interference bands cleared at last. By now the happy couple had moved over to a glass wall, but they didn't seem to be paying much attention to the view. The girl—she was barely eighteen, if that—was abruptly naked. Kelira must have missed her disrobing while descrambling the signal. She was slender, with an olive complexion, dark hair, and dark, narrow eyes. She was quite tall, as tall as the guy, who was removing his shirt with practiced animal grace.

Kelira knew immediately who was acting, and who didn't even know there was a performance going on. Despite her ironic invitation, "Fuck me for the world to see," the girl had no idea there was a camera on her. As it zoomed in for a close-up of her face, her arm was in the way, obscuring her nose and most of her grimacing mouth. The man, on the other hand, was a consummate actor. Even with his back to the camera, and the shot at a rather poor angle, he let the viewer know exactly what he was doing. A switch to a camera on the other side of the glass revealed the essential body parts in action. He was obviously enjoying his role, but his face remained a carefully composed mask of cosmetic ardor, unmarred by clenched teeth or contorted lips.

A young woman landed on a bed in a splash of white gauze drapery. She opened her eyes and looked up, straight into the camera. Her gaze beamed into Rahul's eyes across miles of air and vacuum.

She didn't see the manacles slithering towards her from the four corners of the bed, but Rahul did. He wanted to shout to her, to warn her. How silly. It was only a movie. But when the first manacle attached itself to her wrist, her panic seemed real. Rahul found that he was sitting up, leaning in towards the television, the boredom that had enfolded him a few minutes ago banished entirely.

Kelira had seen more than enough to know she wasn't Rose. Still, his guts twisted as the scenario turned towards slash.

Ordinarily he would switch off now, sparing himself the moral obligation of the passive observer, but this time he kept watching.

When the first restraint attached itself to the girl, her reaction was instantaneous. She got her free hand away from where it could be seized by shooting it in the only safe direction: up. She pulled her legs into her body, out of reach of the two restraints at the foot of the bed. She quickly disabled the manacle seeking her free hand by choking it with the fabric that festooned about her.

Rahul had been mistaken. This wasn't "just a movie." For the young woman, it was real life. He knew because she didn't allow herself to be caught in bondage. This was supposed to be soft-core slash, but as the man began methodically ripping through the gauze with a kitchen knife it started turning into something else entirely.

She rolled onto her back, her knees to her chest. It was a peculiar posture in which to await the arrival of one's paramour. Rahul wasn't sure, but he suspected she had something in mind other than what the standard script provided. He giggled as he thought of Ygrasil and the other VisuAll people he'd met that day. They'd be going crazy right about now, watching helplessly as their finely wrought scenario dissolved at the will of their pawn.

Not taking his eyes from the screen, Rahul reached into his briefcase once again and brought out a blank CD. He slipped it into the aux drive and pressed record.

The man shredded the last of the veils separating him from his intended victim. But as he lunged at her she kicked out with both feet. It was a solid blow to the sternum, strong enough to crack it. He collapsed on the bed, and before Kelira had the chance to rejoice, the girl had taken up the knife and stabbed him twice through the back. The sight of it left Kelira breathless. *She* stabbed *him.* She wasn't very big, no bigger than Rose would be by now, but she had managed to kill her killer, and if she could do it, so could Rose.

All Rahul could see of the young woman now was her hand as she extricated it from the manacle, and then that too was gone, whisked away from his view. She'd be getting the hell out of there now, and well she might. The man seemed to be dead. The VisuAll people would certainly be after her for the murder of their star. Rahul watched him bleed as seconds trickled by in silence broken only by vague and muffled thumps from offscreen. Then there was a flash of white static, then nothing at all. He was alone, staring at a blank screen.

He reached for the phone and punched in Ygrasil's number.

PLATONIC SEX

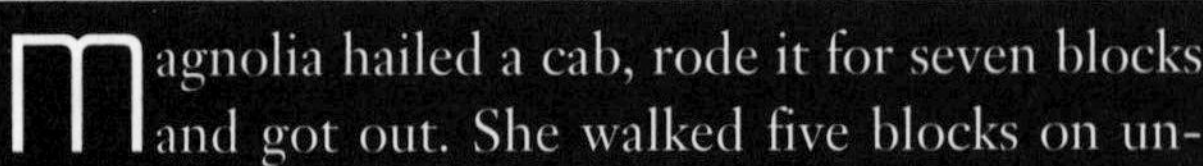

Magnolia hailed a cab, rode it for seven blocks and got out. She walked five blocks on unsteady legs, jumping at shadows and cringing at sirens. At the corner of Fifty-second and Third she caught another cab, and told the driver to take her to Koch airport. She had no idea if that was a good way to lose a tail, or not.

In the cab, she took a deep breath, and forced herself to think. Getting far away from the scene of the crime as quickly as possible seemed like a good idea. She'd take the next available flight out of the country. Magnolia glanced out the window. New York City flashed past her in the periodic illumination of streetlamps. She caught glimpses of people walking, talking. The shop windows assaulted her eyes with a fast-forward replay of all her hungry gazes. Three months didn't seem like long enough to wallow in commercial excess.

She took out her new toy, the Walther-K automatic, and looked at it. She'd heard about this gun; it was all machined plastic, invisible to the scanners at the airport. Of course, lots of guns were plastic nowadays, and airport security knew it. The X-ray machines were all geared to pick up on bullets, not guns. But at the base of the handgrip was a little switch. Magnolia flipped it and felt the thing hum slightly in her hand as it generated its own X-ray field around the ammunition casing. The field would throw off the scanners, confuse them into accepting it as their own, and the bullets would go undetected. Carefully Magnolia tucked the gun inside her purse, burying it underneath a wrinkled pair of panties.

The woman at the ticket counter accepted her cash without comment, and Magnolia walked away a proud passenger on a flight to St. Petersburg, leaving in one hour. She fingered her ticket nervously and made her way to a yellow-tiled restaurant that stood out in the teeming concourse of the airport. A large neon portrait of a fried egg glowed invitingly over the doorway. She took a corner booth and sat facing the entrance.

In the harsh fluorescent light of the diner Magnolia noticed red-brown stains under her fingernails. She tucked her hands discreetly under the table as a waitress approached. "Two eggs, over easy, with hash browns and a side of ham," she ordered mechanically, "and coffee."

Her food had not yet arrived when a dapper old gentleman with a fifty-dollar haircut came in. He was brown-skinned, with a small, round, balding head and wire-framed spectacles. He didn't look much like the kind for ham and eggs at three o'clock in the morning. In fact, he looked exactly the way she'd imagined he would. An unassuming, elegant assassin. He'd probably dispatch her with a poisonous gas emitted from his fountain pen, or maybe a single, deadly blow with his walking stick, only he didn't have a walking stick. He wore a tweed jacket, unmistakably wool, with dark brown dress pants and a crimson tie.

He walked casually to the back of the restaurant and took a seat at her booth, gracing her with the aura of his aftershave. Magnolia got ready to kick his balls into his nose, but he placed a thousand-dollar bill on the table and delicately inched it towards her.

Magnolia eyed him closely. If he wasn't an assassin, then he must be a lonely old man. Only one thing was certain; if he had one thousand-dollar bill, he had more. She sighed. The last thing she wanted to do right now was turn a trick, but her plane fare had left her with only fifty dollars. She really couldn't afford to turn it down. "I've only got a half an hour," she said. "It'd have to be right there in the Hilton." She pointed across the concourse to a commuter's hotel.

He smiled gently and shook his head. "Permit me to introduce myself. My name is Remus Rahul. I had the pleasure of observing your performance this evening. This—" he glanced at the bill that still lay between them—"is merely a token of my admiration."

She narrowed her eyes and stared at him. She felt afraid, but not as if she were in immediate danger. It seemed unlikely that Dano's friends would waste time waving money at her. No, this was somebody else. Probably a danger in his own right, but the threat was subtle. It was something that would wait until she'd forgotten all about it. It might not be so bad, she thought, having a problem she could forget about for a while.

Quickly she took the money and slipped it in the pocket of her jeans. She'd already performed in a porno movie, whether she liked it or not. She might as well get some money for it. "How did you find me? Did you follow me here?"

"Not exactly. But VisuAll, the company that filmed you, had used that apartment before. They were paying off security. The doorman tailed you, but I made it worth their while to let me find you instead."

"You work for this VisuAll, then?" Magnolia's jaw clenched around the words.

"Oh no. I'm an independent businessman. My association with the company is predicated on one thing only. I have something to sell that they wish to buy."

"Women?"

Rahul laughed. "No, not women. I don't deal in human beings."

"Then what do you deal in?" asked Magnolia, curling her lip.

"That you will learn in the fullness of time, my dear." Rahul gazed at her evenly. His eyes were a light, golden shade of brown, like roasted nuts. "What is your name?"

"Magnolia. What do you want with me?"

Rahul reached for the inside pocket of his tweed jacket. Instantly Magnolia had her hand in her purse. She found the handgrip for the gun even as she knew it would be too late. Without bothering to take it out of her bag, she aimed it at his navel.

He had frozen the instant that she moved. His eyes twinkled as they took in her posture, the position of her arm, her hand hidden under the table. "Not to worry, my dear. It's only a cigar. I hope you don't mind if I smoke." Slowly he pulled a thin black cigar out of his pocket and removed the rubberized wrapping.

Magnolia's food came, and hunger overcame her tension. She left the gun in her bag and picked up a fork. "So like I said," she spoke around a mouthful of fried egg, "what do you want?"

Rahul took a pull on his cigar and exhaled a column of purple smoke. "I want to hire you."

She shook her head. "I don't do that kind of work. I didn't know that guy was taking pictures, or I would have stabbed him sooner."

He laughed. "I have no interest in movies, but I do find your reactions fascinating. I'd like the opportunity to study them in greater detail."

Magnolia paused, chewing thoughtfully on a piece of ham. "What do you have in mind?"

"I'd like you to come and live with me, on a strictly platonic basis, of course." Rahul knocked an inch of ash off the end of his cigar.

"What's 'platonic'?"

"It means we wouldn't have sex."

She raised an eyebrow skeptically. "Oh yeah?"

"Oh yeah." He eyed her steadily. "As I said before, I've been in contact with the business associates of the young man you stabbed earlier tonight. As a favor to me they are willing to forego restitution, provided you remain under my supervision for the next several months. Of course you'll be paid. By my calculations, ten thousand dollars a month is adequate recompense for the privilege of your company. What do you say?"

Ten thousand dollars. It was more money than Magnolia had ever dreamed of having at once, and she'd be getting that every month. Carefully she swallowed her hash browns and took a leisurely sip of coffee. She looked Rahul hard in his bright brown eyes and said, "Fifteen thousand."

THE UNIVERSE SPELLS 01

It was night, but the laboratory glowed with the artificial light of row upon row of fluorescent fixtures. The large room, all the more empty for being well lit, was like a vacuum waiting to be filled. Cid would have preferred to be alone, but she heard footsteps echoing in the hallway, and Kelira appeared at the door.

He flopped down in a metal folding chair near her desk. He was a smallish guy, five seven or so, with the finely formed frame of many East Asian men. His hair hung straight and black to his shoulders, framing an oval face with a long, narrow jaw and dark, deeply set eyes. If I wasn't a lesbian, she mused, I'd probably fall for Kelira in a really big way. "Whatcha doing?" he asked.

"A little research." Cid removed the lid from cell culture A. "I inoculated this sample with attenuated melanoma virus yesterday. Now I want to take a look at it."

"What is it?" asked Kelira, leaning forward to peer at the clear plastic dish in her hands.

"It's a skin cell sample from Tumcari. I have another one here that I didn't inoculate. I want to compare them."

She added a top layer of photorefractive medium to the culture dish, smoothly decanting the transparent fluid from a carafe fitted with a flexible pipette.

"It's important to get just the right thickness of medium above the cell sample," she explained, "six millimeters, no more and no less, otherwise I'll have to recalibrate the holoscope's focus, and that could take hours, even days." She discarded the pipette, took another out of its sterile envelope, and repeated the procedure with her control sample, cell culture B. She set culture B down on a bench and turned to face Kelira. "What are you up to?"

A brief shadow crossed his face, but he shrugged, and it was gone. "I was just flicking stations downstairs. I got bored so I thought I'd come see what was happening in the laboratory." He exaggerated his pronunciation of the last word, mugging like an old horror-movie actor.

Cid smiled, but she didn't forget the dark look that had passed so swiftly across his face a moment before. She continued with her explanation, hoping to put him at ease. "The medium has to solidify smoothly, with no bubbles or creases to scatter the laser. I have to wait at least five minutes now for it to set up before switching on the LRH-8000." She nodded at the black behemoth on the other side of the room.

Kelira nodded and stared out the window. He had that look again.

"You were looking for your sister again, weren't you?" said Cid.

Startled, his gaze snapped back to her and he stared, his eyes burning holes through the air.

Cid shook her head. "Why do you torture yourself like that? It wasn't your fault, Kelira. There was nothing you could do then, and there's nothing you can do now."

For a moment she thought he'd jump up and strike her, but his anger was not for her. With visible effort he exhaled and forced a smile. "I guess it's just habit now, Cid. I've been looking for so long. I know I'll never find her, but tonight—tonight I saw something I never thought I'd see."

Cid raised an eyebrow.

"It was a slash scenario. But the girl fought back against her attacker. She killed him." He laughed, and this time his smile was genuine. "It was good to see, even if it wasn't Rose."

Talking about the porn channels Kelira scanned made her uncomfortable. She couldn't help but wonder if looking for his sister was a rationalization for his continued viewing. Cid turned from him and went to the LRH-8000 hulking against the far wall. When she switched it on, its deep-pitched hum resonated through the floor and up her legs.

After placing sample A on the viewing platform, Cid directed the laser beam onto it and adjusted the focus. Kelira peered over her shoulder as holographic images of the cells and their constituents appeared in the blank blackness of the display theater. Cid pointed out the twisting yellow chains that wound between the cells. "Those are melanoma variation antibodies. The presence of the melanoma virus in weakened form caused their production without actually transforming the cells into cancerous ones—just like my college textbooks always said it would. Let's take a look at the control sample." She switched off the laser, removed the cell culture, and replaced it with sample B.

When the images appeared in the theater, Cid caught her breath. Again there were the globular structures of the cells, interlaced with long chains. "There they are! Goddess!" She turned to Kelira. "You see them, don't you?"

He nodded slowly. "Those long yellow things—antibodies?"

"Yeah, they're color coded by the LRH's computer to clarify their structure. They weren't there yesterday, and they shouldn't be there now. This sample has never been in contact with the melanoma virus." The hair at the back of her neck prickled, and she shook her head, as if she could dispel what she saw.

"Something strange is going on. First his mitochondria, and now this. Tumcari's pretty fucking unique, all right. Do me a favor and don't mention this to Rahul, okay?"

Kelira nodded his assent.

"Thanks." She clapped him lightly on the shoulder. "It's just that I'm only supposed to maintain the lab equipment, not use it. He might take umbrage at me playing with his toys, and besides, I'm not certain that he'd use this knowledge for Tumcari's benefit, you know what I mean?"

"Sure. I haven't said anything to him so far, have I?"

"No." Cid turned away from the impossible sight in the laser refraction holoscope and paced the room, her eyes blindly scanning the tables, walls, and floors as her mind searched for an explanation for the presence of melanoma antibodies in an uninoculated cell sample.

She went to the bank of incubators on the wall next to the LRH-8000 and ran each of them through a contamination check. "They're all negative," she said, pointing at the row of doors, each one sporting a green light, "just as they were when I checked them after storing the samples yesterday. The virus couldn't have been transmitted through these."

"Then how did it happen?" asked Kelira, still transfixed by the holograms.

"Bell's theorem," she said, pacing to the windows to stare out into the unending Siberian night. "The quantum principle of nonlocality. It's supposed to be a thing of the very lowest orders of matter, but it's echoed here, where cells stand as universes to the quantum particles they contain."

She turned back to him. "Somehow Tumcari retains some primal connection to the dust from which he sprang. His cells and, it seems, subcellular structures such as his mitochondria know what's going on simultaneously throughout his body, even, apparently, when they're no longer *in* his body." She paused, knotting her hands together. "You know, theoretically the larger structures that these cells form could also benefit from their constituents' awareness."

Kelira abandoned the holograms and faced her. "What are you saying?"

"Well, if all the cells of his body have this nonlocal ability, then his brain cells, the axons and dendrites, would have access to an incredible range of information about what's going on inside his own body, let alone the outer world."

"What would that do?"

"I don't know."

"Well, he is a strange guy," Kelira said, peering into the nearest incubator.

"Yes." She thought of Tumcari swimming in his pond, so fluid and graceful, as if he were another part of the water. Never a false move, an awkward gesture. And his thoughts, though seldom spoken, seemed to reflect the workings of a synesthetic perception; colors and tastes and sounds blended together, superimposed.

"I wonder what would it be like, to have such a complex awareness?"

"It'd probably drive you crazy."

"Maybe." She shrugged. "But maybe madness is just the gateway, the necessary struggle to achieve a totally new state of mind."

Kelira shook his head. "I think you're already crazy."

"Let's check something." Cid returned to the LRH-8000

and stored the image of Tumcari's sample B in memory, placed the sample carefully in its incubator, and then removed the samples she'd taken from herself and Ms. Wujcik. She took fresh images of them and then called all three up into the theater from memory. They hung in blackness together, and she programmed the LRH to focus in on the subcellular level of each of them.

"Tumcari and Ms. Wujcik are human analogues," she said, looking over her shoulder at Kelira. "They possess every feature of human biological functioning, but all on a chemical base distinct from that of humans. They're plant based."

"Rahul used to be a botanist, didn't he?"

"That's right, and I think he's still more comfortable in that field than in human biology. Could be the reason he never picked up on any of this cellular weirdness with Tumcari."

"What are you doing now?"

"I want to compare mitochondria." Three nearly identical ovoids hung in the display theater, side by side. Their colors represented the different proteins in their makeup: hers was mostly blue and red, Ms. Wujcik's mostly yellow and green, but Tumcari's mitochondria were a blend of all four.

"Look, Kelira, when Rahul engineered Tumcari, he must have used human mitochondria. Let's zoom in closer." Tumcari's sample grew until it was lost, and all that could be seen were the color-coded protein molecules; red, green, blue, and yellow building blocks the size of Ping-Pong balls, interlocking with each other, more or less.

"Wow, this is pretty crude." Cid pointed to several gaps between molecules. "No wonder Rahul's never been able to repeat the experiment."

"But this is a magnified view; I mean, they hold together okay in real life, apparently," said Kelira.

"Oh, they work fine. Different, but fine. See, the proteins

aren't really that smart. They'll bond as long as their shapes are more or less compatible, and since the yellow and green proteins are analogues of the red and blue ones, they work together just fine.

"But they don't quite match each other; there's gaps in the bonds. Little spaces that shouldn't be there. They introduce error into the system. The low-level, nonfatal kind of error that often exists in thriving, complicated systems.

"A healthy human heartbeat is slightly irregular. We all live with a thread of chaos winding through our bodies, but Tumcari has a little more of it than the rest of us."

She went to the desk and sank into the swivel chair behind it. "Order and chaos are two sides of the same coin, Kelira. Together, in various combinations, they form every aspect of existence." She picked up a pencil and absently doodled on the blotter.

"Between the crystalline simplicity of the finite and the endless possibilities of the infinite lies everything anyone has ever known." She drew an eight on its side, and a dot. "Each state, isolated, is without meaning. Pure chaos is as rare as unbroken symmetry." She replaced the dot with a numeral one and drew infinity beside it once more. "It is the combination of the two, the endless field of error that lies between two absolute states, that is rife with meaning." Infinity, everything, she replaced with zero, nothing. "Even computer science is based on this; the binary code. Zero and one." She tore off the sheet, holding the symbols scrawled in pencil before him. "Zero and one, Kelira, oh, eye."

He looked at her blankly.

"Oi!" she exclaimed like her Jewish grandmother, "the universe spells oi!" And she broke up laughing, leaning back in her chair and spinning it in circles.

"You're not really a biologist, are you?" said Kelira.

She stopped spinning and looked at him, wiping tears

from her eyes. "Sure I am. I also minored in chaos theory, with a philosophy subunit." She paused and leaned forward, staring at him with wide eyes. "And I do a lot of drugs."

"Yeah," said Kelira, "I can see that." A light above the lab door flashed red.

"We've got a phone call," she pointed out.

He nodded. "I'll get it; you just stay here and tamper with nature, okay?"

"Okay. Bye." As the door swung shut behind Kelira, Cid returned to stare at Tumcari's magnified mitochondria. She wondered if such a hybrid could survive in either of the other cellular environments, and if it would produce nonlocal effects if it did.

She took a blank medium dish from an incubator and crossed to the lab table. She'd need another sample from Ms. Wujcik to test the viability of Tumcari's mitochondria in robot cells, but she already had everything she needed to answer her most pressing question.

Her hands shook as she rolled up her sleeve and picked up a scalpel.

THIN AIR

The fax from Rahul fluttered in Kelira's hand as he walked down the path flanked by robust, shadowy foliage. He was dressed for the rest of the house, not here. By the time he reached the edge of the pond, his neck prickled from the collar of his heavy sweater, and the flannel lining in his jeans was damp with perspiration.

Tumcari looked up as he approached. "Kelira," he said, surprised, "to what do I owe this delightful interruption?"

"Sorry to bother you, Tumcari."

"Not at all. As you can see, I am sorely lacking in personal engagements at the moment."

Kelira nodded and sat down on the gravel beside the pond. "I just got a call from Rahul," he said, waving the fax in the air.

"Ah, he remembers us. How nice."

"Well, he wants Ms. Wujcik to pick someone up in St. Petersburg."

"He does, does he? I wonder why he can't send one of his own lackeys, hmm? Why must he trouble us?"

Kelira shrugged. "We're closer, apparently."

"Mmm. And time is of the essence, evidently. Well, I suppose you want me to ask Ms. Wujcik to attend the good doctor's bidding."

Kelira took a deep breath. He was head of security here, he reminded himself; by all accounts he was in a position of authority over Tumcari, but there was something about the creature's manner which always made him feel as if he were five years old. "Actually, I wanted to ask you—" He held out the fax once again, showing Tumcari the picture on it. "He sent this, so Ms. Wujcik could identify her. I've seen her before. In fact I saw her on television tonight, and I was wondering, What would Rahul want with her?"

Tumcari surged forward until his hands gripped the bank of the pond, pulling the upper portion of his body out of the water so he could get a good look at the fax in the dim light. "You saw her on television, eh? What is she, a movie star?"

Kelira laughed. "Not exactly. She's not anybody, really, that's the thing. She was on a satellite station. It was supposed to be a porn scene, but she didn't know it, and when it got rough, she killed the guy."

Tumcari pursed his lips. "Well, we can probably safely assume she's not a business contact, then."

"You think he wants her for sex?"

He shook his head. "No, Rahul's an old man, he's probably mostly into looking nowadays anyway, and for that he has Althea. He's quite attached to her, I believe."

"Then what does he want with her?"

Tumcari leaned back in the water, staring up into the night beyond the greenhouse dome. "That scenario she was in, you said it went awry?"

"As far as the station owners are concerned, I'm sure it did."

"Mmm. She acted unpredictably, then, you'd say."

"Yeah, I guess so."

He nodded and faced Kelira once more. "Then it's probably her personality Rahul wants, not her body."

"What do you mean?"

"Rahul was never content with me. He wanted to create an autonomous living creature, but apparently I'm not quite what he had in mind. My guess is that he wants to template her personality for a new strain of robots in the hope that they'll be independent, like she is."

"Template her?"

"Yes, distill her personality down to its basic components and program it into a new strain."

Kelira stared at the picture on the fax. The young woman stared up at the camera with dark eyes, her hair fanned out around her on the bed in which she lay. She didn't really look all that much like Rose, but she reminded him of her, just the same. "Tumcari—"

"Yes?"

He hesitated, not sure what to say. He didn't want this woman, whoever she was, to become a tool of Rahul's. She'd defeated her attacker; he felt she deserved better than to be used again. "What if we told Ms. Wujcik to bring her here instead?"

The greenhouse was silent except for the soft rippling of the water as Tumcari moved through it. Finally he spoke. "You must be awfully uncomfortable in those warm clothes, Kelira. Why don't you remove them and swim with me awhile."

Slowly Kelira put down the fax sheet and pulled off his sweater. He had no desire to get in the water with Tumcari, but he sensed that this was a test of some sort.

The water was cool and soothing on his bare skin. Kelira swam the length of the pond, and at the far end he turned around, treading water.

"Come here," said Tumcari from where he floated in the center.

Reluctantly Kelira paddled towards him until they were no more than a meter apart. Something warm and strong wrapped around Kelira's left ankle. Suppressing his instinct to struggle, Kelira concentrated instead on keeping his head above the water.

Tumcari's eyes glimmered a living green in the dim light. "Nothing could please me more than to thwart a desire of Rahul's, but remember this, my man, eventually she will find out that she's not where she's supposed to be, and when she does, it will be up to you to explain it to her." And the thing around Kelira's ankle yanked, plunging him beneath the water. When he surfaced again, sputtering, Tumcari was gone.

WOTROYA HOUSE

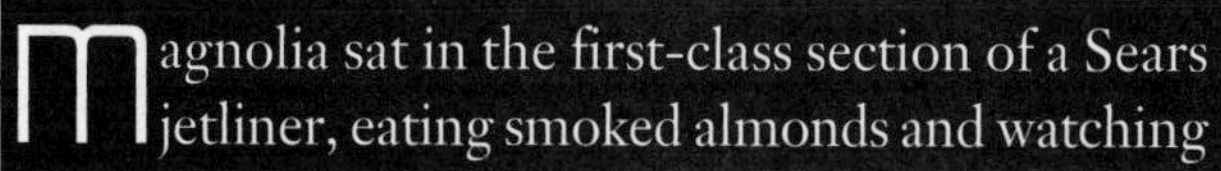
Magnolia sat in the first-class section of a Sears jetliner, eating smoked almonds and watching the ocean slide past beneath her. Eventually she'd end up in Tunis, a city on the coast of North Africa, but first she was taking her previously scheduled flight to St. Petersburg. She and Rahul both felt that it would be better if she left the country as soon as possible. Another employee of his would meet her when she landed, and escort her to Rahul's home by private jet. Rahul had stayed behind in New York. He had some last-minute business to take care of. At least, that's what he said.

A stewardess in a pink latex pantsuit squeaked by taking drink orders. Magnolia asked for a vodka and tonic and returned her gaze to the grey and limitless ocean beyond the window. The rush of adrenaline and coke had left her, and now she began to wonder what was happening to her. She still didn't know who Rahul was or what he really wanted with her. The stewardess returned with her drink. In a halfhearted attempt at cheering herself Magnolia raised it high. "To the big time," she whispered.

The airport in St. Petersburg was indistinguishable from the one in New York. Across the teeming concourse a neon fried egg blared redundantly at her. Magnolia had the disorienting feeling that her jet had never left the ground. She was thousands of miles from any place she'd ever known before; it should look different.

A group of young men dressed in sweaters and flowing skirts walked past, speaking to each other in some incomprehensible language. Reassured, Magnolia made her way to the information counter where Rahul had instructed her to await her contact.

There was a tap on her shoulder, and Magnolia spun around, ready to deck whoever it was. A tall, fair-skinned woman smiled at her with perfect teeth. She wore a dark blue suit, her long, blond hair pulled neatly into a ponytail and fastened with a matching bow. "Magnolia?" she said.

Magnolia blushed and lowered her upraised hand. "Yes."

"Ah good. I am Ms. Wujcik. You will accompany me, please."

They took a limousine to a private airfield and boarded a Yamaha microjet. There was a bar in the back, and Magnolia fixed herself another drink, clumsily spilling vodka on her jeans. Ms. Wujcik put a soft, rounded hand over one of her own. "Are you frightened, Magnolia?"

What a stupid question; of course she was. Magnolia laughed and nodded faintly.

"All will be well, you will see." Ms. Wujcik smoothed the hair back from Magnolia's face and took the drink from her hand. "Try to get some rest."

Magnolia felt like she'd been awake all her life. She lay down on the black vat-leather upholstery of the backseat and closed her eyes. Weariness washed over her as Ms. Wujcik steered the jet into the atmosphere, leaving behind a city she'd never known.

She was shaken awake. "We're almost there, dear," said Ms. Wujcik, leaning around the pilot's seat.

Magnolia gazed at her fuzzily and groaned. Her mouth tasted like polyfoam filler, and her head ached. She leaned forward and made a small, involuntary choking noise as she glimpsed the view through the windshield.

Something was definitely wrong. The world outside the jet's windows was white and altogether empty. They were above a huge snowfield, barren except for a few scattered pine trees. "Where are we?" she gasped.

"This is Polish Siberia," said Ms. Wujcik with evident pride. "A territory donated to the nation of Poland by the Commonwealth as part of the 1998 Cultural Reparations Act, passed by the United Nations in order to ease global tensions."

"But I'm supposed to be in Tunis," Magnolia stammered, still too sleep-groggy to make sense of it. "You were supposed to take me there." A terrible thought occurred to her then. Maybe Dano's people had caught up with her after all, maybe this Ms. Wujcik had gotten to her before Rahul's real employee did. Or maybe Rahul had been lying to her all along.

Ms. Wujcik smiled at Magnolia's panicky tone. "Don't worry, dear, all will be well. You'll see."

Trembling, Magnolia fumbled with the clasp of her purse. She took out her gun and put it to Ms. Wujcik's temple. "Turn the jet around and take me to Tunis."

Ms. Wujcik sighed. "I can't do that."

"Yes you can, and you will, or we both die."

"Then we both die."

There was no sound in the jet's cabin except for the harsh rasp of Magnolia's breathing. Her palm sweated against the plastic of the gun, but Ms. Wujcik seemed utterly calm. "You don't care if you die?"

She shrugged. "Of course I do, but it's not very important."

Magnolia laughed in amazement and flopped back against her seat. Quietly she slipped the gun back into her handbag. Ms. Wujcik didn't seem to notice, or care. Magnolia didn't feel like dying just yet, although she feared she might regret her decision when they got to wherever they were going. "Who are you?" she asked in exasperation.

"I told you, dear, my name is Ms. Wujcik."

"Ms. Wujcik? Nobody's name is Ms. Wujcik; what kind of first name is Ms., anyway?"

Unconcerned, she shrugged. "That's my name."

"Who do you work for?"

"I work for Dr. Rahul. I take care of Mr. Tumcari."

"Mr. Tumcari?"

Ms. Wujcik smiled widely, as if the mere mention of the name gave her great pleasure. "Yes!" she said. In that one syllable she showed more true emotion than she had at any time before.

Magnolia frowned. Things were getting away from her here, already had, most likely. "If you work for Rahul, why aren't you taking me to Tunis like he said?"

Ms. Wujcik was silent for a moment, as if she'd been presented with a paradox of intricate complexity. Finally she spoke up, "He changed his plans." From the seat beside her she picked up a pair of aqua blue, quilted nylon boots with rubber soles and a green-and-white microthin parka. "Put these on. It will be cold outside, and we have to walk to the house."

Grudgingly Magnolia took the gear and put it on. This bitch was about as informative as an infomercial, and apparently beyond threat. Rahul must be a heavy operator, if he could inspire that kind of selflessness. At least she wasn't in the hands of Dano's people, if anything that Ms. Wujcik said was true.

Below them a solitary building came into view, nearly obscured among a stand of pines. Ms. Wujcik banked the microjet sharply, and they began to descend.

When the jet's hatch opened, it let in a wind as cold as the worst of a Detroit winter. Magnolia shrank into her parka and followed Ms. Wujcik, who led her up a gently sloping hill through knee-deep snow. The house was huge and old; brick and timber walls stood in commiseration with the weather. To the left, growing out of the side of the house like a mutation, was a greenhouse, its glass panels supported by an ancient network of copper. The house stood at least three stories tall, and still there were pines whose branches brushed against the grey stone shingles.

Ms. Wujcik handed Magnolia a thin black card and showed her how to insert it into the slot beside the brass handle on the front door. With a quiet click the door swung inward. "Welcome to Wotroya House," she said.

The front hall was paneled in dark wood. Magnolia reached a hand to the carved surface. It was warm and smooth to the touch, without a hint of the cool slickness of synthetics. This was a far cry from the plastic splendor of Dano's apartment. Ten thousand dollars wouldn't buy a square foot of this stuff.

"I'll show you to your room." Ms. Wujcik led her up a curved staircase that swept around the hall like a *Vogue* model.

Magnolia's room was spare and elegant. Hardwood flooring glowed golden in the fading light from the window. A futon pad lay wrapped in grey sheets in the center of the room, directly in front of a closet door. The only other furnishings were a table and chair under the window, and a dresser with a mirror standing against the wall near the door.

All of them were synthetic wood, a reasonably good match with the floor.

"I'll leave you to settle in now," said Ms. Wujcik, and with a click of the door she was gone. Magnolia took off her boots, lay down on the futon, and stared at the ceiling with wide, sleepless eyes.

goon squad

Someone was knocking on a door. Magnolia opened her eyes, and the sight of pale wood and blank white walls brought back the events of the previous day in one long flood of regret. She'd slept after all, apparently, or if it had not been sleep, it was at least some place where this world could not touch her. The light from her window was pale and watery; morning light.

She sat on the edge of the bed and stretched. The knocking persisted. She wasn't too eager to answer it. Whoever was on the other side of the door was going to deliver the punch line to a transcontinental joke that she probably wouldn't get, but that would be on her, just the same.

Suppressing a groan, she stumbled into the bathroom to use the toilet. It was a messy, blue-tiled space, the sink littered with toothpaste stains. She still had on the clothes she'd stolen from Dano. They were stiff and scratchy against her skin, and they didn't smell very fresh. Neither did she. She glanced at the shower stall.

Whoever was at the door could wait; Magnolia was damned if she was going to pass up a good hot shower after the night she'd had. Besides, she preferred to greet her mystery visitor with clean fingernails. She dumped her clothes on the floor and stepped into the shower.

She emerged feeling almost alive again, but the sight of those pathetic garments lying crumpled on the tile was too much for her. She looked in the closet, which was bare. In the dresser she found a pair of navy sweatpants and a red cable-knit sweater. They were clean and approximately her size, so she put them on. She was searching for a comb or brush when the knocking resumed. Magnolia flung her damp hair out of her eyes and opened the door.

Standing in the hallway was a skinny blond-haired girl with bright, blue, bloodshot eyes. "Welcome to the Goon Squad." She smiled and extended a hand. "I'm Cid."

Magnolia folded her arms, ignoring the friendly gesture. She glared at her and announced herself in a monotone, "Magnolia."

Cid was not easily put off. Her smile only faltered a little, and she said, "Nice to meet you. I hope I didn't wake you up."

She sneered. "You did."

She bit her lip. "Sorry, you want to smoke a joint?"

Magnolia laughed in spite of herself. If this was the punch line, the joke seemed harmless enough. She could easily take this girl, and there didn't seem to be anyone else around. "Sure," she relented, and followed her into the room next door.

Cid's room was just like Magnolia's only with a layer of hardware that made it look like a squat in a Holiday Inn. Three different video tubes sat side by side on the desk, along with a battered keyboard. The screen on the left was active; some sort of geometric form blossomed across it in a spectrum of vivid colors. Optical cable and transistors lay in piles on the floor.

A holograph hung over the bed like a prismatic storm cloud, a copy of the image blazing on the video screen. It was constantly changing, growing, sending out spiraling tendrils that reached across the room. Magnolia ducked instinctively as a green-blue-black streak suddenly shot towards her head.

Cid walked to the keyboard on her desk and hit a button. The holo disappeared. Magnolia breathed a sigh of relief and sank down on the bed. "What was that?"

"It's a phase space fractal for a research project I'm working on. It's mapping the electron transport chain of a particularly interesting little organelle I've found." Cid bent down and pulled a plastic shoe box out from under the bed. It was half full of fluffy green buds. Magnolia managed not to stare at it as Cid rolled a joint with absentminded grace. "Where do you come from, Magnolia?"

Here was her chance to make the right kind of impression. She leaned back on the bed and let a slow, sweet smirk spread across her face. "Detroit," she said, quietly pronouncing the skull and crossbones hidden in the word.

Cid looked up at her, her eyes wide. "Detroit? Wow! Do you like music?"

Magnolia frowned. "Sure."

"Did you ever see Kay Baybee or MC20? What's the Scene like in Detroit these days, anyway?"

"The Scene? The Scene!?" Magnolia leaned forward and bared her teeth. "Girl, what do you think this is, '96? There hasn't been a scene in Detroit since before I was born. Those groups, Kay and them, they're from the suburbs, Troy and Birmingham. They just say they're from Detroit so they can pretend they're badasses."

She watched Cid nod her head and light the joint. She was cool, this girl. Just sitting there, listening, her eyes narrowed as she took a hit. It made Magnolia want to keep talking. "I may not know much, but I knew enough to get the hell out of Detroit. I ran to New York, was having myself a fine old time there too, until I picked the wrong dick and got my ass shipped out here. Where the fuck are we, anyway, Cid? What is this place?"

Cid smiled broadly. "This is an old research facility. I don't suppose you've ever heard of the International Bureau of Research?" She handed her the joint, gazing at her with raised eyebrows.

Magnolia shook her head.

"Nah, not many people have. It was one of those glorious, 'global awareness'–type operations. Using an abandoned mansion in Polish Siberia was a stroke of PR genius on the part of the founders. Unfortunately, the project was a disaster; it didn't last more than ten years. Our employer, Dr. Remus Rahul, or 'Uncle Remus,' as I like to call him, ended up with the property. There's a lot of very expensive equipment on the premises, the kind you can't just stick in mothballs and forget about. Most of us are here in what you could call a custodial capacity."

Magnolia took a huge drag, letting the smoke settle in her lungs before she exhaled. "Who's us?" she asked.

"Oh, let's see, there's me and you; Kelira, he's okay. Spider and Dex are a couple of ex–hockey players or something. They're the ones who put the 'goon' in Goon Squad. Tumcari has some interesting things to say, now and then, but you probably won't see too much of him. He spends all of his time floating around in the greenhouse pond. Strange guy. Then there's Ms. Wujcik; she's a fucking robot."

Cid paused and took the joint from her. She hit it, gazing thoughtfully at a cobweb in the corner of the ceiling.

"Let's listen to some tunes." She turned to a dusty portable stereo perched on the bedside table and pushed the play button. The rhythms of techno-funk surrounded them with a wall of sound.

Magnolia hit the joint again, allowing a sense of relaxation and well-being to flow over her. The music, the pot, Cid's room, it all reminded her of the squats; sitting outside on a summer night, toking with Albert and Doralee, the music from somebody's jumped-up sound box reaching them faintly across the ruins. She wouldn't see any of them again, even if she got out of here. Suddenly her chest felt tight, and her eyes stung.

Cid had picked up a length of optical cable and was using it to tie back her shoulder-length hair. She glanced at her, her eyes bright and shrewd. "You got family, back home?"

Magnolia nodded, wishing she could break away from that sharp, intelligent stare.

"Miss 'em?"

"Yeah." Magnolia promptly glared at the wall.

"Oh, well, never mind then. Let's go down and have breakfast."

The kitchen was already occupied when they got there. A man dressed in white canvas drawstring pants and a blue, long-sleeved jersey stood at the sink, cursing, surrounded by stacks of dirty dishes. His dark hair fell across his almond-shaped eyes as he scrubbed vigorously at a frying pan.

He looked up as they entered, and his glower changed to a smile. "Hi. You must be Magnolia." He dropped the pan and dried his hands on his shirt. "I'm Kelira, pleased to meet you." He offered his hand, and Magnolia took it.

He nodded at the pan, half submerged in dingy dishwater. "I thought I'd make pancakes for breakfast, seeing as how we have a new addition and all, but somebody melted epoxy in our last decent pan." He glared pointedly at Cid.

"Hey, it weren't me, Jack." Cid waved her hands in innocence.

Kelira nodded sarcastically. "Yeah, sure." On the counter beside the refrigerator a coffeemaker perked merrily. "At least I can still make ginger coffee. You want some?" He looked at Magnolia.

"Yeah, thanks." She sat at a simulated teak table, doing her best to hide her disappointment. She hadn't eaten since her power breakfast with Rahul the night before, or was it the previous morning? At any rate, she was starving.

"Why would you want to cook something when you can eat like this?" Cid gestured grandly as she opened a cupboard door, revealing shelves stocked floor to ceiling with self-heating entrees. "What would you like? Winter vegetable stew with kelp noodles? Chikken paprika with rice and broccoli? How about tofu stroganoff, a personal favorite of mine?"

Magnolia suppressed a shudder and got up to see what was in the refrigerator. "I wouldn't look in there if I were you," said Kelira. "The fridge has been Cid's territory for weeks now. Apparently she's doing some advanced research with molds." He opened up a cabinet over the sink and pulled down a big glass jar. "How about rice and seaweed? It's very nutritious, and I've managed to keep the pressure cooker out of irresponsible hands."

Magnolia bit her lip. "Do you have any eggs?" she asked wistfully.

"Nah." Cid popped the tab on her tofu stroganoff and dug in with relish. "Ms. Wujcik hasn't gone on a supply run in ages. Most of the fresh stuff went bad weeks ago."

"I'll have the vegetable stew." Defeated, Magnolia returned to her seat. As she slurped noodles from the plastic carton Kelira joined them at the table. He handed her a steaming mug. It smelled terrific, even better than regular coffee. Magnolia took a sip and glanced up at Kelira. "What am I doing here?"

His eyes widened as he stirred sugar into his mug. "Pardon?"

"I was supposed to go to Tunis. I may not know much about geography, but I do know that Tunis, this ain't."

Kelira nodded his head. "Of course, he didn't have a chance to tell you. Rahul decided you should come here for a few months, for training. I've been teaching combat techniques to the gardeners," he said, looking at her seriously. "I'd like to do the same with you. I've seen you in action, and I think you'd be good."

Secretly flattered, Magnolia did her best to disguise her pleasure. "That sounds okay."

"So she's working with us!" A lanky, wiry arm draped itself over her shoulder. Magnolia started and turned to face a tall thin young man who grinned at her, his dark, intense eyes first grazing her breasts and then meeting her eyes mockingly. "I'm Spider," he said. Behind him stood a short guy, thickly built with a round head and a minimalist crew cut. "This is Dex. We train with Kelira. Looks like you will be too. It'll be nice working with a woman for a change." He smirked and glanced at Dex, who grinned malevolently.

Magnolia shuddered and extricated herself from the clinging arm. She was at a loss for words; she'd wasted all her attitude on Cid, earlier.

"You'd better watch yourselves," said Kelira with evident pleasure. "This woman will be wiping up the floor with you boys inside two weeks."

"Magnolia?" Ms. Wujcik appeared at the door of the

kitchen. "Mr. Tumcari would like to meet you. Please, come with me."

Ms. Wujcik led Magnolia down several long, darkly paneled hallways before she stopped at a pair of doors with big, brass handles. "This is the greenhouse. Mr. Tumcari spends a great deal of time here." She pulled open the doors, and Magnolia followed her into another world. They were surrounded by plants; trees dripping with vines, brilliant pink and orange flowers like neon starbursts, mosses and grasses shining with dew. Magnolia struggled for breath in the sudden heat and damp. Above them birds fluttered from branch to branch, their singing filling the air with chaos.

Out of the corner of her eye Magnolia caught sight of movement; something four-legged and sleek darting through the ground cover. "I think you've got rats," she said to Ms. Wujcik, but she only smiled and led Magnolia on towards the sound of running water.

They came to a large pond dotted with round, flat green leaves. A man floated amongst them, his arms sweeping lazily through the water. He caught sight of Magnolia and Ms. Wujcik standing on the gravel path beside the pond, and he drifted closer.

"Mr. Tumcari, this is Magnolia," said Ms. Wujcik, as if she were used to giving introductions from land to water. She probably was.

Tumcari had broad shoulders, blond hair, a magazine-handsome face, and brilliant green eyes. He smiled and folded his arms behind his head. "I'm pleased to have you with us, Magnolia." He nodded faintly. "You show great promise. You'll be working with Kelira, he's training Spider and Dex too. . . . Have you met them?"

"Yes."

Tumcari laughed. "Yes. Well, I've always thought we learn at least as much from our peers as we do from our teachers." He turned and dived beneath the surface of the water.

Magnolia fidgeted uneasily and glanced at Ms. Wujcik. Her round, placid face revealed nothing. A moment later Tumcari resurfaced with one of the water plants in his hand. Magnolia had seen something like it at a garden in New York. "Is that a water lily?" she asked.

Tumcari smiled. "You're very intelligent, aren't you? No, it's not a plant at all, actually. It is, or rather was, an animal. A genetically engineered one. Here, take it."

Magnolia knelt beside the pool and took the thing from Tumcari's hands. It was losing its green color, fading into transparency. A fine network of veins became visible.

Tumcari gestured across the pool. "They eat bacteria, algae, that kind of thing. They keep the pond clean. They're very good at it; it's what they were designed to do. Turn it over."

The underside of the leaf was covered with fine, feather-like membranes. Tumcari continued, "That's where the bacteria is metabolized. It's really a very intricate process."

A thick stem trailed away from the center of the leaf. Magnolia picked up the shattered end. Some sort of fluid oozed gently out of it, staining the gravel at her feet. "Of course, once you break them off from the main stem, they die instantly. Another leaf will grow to replace that one within a few days. But you were right, they do look like water lilies, don't they, Magnolia?"

Tumcari's eyes shone the color of the air in that green, fecund place, and Magnolia, staring at him, became hypnotized. "You know," he said, "sometimes, at night when it's very quiet and the house is absolutely still, I can feel their thoughts moving through the water."

THE FALAFEL STAND

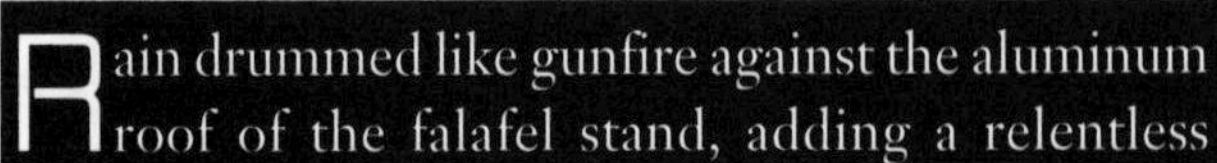

Rain drummed like gunfire against the aluminum roof of the falafel stand, adding a relentless backbeat to the thin strains of Indo-pop from Sheckie's radio. Rose dropped her soaking raincoat on a stack of oil cans and nodded a curt hello to her coworker. Behind her, Antonin struggled with his sodden and fraying windbreaker. Rose knelt to help him, but he pushed her away. "I can do it myself," he said petulantly.

Sheckie wiped the counter with a dingy rag and glanced at the crowds of passersby, coming and going on the busy Tunisian street. "I think it's going to be slow tonight," she said, her broad, brown face damp with perspiration. She frowned as she glanced at Antonin. He was still yanking on the zipper of his jacket.

"You know you're not supposed to bring your kid in here. I've got three of my own that I have to leave with my mother."

"I couldn't find anyone to stay with him," said Rose, getting herself a red soda from the ice chest. She'd only been working here for three weeks, but already this was an old argument. "He won't be any trouble; he'll do his homework. Besides, what do you care? You're off in another hour."

"Four please," said a man on the other side of the counter.

With practiced efficiency Sheckie took his money, scooped four falafel into a cardboard dish, and handed it to him. "Have a nice day, sir," she said without sincerity. She cast Rose a sly, sidelong look. "You could get fired if I told the ownership about this."

"Shit jobs are easy to find." Rose grabbed an oil-stained apron from a hook behind the door and tied it on. Sheckie had been working at this place for two years now at least, maybe three; sometimes she tried to play boss.

Antonin burst from his jacket like a frenetic butterfly. He threw it to the ground and jumped on it. "Die! Die! Die!" he shrieked gleefully, his dark little head thrown back in jubilation.

Sheckie cast Rose a baleful glare and dumped a basketful of raw falafel in the wok. The tiny stand filled with the sound of sizzling oil. "I have a doctor's appointment this afternoon," she shouted over the din. "You mind if I leave early?"

Rose sighed; their shifts were supposed to overlap to handle the rush-hour trade. She handed Antonin his school books and picked his jacket up off the floor. "Okay," she said reluctantly.

"Like I said, it's going to be slow tonight." Sheckie took off her paper hat and threw it in the garbage next to the refrigerator. Bobby pins clung to her frizzy, red-brown hair like crooked antennae. She untied her apron and grabbed her purse. "See you later."

"Wait! At least count out your drawer first, Sheckie!" Rose shouted, but she was cut short by the slam of the rickety screen door at the back of the stand. "Shit," she grumbled, shaking the wok full of sizzling falafel. "Are you hungry?" she asked Antonin.

"Yeah! I want five, with hot sauce."

Rose handed him a dish of falafel and a bottle of Red-Hot. "Do you want pita with it?"

Antonin shook his head. He was preoccupied with covering the falafel with a deluge of hot sauce.

"You don't need to use so much," she scolded.

"Yes, I do." He looked up at her, his dark, Indonesian eyes shining.

Rose smiled despite herself, taking the bottle from his hands and putting it back on the counter. She pulled a magazine off the shelf beneath the cash register and sat down on a folding chair. *American Beauty*, the cover screamed in large block letters, and below the banner a blond woman smiled broadly, showing two rows of perfect, white teeth. Glumly Rose tongued the rotten spot on the back of her eyetooth and flipped through the pages of makeup and fashion ads.

"Excuse me." A woman with gleaming black hair swept up in a turban waited at the counter, tapping her laser-etched fingernails impatiently on the cracked Formica, as if she'd sprung fully formed from the pages of the magazine.

"May I help you?" asked Rose, getting up from her chair.

"I'd like one order with pita bread and cucumbers on the side, please."

Rose pulled a plastic tub out of the refrigerator and opened it. A few pathetically withered cucumber slices clung to the inside, that was all. "I'm sorry ma'am, we don't have any cucumber today."

"It says cucumber on your menu," she countered, pointing a long finger at the ancient pasteboard hanging on the back wall.

"We ran out, I'm sorry. Would you like lettuce instead?"

The woman scowled and shook her head. "No, just give them to me plain, then."

Rose quickly dished the falafel, only to find that she had to open a new bag of pita. The customer sighed with exasperation as she struggled with the plastic tie. At last she opened it, cut one of the round pocket breads in half, and tucked the bread beneath the falafel. "That'll be ninety millimes."

Briskly the woman handed her a sheet of currency and departed haughtily, street-vendor meal in hand. Rose made a face at her back and rang up the order on the cash register. Another customer arrived shortly afterwards, and then another, and then there was a line at the counter, and Antonin wanted a soda, and she had to open a new box of cardboard dishes, and start up the second wok, and haul a fresh batch of falafel out of the freezer.

"One order with pita and sardines, please."

"I'm sorry, sir, we don't have sardines," Rose replied mechanically, glancing at the patron with weary eyes. "Dano!" she gasped.

He grinned broadly, and Rose's stomach turned. He'd disappeared without word a few weeks ago, taking her savings with him. That wasn't so unusual—he was always off on "business trips," often financing himself with the money she'd hoarded away—but this time she didn't wait for him to return. She got herself this job and moved away from the apartment she and Antonin had shared with him. He was the last person she wanted to see now.

"So this is what you've been doing with yourself lately, huh?" He shook his head, lank brown hair flipping into his eyes. "You've come down in the world, Rosie."

Rose curled her lip at him. "I don't think so." She glanced up and down the street, wishing for once that a horde of customers would descend on the stand, but the rush had died off. It was dark now. Most of the people on the street had someplace else to go.

"Aw, c'mon." Dano leaned stiffly against the counter. "You're not telling me you'd rather sling hash in a grease pit than make movies with me, are you?"

Rose glared at him in silence. She didn't trust herself of speak. She knew from experience that arguing with him was a waste of time, and she was so close to tears that she'd probably just humiliate herself, anyway.

"Hey, it's okay," he said, running a finger down her cheek. "You made a mistake, that's all. I'm big enough to take you back."

She flinched away from his touch. "I don't want to come back," she said between clenched teeth. "Besides, if you remember, it was you who left in the first place."

"I'm sorry about that, Rosie, but I had to get out of Tunis for a little while. It was getting hot for me here, you know. Blanks found out I was cutting his stuff with baking powder, and I owed him some money.

"Edgerton had business in New York, and I thought there might be a little project for me there, but it was a bust. Believe me, it wasn't your kind of gig. Those New York guys don't have their shit together. I mean, I had to find my own girl when I got there, can you believe that?

"I've got a new project cooking now, Rosie. You'll like it. We're gonna shoot this one on location. You want to go to Europe?" He pulled a cheap Korean cigarette from a crumpled pack in his shirt pocket and lit it. "I've got some really high-powered backers this time too. Not like those jerks in New York. This is going to be a class operation, right from the word go. I'm doing you a real favor, letting you in on it, especially since you're not getting any younger." He took a drag, gazing at her through half-lidded eyes.

Rose detected the infinitesimal tremor of his hand, magnified in the jagged patterns of smoke that trailed up from the tip of his cigarette. Something was wrong with him, beyond the usual. He needed coke, of course, but there was something else. He held himself stiffly, as if his ribs hurt. He was pale, and even though the night was cool after the afternoon rain, he was beginning to sweat.

This talk about another movie was just patter, designed to win her over to the point where he could hit her up for money. As always, she'd know how much he wanted when she heard how overblown the scheme was. The more grandiose and pompous, the larger the sum he was fishing for, and by the sound of it, this was a big one. Rose had known Dano for ten years, maybe more. Long enough to know how dangerous he could be when he needed money.

"You know, a lot of girls would jump at this opportunity, Rose." He fingered a length of her hair. "I'm just giving you first shot at it because we have a history. I want to do what's right for Antonin, see?"

"Leave him out of this, Dano," she said in a low, quiet voice. He didn't seem to realize that Antonin was in the stand, and she wanted to keep it that way.

"Hey, he's my kid too."

"That never seemed to concern you before," she said hotly, realizing at once that it was a mistake.

He rested his pale forearms on the counter and glared at her. "What do you mean?"

"Did you think of him when you took off with all of my money? I saved that money. It was mine, and you stole it. You steal from me, you steal from your son, it's as simple as that." She picked up a rag and furiously wiped down the counter.

"We're a family, Rose." He spoke in a monotone. "We have to stick together. That's why I'm here, I'm willing to forgive and forget, if you are."

"Hah! Forget what?" she spat, her dark eyes flashing with anger. "You want *me* to forget, you mean. 'This is the last movie you'll ever have to make, Rosie.' How many times have I heard that before? Last time was the last time, do you understand?"

"Okay," he backed off, "I know you want to get out of the business, and we will, but first we have to make enough money to live on. You can't go on like this, working for shit wages."

She knew that this was the point at which she was supposed to give in. From now on, things would only get worse. She knew it, but she couldn't stop herself. Defying him was like a drug, and she was giddy with it. "At least I keep the money I earn, here."

He gazed at the ground for a moment, and Rose held her breath, expecting a blow. But he must have been really hard up, because he just sighed. "Look, I told you I had to get out of town, and Edgerton thought it would be better if I bought my own plane ticket. The project was supposed to bring in enough to cover the ticket and pay off Blanks, but it didn't come off.

"Let me borrow some money so I can get him off my back. If I don't give him something, he's going to kill me, and I know you wouldn't want that." Dano smiled and spread his hands out, palms open.

Rose glared at him in hatred, savoring the words as she spoke, "That would be the best thing that ever happened to me."

He lunged across the counter and slapped her. "Shut up, you fucking bitch," his voice was loud and harsh. "If it weren't for me, you'd still be in that stable in Bangkok. Remember that place? You were happy enough to get out of there, weren't you? You were spreading it for every dick that came through the door. Just another faceless cunt in a whole hotel full of faceless cunts." He leaned closer, his teeth bared in a contemptuous snarl. "Those guys used you like a public urinal. And *I* got you out of there, *me*, *Dano*. I saved your fucking useless life, bitch, so don't go talking about me being dead. If I were dead, you'd be nothing but a whore."

Rose stared at the ground, her face burning with shame and rage. Out of the corner of her eye she could see Antonin, sitting on the ice chest beneath the counter. He had a Cowboys Courageous comic book open in front of him, but he hadn't turned the pages in a while.

The tears she'd held back before welled from her eyes. She looked up at Dano, no longer caring that the streaks they made on her face would make her look ugly. "Why don't you just leave us alone?" she cried.

Dano laughed bitterly. "You want me to leave you alone?" He took another hit off his cigarette and threw it to the ground. She could see his pale, milky blue eyes shake as he glanced around him. "I'd love to leave you alone, you ungrateful cunt, but you owe me. You want me gone so bad, pay me what you owe me." He started walking, fast, around the side of the stand.

"I don't have any money, Dano," Rose shouted, but he was already at the back door.

"Bullshit." He kicked in the rickety screen door and strode across the stand to the cash register. "You've got a whole till full of money, right here." He scanned the keypad, searching for the cash-out button.

"Dano, don't!" Rose grabbed his arm and tried to pull him away.

"Fuck you." He turned and swung a fist at her, hitting her in the mouth.

Tasting blood on her swollen lip, Rose staggered backwards and bumped into the stove. Dano punched a large square key at the bottom of the pad, and the cash drawer sprang open. He stuffed his pockets with tens and twenties, making sure to check underneath the drawer for any larger bills. "Is this all you have?" His voice rose in frustration.

"It's only a falafel stand," said Antonin, huddled on the ice chest. His arms were wrapped protectively about his knees, but he glared up at Dano with pure venom.

"Oh no, Antonin," whispered Rose in terror. Frantically she glanced about the tiny stand for a weapon of any sort.

"You?" Dano turned on him, grabbing him roughly by the elbow. "You're coming with me. I can make some money off you, I bet."

"Dano, he's just a little boy," cried Rose.

"I know." He looked at her, his face a rigid mask of hatred. Only his eyes moved, flickering like the gas flames beneath the wok on the stove. "There's a good market for boys his age in Algiers just now. I can probably get fifty thou for him." He yanked the boy's arm, pulling him off the ice chest. Antonin bit his hand and broke away, scurrying towards the open door.

"You little shit!" Dano shouted, starting after him.

"Run, Antonin!" screamed Rose. On the stove behind her a forgotten batch of falafel sizzled to cinders in hot oil. She picked up the wok, and as Dano lunged after her son she swung it at him.

Oil splashed over his face and left arm, and he screamed; a terrible, screeching howl that spiraled endlessly up into the night. Through a curtain of blistered fingers he glared at her, hatred burning in his remaining sighted eye. Rose backed away in horror, dropped the wok with a clang, and ran out of the stand.

THE ADVENTURES OF ANTONIN

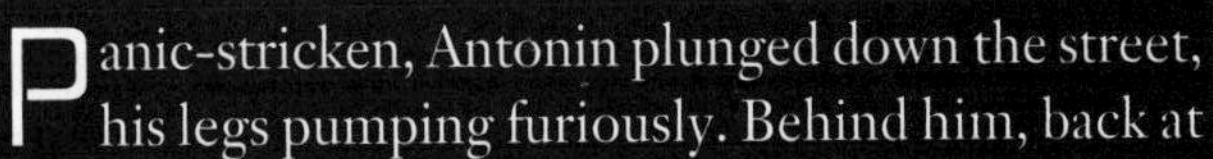

Panic-stricken, Antonin plunged down the street, his legs pumping furiously. Behind him, back at the falafel stand, someone was screaming. He didn't dare stop to find out who it was. He darted down an alley, and then another and another, until he was lost in the labyrinth of the city at night.

He stopped, his chest pounding, his breath rasping harshly against the back of his throat. Weak with exhaustion, Antonin leaned against a crumbling plaster wall. He was in a courtyard; the houses surrounding it were shuttered and dark. His legs threatened to buckle beneath him, and he sank to the ground, huddling in the relative shelter of a dented aluminum garbage can. The damp night air was chilly on his bare arms and legs, and he shivered.

He wanted his mother, but he was afraid to call out to her. Afraid of the sound his voice might make in this dark and echoing place, afraid of who besides Rose might hear him.

Antonin buried his face in his hands and cried. Bitter, salty tears ran down his cheeks. In his mind that terrible screaming still echoed, and Antonin concentrated on it, trying to find some clue as to who had made it. But agony had scrubbed all identity from the voice and deprived it of human tone. He couldn't imagine it being Rose. He wouldn't.

Halting footsteps scraped in the narrow alley that led to the courtyard. Antonin froze, pressing his back into the wall behind him, willing it to swallow him up. Maybe it was Rose, he thought wildly, nearly bawling again at the thought of her rounding the corner and finding him. He bit his lips, choking back his cries.

The footsteps continued in an irregular pattern, approaching. After what seemed an eternity, a figure entered the courtyard. It was neither his mother nor his father. In the dim light cast by the half-quarter moon, he could just make out the figure of an old woman, burdened with a heavy bag. She limped past Antonin, no more than four feet away, but it wasn't until she had passed that she actually seemed to notice him.

She turned, looking right where Antonin crouched in the shadow of the garbage can. Setting her bag down for the moment, she sketched a little wave. "Hi."

Antonin had forgotten to breathe. "Hi," he said with a gasp.

There was a long pause while they stared at each other. Finally the old woman spoke again, "I'll make tea." She headed to the other side of the courtyard, where a plastic sheet had been thrown over a collection of packing crates, forming a makeshift tent. "C'mon," she called over her shoulder as she raised a flap of plastic, "you're cold."

Antonin felt strangely empty inside, as if it didn't matter what he did, which was probably true. He got up and followed the crone, peering dubiously inside the tent. The floor was covered with numerous scraps of plastic, newspaper, and rags, and was reasonably dry.

The old woman lit the stub of a candle and set it in a perforated tuna can. From under a cardboard box she produced a small clay teapot and began filling it with dried leaves from a paper bag. "Come in, come in. I'm Mabel," she said.

"My name is Antonin." The candlelight was soft and inviting, and if he had to hide, at least he didn't have to hide alone. He crawled under the flap and settled himself in a corner beside a stack of Styrofoam packing trays. "I'm looking for my mother," he said.

Mabel nodded abstractly, placing a dented tin kettle over the candle flame. "People who are looking for other people find each other."

Antonin leaned back and pulled a musty pink blanket over his shoulders. "My mother is tall, with eyes like mine. She's beautiful. Her hair is dark like mine too. Her name is Rose." He looked at her hopefully, but got no reply.

Eventually she removed the kettle from the flame and poured steaming water into the teapot. Muttering under her breath, she swirled the water around in the pot and poured it into two cracked and mended cups. She handed one to Antonin.

Antonin sipped the warm liquid, his eyelids drooping. The tent was warm and comfortable, and he felt safe. He finished his cup and curled up on the ground, his head resting against Mabel's knee.

She took his cup in her dry, withered hands and peered intently at the residue of leaves on the bottom. "You'll find your mother," she said, "but lose her again." He barely heard her words as he drifted off to sleep.

* * *

Towards dawn Rose collapsed against a crumbling plaster wall. She'd looked everywhere, all night, and found no trace of Antonin anywhere in Tunis. It was as if he'd vanished into thin air.

She'd gone back to the new apartment and left word with the landlady to keep an eye out for him. Two hours ago she'd checked again. He'd never shown up. She even went back to the place she'd had with Dano, but it was totally deserted. All night long she'd wandered the streets, calling his name, and she never got any answer.

She knew all too well what would become of him, alone and lost in a big city. Dano's threat had not been idle by any means. Children were bought and sold on the black market all the time. After all, it had happened to her. She was the eldest daughter of a family with only one son, her brother Kelira. When she was thirteen, he developed malaria, and the only thing that could save him was some very expensive medicine. They had no money, but they had plenty of daughters.

She still remembered that day with profound bitterness. It was morning, and she'd gone to the well. When she returned, the woman was there, sitting at the shabby little table in their one-room house, drinking tea from their best cup. She reeked of filth and stale jasmine. Rouge highlighted her sunken cheeks, and her lips were painted dark red. She smiled, revealing a mouthful of rotten teeth. Her bony hands were encrusted with rings, their clawlike fingernails encircled with grime. "You say you want six hundred for her?" she said derisively to Rose's father. "She's as scrawny as a chicken."

He stood beside the stranger, gazing at Rose with blank, expressionless eyes. "I can't let you have her for less than five fifty."

On his sickbed Kelira groaned in protest. Her mother washed his forehead with cool water as tears streamed down her face. Rose called to her, but she would not look up. Her sisters sat huddled by the doorway, weeping and clinging to each other.

The stranger grunted, "For that price, I'll have to have a closer look," and in front of her entire family she proceeded to examine Rose from head to toe. She started with her hands, turning them over, noting the length of her fingers, the condition of her skin. She murmured approvingly at the texture of her hair. "Take off your dress," she said.

Rose backed away, shaking her head. She looked at her father; surely he would not allow his eldest daughter to be dishonored before his eyes. "Do what she says," he told her. In shock, burning with shame, Rose removed her shabby cotton dress.

The woman looked her over thoroughly and then stepped closer, until Rose could smell her stale breath. She grasped Rose's breasts in her calloused hands and kneaded them roughly. Rose sobbed and flinched away from her. "Ah, ah," she admonished, digging her fingernails into her shoulder, "you better get used to it."

She left no part of Rose's body untouched. Her dirty hands went everywhere, taking for themselves what had once been hers alone. At the time Rose thought she had been thoroughly violated. She thought she could suffer no greater humiliation. But she was wrong.

She'd been in the brothel three years when Dano found her. Although her customers often refused condoms, she'd somehow managed to avoid testing positive for AIDS. Out of the twenty or so girls she'd come in with, nine had been shipped away to death camps in the hills, never to be heard from again. She was on junk, of course. The only way to survive in a place like that was to lose everything, and live for junk. But Dano took her away from there, and at first she was happy with him.

When he wanted to make movies, she didn't think

anything of it. It seemed harmless enough, and if strangers were going to watch, well, it was better than having to sleep with them. Then she got pregnant, and Dano wanted her to have an abortion. She refused and secretly went to a doctor, who told her she'd lose her baby if she didn't get off heroin.

She quit her habit. She had to go into the hospital to do it, and she had to lie to Dano about it, but she did it. She could never decide which had been harder, getting off junk or going through labor. In her memories the two became one, an all-consuming struggle in which she won the only thing she'd ever cared about in her adult life, her son.

She remembered when he was born. After the toil and agony she'd held her little child in her arms. He was slimy with blood and mucus, but she clutched him to her, and he'd taken her breast. She'd laughed out loud, she was so surprised by her joy. She was proud of him, and of herself too.

Antonin changed everything. For the first time she understood why Dano had pressured her to have an abortion. When it was just her, it was easy to say, So what? and do whatever he wanted her to do, but everything she did affected her child, and she could not say, So what? about him.

Having someone to defend made it easier for her to stand up to Dano, and gradually she began to see him for what he was. He wasn't really any different from the woman who had bought her from her family. A little more charming on the surface perhaps, but still a bully. He had bought her from the brothel, and to him that meant she was his property. She never saw any of the money from the movies they made. He expected her to sleep with whoever he told her to, he beat her if she didn't, and when it suited him, he abandoned her for weeks on end.

Leaving him had been like kicking another habit, but this time the cost was more than she was willing to pay. Her son was the only person in the world she cared about. Now she'd lost him, and she had nothing else.

Rose leaned against a wall and wept with exhaustion and grief. It was too much. The world was too much. In fury she pounded the brick wall of the restaurant with her fist. "No!" she cried. "You cannot have my son!" she screamed at the sky, at the world. "I will not let you have my son!"

Antonin awoke to the sound of his mother shouting somewhere nearby. Beside him Mabel slept, snoring softly, her mouth hanging open. Carefully he sat up, rubbed the sleep from his eyes, and crept away, fearful that if he awakened her, she'd make him stay. He was grateful for her hospitality, but he wanted his mother, and she could only be a block or two away.

It was just barely dawn. In the dim, early light he saw a pair of dogs nosing around the garbage cans where he'd hidden the night before. He ran down the alleyway, hoping his mother had not moved on. He hadn't heard her voice since the shouts that woke him.

Towards the mouth of the alleyway he slowed. He'd been too groggy with sleep to discern her words, but it sounded like she was yelling at someone. Perhaps Dano was still with her. Uncertain, he peered around the corner and saw his mother alone, squatting against a wall.

She looked up, and her face was red with tears. "Antonin!" she cried, rushing forward to take him up in her wonderful arms. She clutched him to her, sobbing with relief. "I was afraid you were lost, that I wouldn't find you. Are you all right?"

"Yes," he whispered in her ear. "What happened to Daddy?"

She set him down again and knelt before him, her hands gripping his shoulders. "Daddy's not going to bother us anymore, darling. We're going to leave this place. We'll go some place where we can start a whole new life."

"Where will we go?"

She paused with that thoughtful look on her face. Antonin knew that whatever she decided, it would be practical. His mother was very smart, and practical. "I have enough money for plane tickets to Europe. We'll go to Amsterdam. A lot of Indonesians live there, and it's close to France and Belgium, even Italy is not that far. If we don't like it, we can go to one of those other places, okay?"

He nodded, and she stood up. Taking his hand, she led him down the street as the sun rose, its golden light painting the cracked pavement with brilliance.

FIX

Like an animal afraid of the light, Dano scurried into the darkness of an abandoned alleyway. Out of the scrutiny of the halogen streetlamps, he leaned against a wall, gasping for breath, trying in vain to quell his panic. He couldn't see a thing. His left eye was clouded with tears, which spilled down his face to work like acid on his burns. His right eye . . . *Oh God.* He sobbed silently as he lifted his burned, trembling hand to his ruined face.

One small corner of his brain, still untouched by the pain that ate away at his consciousness, was still thinking. Like a conversation that he was not part of, Dano heard his thoughts from a distance. He didn't know what they were saying. With his good hand he felt his way along the damp, crumbling concrete wall and walked onwards.

He became aware of the sound of trickling water and of his own scorching thirst. He tried to hurry a little. His foot caught on a pile of rotting garbage, and he tripped, barely saving himself from falling by grasping a drainpipe that had broken away from the wall. Runoff from the pipe trickled into a shallow, muddy pool in the center of the alley. Whimpering, Dano knelt beside it. The water was filthy, and it stank, but he drank it anyway.

Shaking, he removed his fine linen shirt, soaked it in the foul water, and wrung it out. Gingerly he wrapped the wet shirt around his face, biting his lips and crying out as the cloth came into contact with his burns.

He slumped against the wall and tried to stop his body from shaking. This was bad. His face was messed up. His eye . . . He was hurt bad. She'd gotten him right in the face with that oil.

Her face came back to him clearly now: round and soft, a moon face. Her eyes dilated with fear and anger. Dano shivered inside, remembering the way she'd looked at him, like you'd look at a roach or a rat. Something to be gotten rid of.

There was still a part of him that couldn't believe it had happened. How could she do something like that to him, after all he'd done for her? She knew he needed the money for coke. Cocaine. If he had some right now, he'd be able to handle this. He'd think of something clever and pay that bitch back. But it was hopeless. He owed everybody money, and now he looked like the Phantom of Hollywood.

It was no use. He'd have to go to Edgerton and hope for the best. He'd helped him out before, wired him money after he got knifed in New York. It was a long shot, his only chance. He struggled to his feet once more and made his way gradually through the backstreets and alleys.

It was almost morning when he reached the warehouse. His mind was numb with pain and weariness. Dano staggered to the side door. It was sturdy and anonymous; metal painted white. Bolted to the wall above it was a floodlight, and next to that, a security camera. As he approached, the flood came on, bathing him in white radiance. Instinctively Dano hid his face from the gaze of the camera. He took a ragged breath and knocked on the door.

It opened, and a tall, wiry guy in a leather jacket stepped through and grabbed Dano by the front of his T-shirt. His other hand swung back, ready to deliver a hideous blow to the side of his face.

"Wait!" he screamed, "I'm Dano, a business associate of Edgerton's. Please, just ask him if he wants to see me. If he doesn't, then you can do whatever you want to me." Dano looked frantically into his dark and expressionless eyes. "Please."

The doorman released Dano with a smirk and a shove, and shut the door on him. As he waited, sweat trickled down the side of his face, stinging his blisters. He had no idea how long it had taken him to walk here; it had seemed like days, the longest days of his life. He would be in Edgerton's hands now; there was nothing Dano could offer him, no deal to be cut. Nothing Dano could do to save his life, but this.

The door opened again, and Dano was ushered down a long, narrow hallway to a tiny office crowded with stacks of videodiscs. Behind a large, Formica-topped desk sat Edgerton. He was a big guy, maybe six five, and he weighed at least two eighty. He had a large, round head, covered with closely cropped grey stubble. He watched placidly as Dano stumbled into the room and took a seat. His hairless face was patient and bland, but his eyes burned with anger at this inconvenience.

He nodded to the doorman, who stepped behind Dano and began to remove the dirty cloth from his face. In some spots blood had soaked into the shirt and dried against his burns. Dano could not prevent himself from whimpering as it was pulled off.

Edgerton whistled. "You're a real mess, Danforth. Who did this to you, or did you go bobbing for french fries?"

Speech was painful. "Rose," Dano mumbled. "She fucked up."

Edgerton raised his eyebrows. "Did she? Or did you? You know, you're becoming a real pain in the ass, Danforth. First you tag along to New York and cause a ruckus there—"

"That chick didn't know what she was doing," said Dano.

"Why is it every time a broad is too tough for you, you say she fucked up? Christ! If I wanted a problem child, I'd adopt a Lithuanian. This is ridiculous!"

Dano shook his head. "Don't worry, Rose is out of the project. I won't work with her."

For a moment Edgerton stared at him in amazement, and then his broad face dissolved into laughter. "*You* won't work with *her?* I got news for you, Danforth, ain't nobody gonna be working with you. I'd have to pay the customers just to look at you! I mean, we are talking ugly, and that's after those burns heal. Right now you're a passable imitation of a creole gumbo." He shook his head. "Shit, what am I supposed to do with you, huh?"

"My face hurts."

"Yeah, I bet it does."

Dano started to cry. "Please."

Edgerton threw his hands up in disgust. "Ah, fuck. Clyde, poke him, and then take him to the doctor. I want him out of here."

The doorman left, returning quickly with a hypo kit. He tied a rubber tube tight around Dano's upper arm.

"What are you giving me?" asked Dano, although he didn't really care.

"Heroin," said Edgerton. "You're about to start on a whole new brand of desperation, my boy. If you think things are looking up, you're wrong. But Clyde here is gonna take you to a doctor friend of mine." He smirked. "Guy owes me a favor."

The needle bit into his flesh, and immediately Dano felt better. The pain faded away, and he felt a deep sense of relaxation, as if he were floating up above the world, too far away for it to reach him. He wasn't worried about his face anymore. The doctor would take care of him, that's what Edgerton had said. He gazed at him with half-lidded eyes. "You have to get another girl," he murmured.

"No. No, we don't even need girls anymore." Edgerton's voice rippled over him like warm water. "I just made a deal with the gentleman you're going to see. He makes robots that fuck. They're just like real girls, Danforth, but they smile all the time, and they don't lip back. Ain't progress grand?"

Dano found himself in a small white cubicle, his face wrapped in bandages. He sat on a cheap plastic chair. An examining table stood on the opposite side of the room, its vinyl cushion only partially obscured by sterile tissue paper; by all appearances the same kind as he was wearing. Through the diminishing fog of Edgerton's heroin Dano felt the coldness of the chair beneath his butt. There was a draft in this room, no question about it. He shut his legs and folded his arms across his chest.

The pain in his face was returning as well. To distract himself he planted his bare feet firmly on the cold, slick tile of the floor and studied a faded plaque on the wall. "Love is . . . ," it said in flowing script, and in the picture a couple walked along the beach at sunset. It reminded Dano of the next film he'd been planning to do with Rose. It was going to start with a sweeping montage of her wading naked in the ocean, the camera panning across the landscape, arriving at her revolving body from a different angle every time.

The door to the cubicle opened, briefly admitting the gurgle and hum of the laboratory outside. A small man in a white coat entered. He was bald and aging, probably about seventy, with brown skin. He wore round spectacles, and a stethoscope hung around his neck in useless reassurance. He smiled at Dano and offered his hand. "Hello, Dano, I'm Dr. Rahul."

Dano nodded silently and shook his hand. He wanted to ask the doctor if he could help him, if he could make him handsome again, if he could fix his eye, but afraid of the answers, he didn't ask any of the questions.

"Well, let's take a look at you. Hop up onto the examination table, please."

Dano did, and the doctor took his pulse and listened to his heart. "I was told you were given sedation a few hours ago, but I think it might be advisable for you to have another shot now. I have to remove these bandages, and in order to examine your burn thoroughly, I'm going to have to do some poking around."

Dano nodded his head and watched as Dr. Rahul prepared his injection. "You'll be in a relaxed state, you won't feel any pain, but you'll remain conscious, so I can ask you questions if I need to." He made Dano lie down and rubbed the inside of his elbow with alcohol. The quick sting of the needle was soon replaced by a flood of euphoria. Dano felt as if he were floating, and it was only the particleboard tiles of the ceiling above him that prevented him from disappearing into the sky.

Vaguely, as if from another room, or another life, Dano heard the soft clucking of the doctor as his bandages were removed. "Hmm, this is quite serious. Most of the facial tissue can be repaired with skin grafts; the eye, however . . ." His words drifted through Dano, leaving no impression at all. He felt him prodding at his face, knew it should be hurting him, but he didn't care. He didn't care at all. He was looking at the plaque upon the wall. He was on the beach with Rose, the surf caressing their bodies as they rolled across the sand.

Sometime later—it seemed he'd been hours upon that eternally sunset shore—he became aware of the doctor once more. He'd asked a question, and it was the expectant silence that followed it, rather than his voice, that roused Dano from his dreaming. "What?"

"I'm afraid your eye is beyond repair, but if you like, I can provide you with a prosthesis."

"Prosthesis? Then my eye—"

Dr. Rahul nodded. "It's inoperable, too much damage."

"I'll be half blind."

"Au contraire, mon ami. You'll see very well. Of course, it's up to you; I could simply clean out your socket and fit you with a glass eye, if you prefer."

Dano shook his head. "No. If I can see . . ."

"Yes, you will. It's a surgical procedure to implant the prosthesis; I'll need you to sign a consent form." He moved to a cabinet standing against the wall and took out a clipboard and pen. Dano could hardly hold the pen, and the doctor had to support the clipboard for him, but he managed to scrawl his name across the bottom of the form.

"Excellent. Now if you'll excuse me, I'll be right back." And he disappeared once more into the gurgling place beyond the door.

When he returned, he carried something pale and wet in a Plexiglas tray. "I'm afraid there's been a run on blues in the last few weeks. The closest I could get is green. I hope you don't mind."

Mutely Dano shook his head.

Dr. Rahul stepped closer, lifting the thing out of its tray with tweezers and holding it up to the light. "You're a very fortunate man, Dano; this is an expensive procedure. Of course, I'm only too happy to help out the friend of a business associate, and then, one never knows, perhaps someday you will be in a position to do me a favor in return, eh?" Pale fluid dripped from the eye as the green iris, pierced with its black pupil, swiveled around to stare at Dano with a cold, unblinking gaze.

THE CHARNEL HOUSE

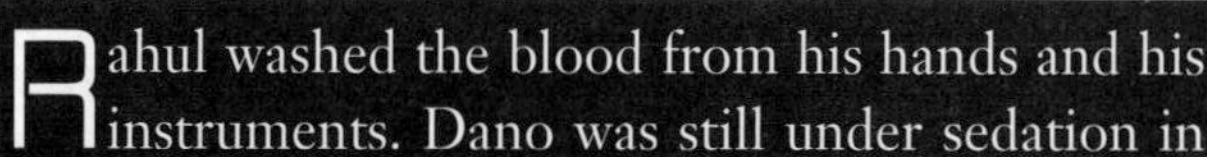
Rahul washed the blood from his hands and his instruments. Dano was still under sedation in the operating room. It would be hours before he came out of it, and then there would be a period of recuperation that would last several weeks.

The skin grafts had gone well. Of course, he would never look exactly as he had before being burned, but he'd get used to that, as well as to other things.

Despite Dano's disfigurement, Rahul recognized him as the other player in that VisuAll fiasco. He took a perverse satisfaction in giving him the eye he did.

He'd lied to him. He had plenty of blue eyes, but the one he had given him was an experimental prosthesis, designed to equip its wearer with telescopic sight.

He'd been working on it off and on for several months but had needed a test subject. Edgerton had asked him to treat Dano as a favor in return for VisuAll letting him have Magnolia.

But Rahul did not have her. He'd lost her in St. Petersburg. As far as he could tell, VisuAll had had nothing to do with that, but just the same, this was a favor asked in return for one that had never really been received.

Edgerton had let it be known that Dano was of no great significance to him, and had in fact expressed gratitude to Rahul for getting him out of his hair.

Under these circumstances it seemed fair, even politic, for Rahul to take what advantage he could of the situation. And the fact that Dano was Magnolia's aggressor and victim added a delightful note of irony to the entire situation.

He had watched the tape of their rendezvous many times, often freezing the picture at the point when she looked up into the camera lens above the bed and out, into the eyes of her viewers.

He had received a gaze like that once before, when he was a child in Calcutta. He used to run about the streets of the city, for which his mother was forever admonishing him, but he could not be prevailed upon, through words or blows, to stop.

There was simply so much to see. Around every corner something was happening, an argument or a crime, and Rahul stuck his nose into everything. He was at least as intimate as his grandmother with the gossip of the neighborhood, and often he ranged farther, to markets and docks and, once, the temple of Kali in the south end of the city.

It was a considerable distance from his father's house, and in truth he had not meant to go there. He'd been watching a beggar extort money from a shopkeeper by refusing to remove his diseased body from beside the door or to desist in haranguing all potential customers as they passed, until the man paid him off. After witnessing this spectacle of enterprise, Rahul had boarded a bus, which would have taken him back home, but it was a warm day, and he'd been walking about for many hours, and the lurching gait of the bus lulled him to sleep.

When he awoke and realized he'd missed his stop, he got off the bus and found himself in a part of the city he'd never been to before. He wandered aimlessly among the streets, where he found many of the same spectacles that greeted him on a daily basis in his own neighborhood—market women arguing with customers, children cajoling recalcitrant oxen, and pickpockets shadowing marks—and then he rounded a corner and saw the temple.

It was a large complex of buildings, its stone walls carved with images of deities and heroes. Rahul went up the broad, shallow steps to the archway of the main building and stepped inside.

It was a charnel house, where people brought their animals to slaughter them and offer the entrails on the altar, which was caked with the ashes and fat of previous devotions. The stench of the place was a palpable thing, an invisible wall that greeted him beyond the wall of darkness.

Someone was slaughtering a goat, slitting its throat with a long knife, and as the death scream of the animal stabbed his ears, his eyes were riveted by something else, the figure of the goddess in the alcove above the altar.

Here, finally, was a sight that brought him up short, that stopped his eyes in their endless gobbling of spectacles.

She was black, her form shadowed and kindled by the light of the fire. She was dancing balanced on one leg, her four arms outstretched. Four hands, one brandishing a knife, one proffering a bowl, one dangling a human head by its hair, the fourth raised in benediction.

She looked at him with eyes of lifeless plaster, but her blessing burned through them, and into him, to sear his heart with the terrible truth of what life is.

He had not imagined that there was anything else but the succession of events that was life. A parade of experiences following one another like a string of pearls, marking segments of time. He had believed it would go on forever, but as he hung in the darkness of her eyes he felt the end of the thread, felt the pearls of existence slipping off it to disappear into the darkness outside of time.

That was the message of the goddess in the temple. A message also delivered to him more recently, through the gaze of a girl in a slash porn flick.

He was still bitter at her loss. She had worn the fierceness of death on her skin. Her template would have made a fine assassin, but even more, the unpredictability of her behavior held the promise of something that had been absent from all but the first of his efforts with humanoid life-forms—individuality.

THE NATURE OF SMOKE

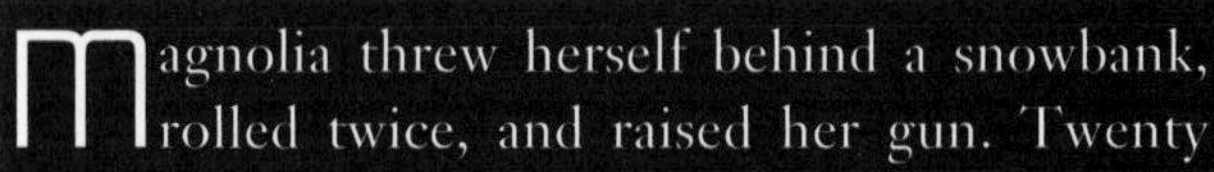

Magnolia threw herself behind a snowbank, rolled twice, and raised her gun. Twenty yards to her left, Spider darted through the trees, no more than a shadow among the twisted branches. She tracked his movement and fired. The shell exploded on impact in a burst of red paint. She'd missed, and a young pine wore a splash of crimson on its trunk at chest level.

A footstep crunched in the snow behind her. She rolled to the right, and an explosion of blue soaked the snow where her head had been. It was Dex; a streak of yellow on his shoulder and another on his thigh testifying that he had already been hit twice by Spider. Magnolia fired at him. Red paint splattered across the front of his armored snowsuit. "Urk!" he croaked, clutching his chest dramatically. His eyes rolled back in their sockets as he staggered and fell backwards in the snow, arms and legs outstretched.

Out of the corner of her eye Magnolia caught movement.

She spun to face Spider, but he was nowhere in sight. Crouching behind her snowbank, she scanned the trees. Spider loved to fight among the trees, and with his snowsuit dialed to dark he virtually disappeared among them. To her left, from behind a midsized pine, drifted a wisp of vapor. Magnolia smiled to herself. In this cold, not even Spider could hide his breath.

Slowly, silently, she sidled to the left. There, a thin wedge of Spider's body was just visible behind the trunk, his long nose and angular cheek pale against the bark. He leaned forward, preparing to fire, and in that instant Magnolia fired on him.

She missed again. Somehow Spider had managed to fade behind the tree just in time to avoid her shot. Cursing, Magnolia dived and rolled as yellow paint smeared the snow just to the left of her head. Looking over her shoulder, she saw Spider running through the stand of pines. He was changing position; this was her chance. She got to her knees and steadied her aim for a volley of shots designed to herd him out into the open.

The minicom in her ear squawked, and Kelira's smooth voice spoke, "Okay, that's enough for now. Come on in for debriefing." Dex picked himself up out of the snow and joined Magnolia as she trudged towards the house. They'd been out here for almost two hours. She knew she should be tired, but her thwarted attack on Spider had her pretty keyed up.

As they approached the house he filtered out of the trees and ambled towards her, his eyes gleaming with insolence. "Not bad, baby, but you still couldn't peg me!" he crowed. "You know, I really liked the way you took that dive there at the end." He flung a long wiry arm around her shoulders. Magnolia's jaw clenched, and her hand strayed wistfully to the butt of her paint gun, but Spider was, as always, oblivious to the very thin ice upon which he walked. "Maybe when we hit the showers you can show me a few pointers." He grinned as his hand slipped down her side and around, cupping her breast through the padded snowsuit.

Magnolia pulled her gun. Turning, she struck Spider across the jaw with the muzzle. He reeled under the unexpected blow, his face gone slack and stupid. At this range, and on unarmored flesh, even a paint bullet could do considerable damage. Magnolia aimed at his long skinny nose and fired.

Dex gasped, and Spider staggered, putting his hands up to his face. It was difficult to distinguish between red paint and blood, but she was almost certain that she'd broken his nose. Magnolia turned her back on them and went into the house.

On her way upstairs she passed Kelira, who was running down the broad, red-carpeted steps with a medical kit in his hand, his face tight with urgency. Of course, he'd seen the whole thing. He'd wired miniaturized cameras to their suits and watched the melee from a portable monitor. Kelira saw everything that happened out there from three different viewpoints. He glanced at her, his eyes clouded with a mixture of admiration and dread. "I guess you've made your point," he muttered, and hurried on to repair Spider's face.

After showering, Magnolia paced restlessly around her sparse bedroom. The walls stared blankly at her, offering no suggestions. Music from Cid's stereo reached her ears faintly; a soft, soothing pulse of rhythm. Magnolia threw on a shirt and a pair of jeans, went out in the hallway, and knocked at Cid's door. "It's me," she said.

"C'mon in." Cid was lying on her bed with an incense burner balanced on her stomach. A wisp of smoke trailed delicately up towards the ceiling.

"What are you doing?"

"I'm watching smoke." She waved Magnolia over with

one pale, skinny arm. "Look at that." She pointed to a corkscrewing plume of smoke. "See the way it spirals? It turns in upon itself and spreads itself outwards, until it fills all the available surface area, which, given the nature of smoke, is infinite." She picked up the incense burner, placed it carefully on the nightstand, and rolled over to face Magnolia. She had ashes on her T-shirt, and her eyes were shining. "Smoke fills the boundaries of the air and maps the surfaces that are not there."

Magnolia laughed. "Who said that?"

"I did." Cid smiled. "How was your melee?"

"I broke Spider's nose."

Cid gasped and hid her smile with a hand. "On purpose?"

Grinning, Magnolia leaned against the wall. "Of course on purpose. You got a joint?"

"Yeah, here." Cid reached into an ashtray on the floor and came up with a half-smoked joint.

Magnolia lit it. "I got him at close range with the paint gun," she said, speaking through a haze of smoke.

"Dang!"

"Yeah. I passed Kelira on my way up here. He had the med kit with him."

Cid leaned forward, looking up at her eagerly. "So what did he say to you?"

"Nothing." She shrugged. "I think he's afraid of me."

"I don't blame him," Cid said. "I'm glad I'm not involved with that combat stuff."

Magnolia laughed. "Oh, yeah, you'd rather lie around and watch smoke."

"Hey." She smiled, her blue eyes dancing. "Smoke is a turbulent, dynamical system. It adheres to the laws of chaos."

"How can chaos be a law?" Magnolia asked before she could stop herself. She didn't like to show her ignorance around Cid, but Cid made that very difficult to do. She knew so much, about things Magnolia had never even dreamt existed. That was why she hung out with her so much. Being with Cid was like being in another world. "Have you ever heard of chaos theory?" asked Cid.

"What?"

Cid sat up and brushed the ashes off her T-shirt. Patting the bed, she said, "Sit down, I want to show you something."

Magnolia sat on the bed, leaning her back against the wall. Cid opened a drawer in her desk and rummaged around until she came up with a CD in a plastic envelope. "This is a hologram of the Mandelbrot set." She slipped the disc into one of her computer's drives, powered up the monitor, and tapped out incantations on the keyboard for a few minutes.

A squat white box perched atop her dresser came to life with a low hum and a single red light on its front. And the next thing Magnolia knew, she was looking at a bulbous black form, its edges ringed in fire, hanging in the air before her. The shape was vaguely reminiscent of a bug. Its main body consisted of a large cleft circle, like a heart lying on its side. Only instead of a point on its other end, there was another, smaller circle attached to it, and attached to that circle, yet another circle, smaller still. As Magnolia continued viewing the shape, she realized its fuzzy edges were really countless smaller stacked circles, sprouting off of the sides of the main form.

"This graph is formed by feeding a simple equation of the complex plane in upon itself about a gazillion times. Even though the equation itself only contains two variables, it produces the most complex object in mathematics. Watch what happens as we get closer to it." Cid tapped away at the computer again, and the view shifted, moving closer to one of the set's fuzzy, fiery edges.

The stacked circles grew larger, until Magnolia could see that they were all versions of the two circles attached to the end of the nonheart, complete with circles of their own, sprouting off their sides.

But something even more interesting was happening in the fiery border that surrounded them. Colors bloomed in intense profusion, ranging from yellow to red to blue. They formed twisting patterns unlike anything Magnolia had ever seen before.

Cid continued to guide their view, focusing first on a spiraling, red-orange tendril fringed with cresting waves, and then on a vast, blue-green peacock feather with the blackness of infinity at its center. Magnolia saw flowers, stars, and networks of branching nerves, and still they fell into the brilliant complexity of the thing. It seemed to go on forever, constantly changing, but always recycling itself. Each detail was somehow constructed of numerous tiny versions of itself, and each of those presumably made up of still smaller but similar patterns, going on forever, smaller and smaller.

Eventually they wound up in a circle of undulating palm trees, their starting point far behind them and forgotten in an infinity of detail. But as they descended the curving trunks a pool of blackness became visible in the center of that charmed grove, a cleft circle with other circles, large and small, bulging off of it on every side. The bug that they had started with was back somehow, smaller, but containing in miniature every detail they'd explored and the countless ones they hadn't.

Magnolia was surprised by the overwhelming sense of reassurance its appearance brought, as if she'd been wandering lost, had finally spied a familiar landmark, and now knew the way home.

Cid gave a final few taps to her keyboard, and the image disappeared.

"Wow," said Magnolia. If there really was another world that Cid lived in, she had the feeling she'd just seen it.

Cid switched off the power on her computer and came back to sit cross-legged beside Magnolia. "That's one example of a chaotic system. The mathematical term for it is a fractal. There are lots of other fractals, and even more examples of chaos in the real world. As a matter of fact, that's what the real world is mostly made up of—chaos."

"You're telling me," Magnolia said, laughing.

"But did you notice, no matter how strange the pattern got, there was always something familiar about it?"

"Like at the end, when the bug showed up again?"

"Exactly. See, no matter how complex things get, there's always a pattern. It's just that most of the time we don't have the equipment or the perspective to recognize it." Cid's eyes glittered in a manic, unfocused way, as if she were seeing those glorious patterns once again. "In fact, I think that's what beauty really is. It's symmetry. Adherence to a pattern. If there is an inherent morality to the structure of the universe, it's probably aesthetic."

"So if you can use a computer to describe how something works, then you can predict what it'll do next, right?"

"Actually, no. Chaotic systems are unpredictable because they're so sensitive. Take the weather, for instance; the fluttering of a butterfly's wings in Australia can cause a hurricane off the coast of Florida a month later. Because of the way these systems feed off of their own output, even the most minor change to the input will multiply rapidly, producing wildly divergent results."

"Then they're random," blurted Magnolia, thinking she was beginning to get it.

Cid shook her head. "No, because no matter what those results are, they will fit the overall pattern of the system. Even though the equations that govern it never produce exactly the same values twice, those values still fall within certain parameters."

"But if it's never the same value, how can there be a pattern?"

Cid picked up a piece of orange-and-green telephone wire and started bending it into a spiral. "It's simply ordered in a way that our unaided senses are unable to perceive. In fact, until the advent of computer graphics, phenomena that didn't conform to linear solutions were considered just too difficult to examine in detail. They were approximated or ignored. Now, whole fields of research that were out of reach are open for exploration, and even if we can't predict the behavior of weather, or the stock market, or insect populations, at least we can gain an understanding of each system as a whole. Know what its shape is."

Magnolia was lost. She could hold her own against creeps like Spider and Dano, she could survive the squats, and even escape, but she couldn't grasp what Cid was talking about. She felt as if she were being asked to repair a transistor with only a hammer for a tool. She was out of her depth, marooned in a world she knew nothing about. "You said that the real world is chaotic."

"Yeah."

"Can you find out the shape of life?"

Cid smiled at her in silence for a moment before answering. "Not yet, but I'm working on it."

Magnolia lit the roach again, took one last hit off of it, and tossed it back into the ashtray. The world Cid lived in seemed to have different rules for the way people lived their lives. Rules that ran along the lines of "Do what you want."

What she wanted was not something Magnolia had really asked herself much. She didn't know how. But Cid always seemed to be doing just what she wanted, and nothing else, either. It fascinated Magnolia, even more than this strange chaos she described.

Cid was still playing with the telephone wire, her hair, soft and fine, falling across her face as she worked.

Magnolia wanted to understand the things Cid talked about. She wanted to know what made them interesting in the first place. She wanted to know more about this world that Cid was living in. She wanted to live there herself. Magnolia couldn't imagine saying any of these things and being understood, so she leaned over, took Cid's warm, golden face in her hands, and kissed her.

gauze and sympathy

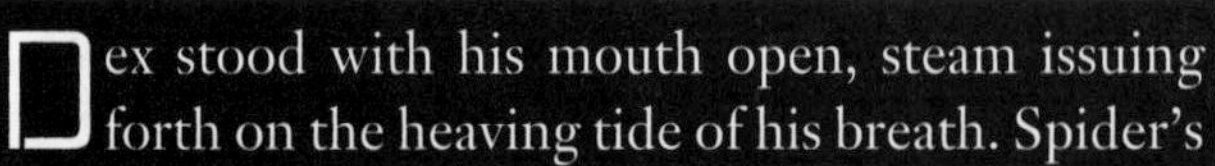

Dex stood with his mouth open, steam issuing forth on the heaving tide of his breath. Spider's face was splattered with red paint and blood. His hands covered his injured nose, so Dex couldn't see how serious the damage was. Spider took an unsteady step towards the house, and Dex was by his side, guiding him with an arm around his waist.

Kelira met them at the door, and together he and Dex ushered Spider into the kitchen. They seated him at the table, and Kelira opened up the med kit and took out several packets of sterile gauze. "Put your hands down, Spider. Let me take a look at it."

Reluctantly Spider took his hands away from his face. He flinched as Kelira dabbed at the wound, clearing away the paint and excess blood. It suddenly occurred to Dex that it would hurt a lot, to have paint in an open wound.

"Well, at least your nose is still there," said Kelira. "It's broken, and the left nostril is torn, but there's no irreparable damage."

None to his face, thought Dex, but his pride was wounded, and knowing Spider, it would take a lot more than gauze and sympathy to heal that.

"I'll have to straighten it out, and you'll need stitches, but I should be able to sew it up in a way that won't leave much of a scar. You won't be very pretty for the next month or so, but after that you'll hardly know it ever happened."

Kelira was wrong. Spider wouldn't forget it until the score was evened. Magnolia may have thought she'd taken care of her problems with him, but Dex knew this was only the beginning.

Carefully Kelira laid his thumbs on either side of Spider's crooked nose and pushed it back into position with a sudden jerk.

Spider screamed, a short, shrill sound, strangled off at the end. Tears streamed down his face. "I'm going to kill that bitch," he muttered, his speech muddled by the swelling of his jaw.

"I know you're in pain," said Kelira, "and I'm not trying to justify what Magnolia did. But you pushed her. You know you did."

Spider's dark eyes glistened with tears and hatred. "It was a joke for chrissakes! I wasn't going to hurt her or anything."

"Oh come on, Spider. You knew she didn't like it, but you kept it up anyway. Last week, when you grabbed her ass during that sparring match, did you think she was amused?"

In spite of his pain, Spider cracked a grin and shrugged. He was quite a sight, his face wet with tears and blood, his jaw swollen and bruised, and through it all, that maniac grin. He wasn't a bit sorry; he didn't begin to conceive that his injuries were in any part due to his own actions. He wore them proudly, like a badge. Just like when they played hockey in

Saskatoon, and he'd do time in the penalty box for fighting. Dex always suspected he was disappointed when he didn't have any marks from a fight, as if he wanted the proof of his courage carved upon his flesh for all to see.

"You've been up here with Ms. Wujcik too long," said Kelira, continuing his lecture in vain. "You've forgotten what real women are like."

Spider's defiant grin faded, and he eyed Kelira coldly. "At least I still know the difference between pussy and my hand."

Kelira frowned in annoyance. "I've got to sew up your nose now. I don't suppose you want any novocreme on it before I start?"

"What, do you think I'm crazy?"

"Could be."

Apparently even macho demonstrations had their limits, because Spider allowed Kelira to smear his nose with anesthetic before sewing it up. When he was done, Kelira handed him a tube of antibiotic ointment. "Put this goop on your nose at least twice a day and try to keep it clean, okay?"

Spider hung his head and nodded in false humility. "Whatever you say, boss."

Without another word Kelira gathered up his medical supplies and split.

"Well." Spider's stitches made a blood black line curving from the outer corner of his nostril to the center of his nose. Somehow it gave the illusion of that nostril being perpetually flared in anger. "Looks like our boy is sweet on one of his trainees, and it ain't either of us."

"Maybe." Maybe he's just trying to give her an even break, thought Dex, but he knew enough to shut up after the maybe part.

"What's she doing here, anyway?" Spider unscrewed the

cap on the tube of ointment and squeezed a dollop onto his finger.

"What do you mean?"

"I mean she doesn't have a job." He winced as he gingerly applied antibiotic to his stitches. "Oh, she's training with us, but that's strictly extracurricular. It's just something we do because there is absolutely fucking nothing to do up here. But we were hired as maintenance men. That's why we're here, to maintain. What's she supposed to be doing, huh?"

"You have a point, Spider."

"Damn straight I have a point. There's something fishy about that chick. I mean, Kelira tells us she's coming, and then 'Bam!' she's here the next day. Just like that, and we never hear a word about it from Rahul."

"Kelira said that Rahul wanted her here so she could train with us."

"Yeah, 'Kelira said.' I'm willing to bet that Rahul doesn't know dick about it. Kelira's got her here so he can fuck her, or something. I'll find out. And then we'll see how Rahul feels about his security chief sneaking around behind his back. Could be some room for advancement in this organization after all."

"You're brilliant," said Dex.

"Yes, but I'll need your help, buddy."

So here it was. The point in the conversation when Spider would ask him to do something. He'd known it was coming. It was inevitable in a situation like this. Just as it was inevitable that Dex would do what Spider asked, whatever it was. He always did. It was probably what their whole association was built upon. Dex had long ago given up pretending, even to himself, that things were any other way between them. "What do you need me to do?"

"Keep an eye on her. See where she goes, who she hangs

out with around here. I can't do it, because if she comes across me in the hallway, or I happen to wander into the video room while she's there, she'll think I'm harassing her. But you can get away with it. She won't think twice about running into you."

Of course not, Dex thought bitterly. After all, who was he?

Spider went on, oblivious to his friend's chagrin. "Then, once we know her habits, we can best decide where to plant this." He pointed at the minicam still attached to his snowsuit.

Dex laughed. "You're a sick motherfucker, you know that?"

"You're too kind."

"But won't Kelira notice it's missing?"

"I'll tell him I lost it in the snow."

Dex contemplated that for a moment. "Still, it's just an eyeball. You need the monitor to translate the signal."

Spider's sly smile spread across his face like oil on water. "I think I can manage that. It strikes me that Kelira has a few things on his mind lately. I'm willing to bet he won't notice it missing for a couple of days, and hopefully that will be long enough."

GODDESS 101

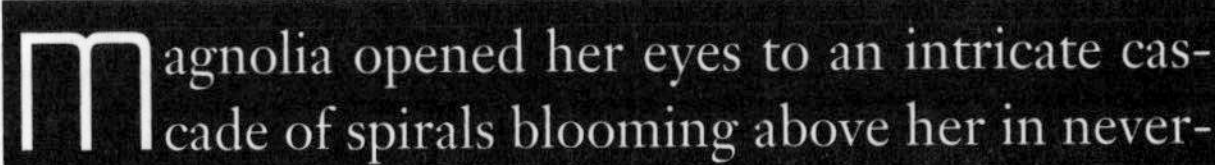

Magnolia opened her eyes to an intricate cascade of spirals blooming above her in neverending variations. It was the phase space holograph for the work Cid was doing with Tumcari. She must have turned it on sometime during the night. It looked like an orgasm, she thought, and she rolled over to face Cid.

She was still sleeping. Her eyes darted behind the delicate veils of her eyelids, dreaming. Magnolia wondered what sorts of dreams *Cid* had; someone who talked in dreams, someone who coaxed them to hover in midair, who wove them with her fingers and strewed them with her mind. She must go to the place that she came from, thought Magnolia, to the Land of Only-Doing-What-You-Feel-Like. She reached out and carefully laid her fingertips on Cid's closed eyes, as if she could feel what they saw.

Cid sucked her breath in sharply and jerked backwards,

suddenly awake. "What are you doing?" She laughed sleepily.

Magnolia blushed. "I touched your eyes. You were dreaming."

Cid smiled and drew her close. "I was dreaming of you."

Magnolia squirmed happily in the warm, astonishing tangle of Cid's arms and legs. "That's dumb," she protested.

Cid laid her head in the hollow of Magnolia's shoulder and gazed up at her in innocence. "Why?"

"Because I'm here already."

"Mmm. I suppose that makes sense." Cid's eyes seemed to look right inside Magnolia's head, to see her thoughts and ask her questions she didn't know how to answer. She reached forward and ran her fingers along the side of Magnolia's face, over a bruise on her cheekbone she'd gotten sparring with Kelira. "I dreamt you were the Goddess Kali," she said.

"The who?"

"An Indian deity. She's known as the creator and destroyer of all life." Cid glanced at the fractal that seethed above them. "The formless ocean of blood that exists between the destruction of one world and the creation of another. The primal embodiment of chaos."

Magnolia smiled ironically. "Chaos again, huh?"

"Here." Cid squeezed her thigh. "I'll show you something." She got up and crossed to the desk, her naked body gleaming in the multicolored light of the holo. She rummaged around in one of the desk drawers and pulled out a disk. She inserted it in a drive, switched off the holograph, and turned on the middle monitor on the desk. "Come here." She held the chair out for Magnolia. "This is a picture of Kali."

Magnolia sat down, her eyes fixed by an image of a naked woman with blue skin and four arms, wearing a string of skulls around her neck and a string of severed hands around her waist. The blue woman crouched over the body of a man, engulfing his penis with her vagina and eating his intestines. "Shit, Cid, whose guts was I eating?"

"Oh, that's Shiva, he's dead. I'll call up the text for you, and you can read about it."

"That's okay, I've seen enough." Magnolia stood up quickly, her face burning. She didn't want Cid to know that she could barely read. To cover her embarrassment, she wrapped her newfound lover in her arms and kissed her passionately.

Cid's mouth was open and wet, her hair like soft, spring sunshine streaming through her fingers. Magnolia ran her tongue down the silky, tan-gold skin of her neck to her small round breasts. Her shame eased, and the heat in her face traveled down her body like a warm river. As they stumbled backwards to the bed together, she glanced once more at the image that glowed on the screen. "People used to worship that, instead of God?" she asked, her breath hot in Cid's ear.

Cid lay back on the rumpled sheets of the bed, pulling Magnolia onto her. Her half-lidded eyes glittered as she spoke. "Before there were any gods, fertility goddesses were worshiped all over the world."

Her voice made her belly vibrate against Magnolia's clit. Magnolia shivered and leaned forward, pleasure mounting through her body as Cid sucked at her raised nipples.

They rolled over in unison and Cid circled Magnolia's navel with her tongue, bit at her belly, and kissed her thighs. "Women were revered because we have the power to give birth and take life." She looked up from between Magnolia's legs, her eyes shining. "We were worshiped as Goddesses."

Her touch was sweet, her tongue was warm. Magnolia

closed her eyes and sighed. “That must have been fun,” she said.

“It is,” said Cid, biting the soft flesh of her inner thigh.

“What do you mean, ‘is’?” Magnolia laughed.

“I’ll show you.”

THE DEAL

Kelira shuffled the cards and handed the deck to Magnolia. She cut the deck close to the bottom, slapping the upper three-quarters down on the glass surface of the patio table. "I don't know why we have to play this idiotic game; I can't keep the rules straight. Poker's a lot better."

"You can't play poker with just two people," Kelira observed as he dealt them each seven cards.

Magnolia glanced towards the pond. "Tumcari could play with us."

Without looking up from his deal, Kelira shook his head. "He'd get the cards wet."

"So give him a towel."

Kelira smiled and turned over the first card from the remaining pile. It was the four of clubs. "I dealt, you start."

Magnolia discarded the queen of diamonds, and Kelira

picked it up, but he had no set yet, apparently. He discarded the seven of clubs, something she could use.

Even if there were enough people for poker, she couldn't bet anything but the money she brought with her. She'd been here for over a month now, and she still hadn't seen a paycheck. "Hey Kelira," she said, picking up the card, "shouldn't Rahul have paid me by now? I came here on the sixth of November, and if I'm not mistaken, today is the twelfth of December." She put down her first set, the five, six, and seven of clubs.

He hesitated. "Maybe he's planning to pay you back wages for the time you're here, once you get to Tunis. There's nothing you could spend it on out here anyway."

"Well, yeah, but it's still my money, and I'd like to have it. Didn't he make any arrangements with you about my salary?"

Kelira pursed his lips and drew a card from the facedown pile. "Nope."

Tumcari swam up to the edge of the pond. "Maybe he's just not sure where to send the check."

"What?"

"Tumcari, please," said Kelira.

"No, what did you mean by that?" asked Magnolia, laying her cards facedown on the table.

He shrugged. "Only that maybe the reason Rahul hasn't paid you yet is because he doesn't know where you are."

"You're crazy," Kelira said to him. "You know that, don't you?"

Tumcari smiled. "I simply think it's high time the young lady was apprised of her situation. She's bound to find out eventually, you know."

Magnolia looked at Kelira. "Find out what?"

She saw the panic in his eyes before he could recover with

a laugh and a grin. "Nothing, Magnolia. Tumcari's just trying to stir something up for his own amusement."

She shook her head. "I don't think so, Kelira." She turned to face Tumcari. "Are you saying that Rahul doesn't know I'm here?"

His green eyes glittered like the water around him. "Yes."

"Why?"

"Under the circumstances, I think Kelira is the best one to explain that to you. Kelira?"

Kelira glared at Tumcari with unexpected anger. "You bastard," he said between clenched teeth.

"Well?" said Magnolia, crossing her arms.

He didn't look at her but shifted his gaze from Tumcari to the jungle growth surrounding them. "Rahul thinks you ditched him at the airport in St. Petersburg."

Magnolia stared at him in disbelief. "Because—"

He nodded slowly. "Because I had Ms. Wujcik bring you here, instead of Tunis."

She snorted with disgust. "Why?"

Finally he looked at her with a lost expression. His dark eyes searched hers for an answer. "I don't know, I—" He sighed. "I saw you too, just like Rahul did. I knew what he wanted to do with you and . . ."

A twinge of dread imposed upon her righteous anger. "What did he want to do with me?"

"He wanted to template you," said Tumcari. "Distill your personality down to its basic components so that he can design a new line of robots, all of which will look and act exactly like you, except that they'll have no real minds of their own, no free will. They never do."

"Robots?"

"Bio-organic automatons," he said smugly. "Like Ms. Wujcik for instance. Ever notice that she seems awfully suggestible? Even to the point that she'll sleep with Spider or Dex whenever they want her to?"

Magnolia remembered when Cid told her that Ms. Wujcik was a 'fucking robot.' At the time she'd thought she was joking.

"The robots are designed to look and act like human beings, up to a point. But their thought processes are too linear, they're too predictable to really be people, and they have no initiative of their own. Since they're incapable of forming their own personalities, they have to have one given to them, and that's where the templating comes in. Rahul wanted to use your personality for a new strain of robots. They'd act like you, sort of, but they'd never change or grow. They'd just be a static representation of you as you were at the time of the templating. They're not capable of the dynamism of a true evolving person."

Magnolia chewed her lip thoughtfully. "How is this . . . templating done?"

"He uses video equipment to record your responses, body language, and speech patterns. Then once he has the data, he encodes it into a new robot strain."

Magnolia wasn't sure how she'd feel about a bunch of duplicates of herself running around, doing other people's bidding, but it would have been nice if the decision had been hers. Besides, the money Rahul had offered her was good, very good. "So what's to stop me from just walking out of here and blowing the whistle on our friend Kelira here?"

Tumcari leaned back in the water, his eyes glittering. "For one thing, my dear, you *would* have to walk. It's two hundred and fifty miles to the nearest road."

"I could just tell Ms. Wujcik to fly me in the jet."

He shook his head. "No, I wouldn't let her do it. You see, over time each robot develops an attachment to whomever they're around the most. Rahul mistakenly thinks that he controls Ms. Wujcik. He doesn't. Kelira had to get me to countermand Rahul's order; he couldn't do it himself."

Magnolia remembered Ms. Wujcik in the microjet with a gun at her temple, calmly refusing to turn it around. "So you had a part in this as well, then."

Tumcari nodded. "Anything that goes against Rahul's wishes is amenable to me. And I don't think you're really that unhappy about being here, Magnolia. You and Cid seem to have something quite special between you, if I'm not mistaken."

Anger boiled up inside her at the mention of Cid's name. Fury pounded behind her eyes, coloring her vision in blood red waves. Magnolia stood up, her hands clenched into fists at her sides. "I'll take her with me."

"Mmm. I doubt seriously that she'd go, even if it were a possibility. You see, she's been conducting some research of her own, using the facilities here. She's quite as passionate about the discoveries she's making as she is about you, believe me. And of course if you attempt to contact Rahul by vidphone, she'd surely be implicated in Kelira's treachery, purely by virtue of the relationship between you two.

"If you caused her to lose her job at such a critical point in her work, I doubt very much that she'd be willing to follow you anywhere, let alone to Rahul's house. So you see, my magnificent Magnolia, you really are better off here with us."

"Not if you're dead," she snarled. Through a curtain of rage she saw Tumcari afloat in the sparkling pool, his smile mocking her.

"Come on in, darling, the water's fine."

"I want my money, goddamn it!" she shouted, plunging towards the edge of the pool.

Kelira was instantly by her side, grabbing her arm. He twisted it behind her painfully, his other hand on her shoulder, pulling her up hard against his chest. Magnolia lifted her foot to stomp on his instep, and Kelira tightened his grip, bringing the arm that pinned her shoulder up around her throat, ready to choke her. His face close to her ear, he whispered, "Don't."

Tumcari's green gaze was as cold as stone. "You don't know what you're dealing with, child." He turned and dived, this time revealing the long, green-spotted and sinuous tail that tapered away smoothly where his legs should have been. He slashed it angrily against the surface of the pond, sending water everywhere.

For an instant Magnolia caught sight of the end of his tail as it slid through the waves. Sharp black ridges like blades ran down to a keen point, and then he was gone, disappearing beneath the turbulent water like a dream.

Magnolia lay awake in bed, staring into the darkness, her final glimpse of Tumcari playing over and over in her mind. A man with no legs, only a great sea monster's tail, as if Rahul had only bothered with his head and upper body, leaving the rest to chance. At least she had the satisfaction of knowing that he was more of a prisoner here than she could ever be.

When she'd returned to their room this afternoon, Cid was in the laboratory, working on her project. She was there still. Magnolia felt secretly relieved. She needed time to think about some of the things Tumcari had said. Like it or not, it wasn't only Kelira and he who held her trapped here, but her feelings for Cid as well. Even if there was a way out of here, a way to contact Rahul, did she really want to? What she had with Cid was something she'd never experienced before. She felt comfortable with her, right somehow in a way that she'd never realized had been wrong before; almost as if she'd found a missing piece of herself. Although still angry with Kelira for cheating her out of a soft and lucrative gig, she also felt a twinge of gratitude to him for bringing her here. And that infuriated her most of all.

Why? she wondered for the umpteenth time, Why did Kelira bring me here in the first place? She never had gotten a complete answer, thanks to Tumcari. She peered at the clock on the bedside table. It was three minutes after two in the morning. As good a time as any to pursue unanswered questions.

Magnolia got up and quietly dressed herself in black jeans and a black sweatshirt. She padded out into the hallway on bare feet.

In the darkness she switched on a penlight and crept soundlessly upstairs to the fourth floor, where Kelira kept his room. The staircase narrowed here, no longer the grand, sweeping spine of the house. At the top the doorway hung open. Magnolia's penlight picked up the dense, interlocking patterns of the woven rug that ran down the center of the hallway.

Kelira's room was on the left, two doors before the gymnasium. The door was shut. She leaned against it, listening. It was quiet. She crouched on the floor and peered underneath the door, but all she could see was the gleaming reflection of the moon on the wooden floor. Magnolia switched off the penlight and tried the doorknob. It turned easily in her hand, and the door swung silently open on well-oiled hinges.

The silence was punctuated by the soft rhythm of Kelira's breathing. He lay on the bed, sprawled beneath a batik bedspread, one arm flung across his chest. His face was slack with the mystery that all sleepers possess. Magnolia smelled incense floating in the silvered air like a memory.

The moon hung outside the window, full and bright, inundating the little room with pale radiance. She had no need of the penlight, and her dark clothing was in vain. She'd have to make this quick. Magnolia cast an appraising glance about the room.

She had no idea what she was looking for. Some sort of clue; a telling artifact she hoped she'd recognize when she saw it. The room was neat, especially compared to the chaos she shared with Cid. In the center of the room stood a broad wicker pedestal topped by a black cushion. Against the wall near the window was a large dresser. Beside it a stack of magazines had slid over; images of smiling, naked women lay scattered in the shadows.

Apparently he didn't go for pinups; the walls were bare. Next to the bed where Kelira lay sleeping stood a small bookcase. Its top was the only cluttered place in the room. A small lamp fought for space with a glass of water, an incense burner, and a photograph in a synthetic teak frame.

Magnolia moved closer to investigate. The photo was of a young girl, maybe fourteen years old. Tall and dark; an oval face with an olive complexion and large, dark eyes. In the dim light she resembled Magnolia herself at that age, but she leaned against a bamboo post supporting the porch of a tiny hovel that would never have withstood a Detroit winter.

Magnolia glanced again at Kelira's sleeping face and wondered what secrets mixed with his soft breath and the slight dew of sweat that collected in the creases of his skin.

It would be here, she thought. Anything he had to hide would be here, beside him. She knelt to examine the contents of the bookcase, scanning the spines of books whose titles she could not read. From the corner of her eye she caught a flicker of movement, and suddenly her arm was caught in Kelira's iron grip. Magnolia gasped as he hauled her up painfully by the arm.

"What are you doing?" he growled, his voice still rough with sleep.

Magnolia shook her head, speechless in the face of his sudden fury. He was kneeling on the bed, half-naked. The sparse hairs of his chest were darker than his dark and angry eyes. She tried to pull away from him, and he jerked her closer, twisting her elbow against the joint so that she bent over, her face against the bed.

"Why are you in here?" He didn't release her but kept the pressure on. Just enough to prevent her from moving.

"Jesus, Kelira, let me go." Magnolia shot her free hand up and over his, bending his thumb back until his grip loosened. She stepped back and released him, half expecting him to come at her again. But he only sighed and sank back down on the bed, glaring at her.

She stared back at him in indecision. She should leave, she knew, but curiosity held her. She walked to the bookcase, and Kelira's dark gaze followed her intently. She picked up the picture and held it towards him. "Who is this?"

He flinched and crossed his arms. "It's my sister Rose. That picture was taken a long time ago."

Magnolia glanced at it once more. "She looks like me."

"A little bit. About as much as an East Asian can look like an Anglo." He wasn't looking at her, or at the picture, either. Kelira's eyes were focused on the middle distance, seeing something very, very far away.

She set the picture back down on the nightstand and perched on the edge of the bed. "Kelira," she said, and he looked at her again. "Why did you bring me here?"

He laughed a little and edged away from her on the bed. "Why don't you get out of here now, anyway? I caught you sneaking through my things; don't you have the decency to skulk away in humiliation?"

Magnolia shrugged. "I guess not. Besides, you could have made me leave before, but you didn't." A sly smile spread across her face. "I think you like it like this; me and you alone in your bedroom at night. Is this why you kidnapped me, Kelira, because you want me?" She laughed softly and ran a finger teasingly down the side of his face.

He recoiled from her touch, gasping as if stung. "No! You don't understand!"

"I guess not." She leaned back against the wall, one eyebrow raised in skepticism. She turned to look at the picture again. "Your sister . . ."

"I haven't seen my sister in fifteen years. She was sold from the family when I was twelve. A couple years later I ran away to look for her. I joined the Red Army Mercenary Fleet, and I searched all the port towns in Southeast Asia, but I never found her." He spoke mechanically, as if he had rehearsed these lines before. "When I saw you—"

"You thought I was her," Magnolia interrupted.

"No. No, I knew you weren't her, but you were in her situation. She—she was sold into prostitution, but there's always the chance that she got into porn. So I keep an eye out, you know." He glanced at her sidelong, then shrugged. "Anyway, there you were, and that guy was coming for you with a knife. I was going to turn it off, but then you kicked him, right in the sternum, broke a couple of ribs by the looks of it. You had the knife in your hand so fast I could barely follow the motion. You stabbed him. *You* stabbed *him.*

"It's what I've always hoped that Rose could do, and seeing you do it, I knew she could. I knew she was like you." He stared at her, his deep brown eyes looking past her, through her, searching for the someone else she represented. He caught himself and laughed. "I guess it doesn't make much sense."

Magnolia shook her head. "No, it does make sense." She looked down, frozen in the face of Kelira's feelings. She felt like an intruder now in a way she hadn't when she came here. "I'd better go," she said, standing up.

"Yeah." He nodded. "Good night."

At the doorway she hesitated, looking back over her shoulder to where Kelira sat on the edge of his bed, his hands clasped between his knees. "I hope you find your sister," she said, and closed the door behind her.

FOOLED ON THE HILL

The morning sun was just beginning to shine through the east window of his bedroom. Rahul opened his eyes, blinked in remembrance that he was still alive, and began the slow process of sitting up.

He could not understand why, when he slept so little, it should be so difficult for him to get out of bed. With patience born of experience, Rahul persuaded his body to stand.

He walked to the window and lifted a cloth from the large wicker birdcage that housed his finches. The little birds stirred in the dawning light, slowly bringing their heads out from under their sheltering wings, ruffling their feathers, and performing their morning ablutions.

Rahul padded slowly to the bathroom adjoining his bed-chamber. He turned the chrome-plated knob of the shower faucet to hot and let it run, filling the room with steam to loosen his stiff joints.

When he stepped out of the shower, the first thin strains of birdsong reached his ears. He opened the door to hear them better and turned to a broad antifog mirror for his shave. Scraping the foam and white stubble from his face with an old-fashioned razor was like participating in an archaeological dig. Carefully he unearthed this relic of the past, his face.

There was a soft knock at his bedroom door. Rahul put on his robe and answered it. Henri stood in the hallway. "There is a call for you, sir, from Wotroya House."

"Thank you, Henri. I'll take it in the sunroom. Ask them to hold a few minutes, would you please?"

Henri bowed and retreated silently down the hallway, and Rahul opened his closet, selecting a pale salmon-colored shirt and brown linen trousers. Ordinarily he checked in with Kelira once a month, and that was that. It was highly unusual for anyone from Wotroya to contact him. Something must be wrong.

Despite his uneasiness, he carefully fastened the tortoiseshell buttons of his shirt and selected a russet paisley tie from the rack. Knotting it as he made his way down the hallway, he wondered if this were some ploy of Tumcari's.

In the sunroom Henri had placed the vidphone on the inlaid mahogany coffee table. Rahul seated himself on the love seat across from it and released the hold/veil button. The face of a dark-haired, Caucasian young man with a bruised jaw and stitches in his nose materialized on the screen. To his surprise Rahul realized it was Spider Picardi, one of the boys he'd hired as maintenance workers at Wotroya House more than two years ago. "Good morning, Dr. Rahul."

"Good morning, Spider. What can I do for you?"

"Actually, sir, it's more the other way around. I have something here I think you should see."

Rahul raised an eyebrow. "What is it?"

"It's a tape that was made last night at approximately twenty-one hundred hours, featuring a recent addition to our staff here who might interest you."

"Spider, I haven't hired anyone new for Wotroya since Cid joined you."

Spider grinned and nodded his head. "I didn't think so; check this out." His face disappeared in a moment of transmission noise, and then the screen resolved into the interior of one of the bedrooms in Wotroya House. There were two figures in the bed. Cid, her blond hair drifting across the pillow, and someone with dark hair who was lying across her, her face hidden in the crook of Cid's arm.

"Yeah, I have a brother," Cid was saying, "but he left home when he was about sixteen. He was always getting in trouble. What about you?"

"I had eight brothers and sisters when I left. Well, seven, actually," the other figure answered, rolling over. Rahul jerked as if splashed with ice water. It was Magnolia, the young woman he'd found in New York.

How she had made her way to Wotroya House was an intriguing question, almost as intriguing as she herself was. Despite its troubling nature, Rahul welcomed this news. He'd thought she was gone forever, and yet here she was, right under his nose.

"We squatted in the River Rouge Partition, one of the sections of Detroit that the city fenced off so it wouldn't have to pick up the garbage or have police patrol it. They did it because the buildings were all vacant anyway. There wasn't anyone there who was supposed to be there, so fuck 'em.

"They put up these big wire fences, and the thing is that weeds and tree of heaven and all grew up around these fences that were, like, twenty feet tall. For a while the only way you could get in and out of there was through holes people cut in the fence, and you had to crawl through these teeny little spaces between the trees. So at first it was mostly kids there.

"But that was all way before I was born. Most of the fence is gone now. Nobody needs it. The partitions have made their own borders."

"What's it like there?" asked Cid.

"The Rouge Partition had a lot of factories in it before it fell vacant, so we mostly lived off of scavenging, or once in a while Drew would sneak into the suburbs and loot some businesses."

"Who's Drew?" asked Cid.

"Drew is my father. He and my mom had about ten kids together, but by the time I left home, two of them were dead, and one, Manus, was a half-wit cripple."

The screen went blank again, and Spider's face returned. "We've got more, hours of it, in fact, but that clip should give you an idea of whether you're interested in the rest or not."

Rahul laughed. "Oh, I'm interested. Tell me, how did the young lady come to be with you?"

"Well, Ms. Wujcik brought her in on the microjet about a month ago. Kelira said you sent her here for training."

"Did he?"

"Yeah. At first I didn't think much of it, but then I noticed that all she does is train with us, and that's strictly extracurricular. She doesn't really have a job around here, and of course, when Cid came, you personally introduced us to her. So I just got to wondering whether you knew about this."

"Yes, well, that's very thoughtful of you, Spider. I appreciate you looking out for my interests. But tell me about this training you mentioned."

Spider paused, then broke into an embarrassed smile. "Well, I mean, there's not that much to do up here, you know, umm. I mean, we keep up with the maintenance and all, but, since there's no town nearby or anything . . ." He took a deep breath and plunged on through his explanation. "It's just something we do to keep busy. You know that Kelira was in the Red Army, right?"

"I am aware of that, yes."

"So he shows us a few things, that's all. We play war games outside in the snow or spar in the old gym upstairs. It's more of a game, really."

"I see. Well, thank you, Spider, your vigilance will not go unrewarded, I assure you. Now, would you be so good as to download the rest of your tape, so that I can view it at my leisure and decide upon a course of action?"

"Absolutely, sir. And if there's anything you need done on this end, I hope you'll think of me."

"Yes, I'll be in touch. By the way, what happened to your face?"

He looked surprised. "Oh, one of the paint guns went off accidentally."

"During training, no doubt."

"Uh, yeah."

Rahul nodded sagely. "Well, I hope your injuries aren't serious."

"Oh, no. Just a few stitches." Spider laughed, peering anxiously at him through the vidphone screen.

"That's good. Take care of yourself, Spider, and keep your eyes open, eh?"

"You bet." He nodded.

"Good-bye." Rahul toggled the disconnect switch. He leaned back in the love seat, closed his eyes, and rubbed his forehead. Three impossible things, all before breakfast. Magnolia was at Wotroya House, Ms. Wujcik had betrayed him, and Kelira had not notified him of any of it.

And Rahul had the feeling that he had barely scratched the surface of what was going on at Wotroya. That Ms. Wujcik had disobeyed his orders and then lied about it was excruciatingly plain. But just as surely, she had not done it under her own initiative. She didn't have any.

He spent the next several hours watching the activities of Cid and Magnolia in their bedroom. It was certainly a side of Magnolia he hadn't seen before. For that matter, he was treated to several sides of Cid he'd never seen before, either. This thing needed a massive edit job—there were hours where they were just sleeping, or the room was empty—but cut down to an hour and a half, it'd make a pretty passable porno flick. He laughed at the notion of passing it on to Edgerton. He'd probably get a kick out of it.

What Rahul liked best was the dialogue, which swerved uncontrollably between the mundane and sublime. One moment it was Magnolia, her eyes as wide as a hand-painted urchin's, giving the obligatory "I've never been with a woman before" speech; the next, Cid was describing the cycles of the tides and relating them to estrogen levels in the human body. One thing was certain. Those girls smoked a lot of pot.

There was often an obstruction in the upper part of the frame. An undulating blob pulsing with colors. At first he'd taken it for signal noise or transmission damage, but soon he realized it was something actually in the room with them. It was a holograph of some sort of fractal, possibly a strange attractor. For all its unpredictable changes, there was a consistency about it. Its colors did not swirl madly; they moved in madly swirling patterns. And as for the shape of the thing, it was always roughly the same, although never exactly the same.

Cid referred to it as a phase space model of an electron transport chain. From her frequent remarks about the LRH-8000, he surmised she'd been using the equipment in the genetics lab to conduct a little research of her own.

She spoke of nonlocality in Tumcari's cellular functioning, and increasingly of a world without the boundaries of space and time.

Althea entered with a tray bearing a plate of sandwiches and a silver-plated teapot, steam issuing invitingly from its spout.

"I thought you might like to take tea," she said with a demure smile.

Rahul smiled at her with proprietary satisfaction. She was one of his best strains, very popular with the wealthy executives who could afford her. Rahul recalled the woman he'd modeled her on. He had not yet become an old man when he met her, and together they'd spent the stillness of his middle years isolating the patterns of congenial servitude. "Thank you, Althea, that's very thoughtful of you."

Actually, it was nothing of the kind. Thoughtfulness implied spontaneity, free will—qualities that he had failed to produce in any but the very first of his experiments with bio-organic automatons. Althea's thought processes were carefully ordered and wholly predictable, her motivations ready-made and installed in the gene code of her strain. All the same, a little falsehood was a small price to see her blush so prettily at his compliment.

"Sit down beside me, Althea. I have a problem I wish to discuss with you." Robots were good listeners, and talking to them allowed him the illusion that he was not alone. "A robot out at Wotroya House—one of your own strain siblings—seems to be malfunctioning. She lied to me."

Althea's china blue eyes turned round as saucers. "How could she do that?"

"Well, it's my fault, probably. I visit Wotroya so seldom, her primary attachment must have switched from me to someone there." Tumcari, of course. Tumcari, whom she waited on day after day, who was nearly one of her own kind.

Of course Tumcari would be behind this. Damn the creature.

He'd been resentful right from the start, when he was first made. Gifted through Rahul's science with a mind equal or superior to that of any human being, he was furious at not *being* a human being. Rahul remembered the first thing he ever said: "What am I?"

He had already destroyed Rahul's research once. Now he had sabotaged his efforts to template Magnolia. There could be no reason behind it except for a personal one, except for sheer spite.

And he had infected Kelira with his insubordination as well. Kelira knew that Magnolia was supposed to be brought here, to Tunis, but he did nothing to remedy the situation. In fact, if what Spider said was true, he lied to cover it up. To what extent he cooperated with Tumcari of his own free will was questionable, however. The creature could be most persuasive.

Rahul remembered the time Tumcari talked a technician into bringing some of the lab rats down to the greenhouse for him to play with. Of course the rats got loose, and some of them were never recovered. They had all been inoculated with Chorus II antibodies as part of a disease-control project. The incident set the project back months. When the tech was questioned as to why he'd taken the rats from the lab, all he could say was, "He asked me to."

Rahul sipped his tea and sighed, looking at Althea. She smiled and patted his knee. "It will be all right, you'll see," she said.

He smiled thinly. That was bullshit, the kind of preprogrammed pablum she was designed to spout. He knew better. Where Tumcari was concerned, nothing would ever be all right.

THE MOTION OF FROZEN WATER

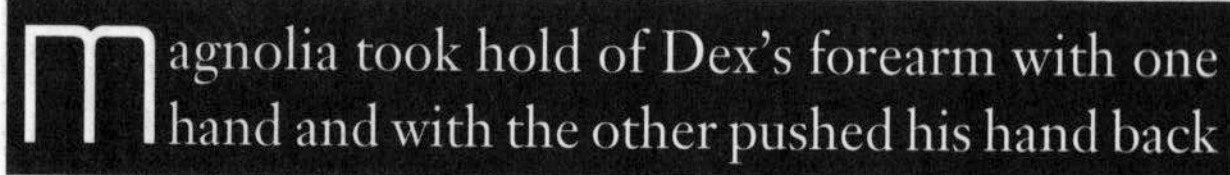

Magnolia took hold of Dex's forearm with one hand and with the other pushed his hand back against the wrist joint. She stepped closer to him, positioning her leg behind his. She used her weight and momentum to unbalance him and send him down onto the padded mat. She kept up the pressure on his wrist as she knelt, then switched her hold to an armlock, and rolled him onto his stomach. She placed her knee in the small of his back to further immobilize him. Dex slapped the mat with his free hand, and she released him.

"Okay," he said, standing up. "Now I get to try it out on you."

When Dex grabbed her arm, she grasped his thumb and peeled his hand off of her. He twisted his hand out of her grasp and captured her wrist, putting her in an armlock. He stepped behind her, but as he did, Magnolia got her foot behind his knee and rolled him over her back, onto the mat once more.

"Good one," he said, getting up again. Dex was all right, as long as Spider wasn't around.

"Want another try?" she asked him.

"No thanks, I think I'm getting premature arthritis from all this stress to my joints." He glanced to the other end of the gym, where Spider and Kelira danced around each other in the ring, wearing gloves and padded helmets, boxing. "Besides, they should be done soon, and then we can box."

Since the paint gun incident, Magnolia and Spider were not allowed to spar together anymore. She wandered over to the ropes and leaned on them, watching.

Spider buffeted Kelira's head with a hail of blows. Kelira bent under the onslaught and then stepped back and caught Spider on the chin with an uppercut. It bought him some space, and he needed it. Every time he got in the clinch with Spider, he got nailed. The time went off and they separated, pulling off gloves and helmets. Spider walked towards her, waving his mouthpiece by the tab. It bounced up and down, slick with saliva. "Want me to rinse it out for you?"

"I've got my own, thanks." He didn't try to touch her anymore, and his remarks had become pretty vague, but when he looked at her there was a hard black lump of hatred in his eyes, and she thought he must be saving it up for something big.

After her bout with Dex, Magnolia took a shower and then wandered downstairs to the video room. Cid sat curled up on the couch, cradling a bowl of popcorn in her lap. She smiled when she saw Magnolia come in and pointed at the screen. "*The Lone Ranger*," she said, "in Russian."

"How can you follow what's going on?" asked Magnolia, sitting down beside her and plunging her hand into the bowl.

"I can't, but who cares?"

"We should get Kelira; he speaks Russian, doesn't he?"

"Huh-uh, Chinese."

"Oh. Oh, well." She slid closer to Cid and leaned her damp head on her shoulder, staring absently at the television. "I'm bored," she said at length.

"What, Kelira isn't keeping you busy enough being macha?"

"Eh, I don't know. Dex is too easy. Kelira's better, but he mostly works with Spider now."

"So in other words you're not fighting anyone you really want to hit."

"I guess."

"Ever think of going back to Rahul?"

"Yeah, 'cause of the money, you know? But what he wanted to do didn't sound all that interesting, either. Standing around being filmed, oooh, how exciting. Besides"—she turned her head to nuzzle against Cid's neck—"I couldn't leave you."

"Really? Not even for fifteen thousand a month?"

Magnolia shrugged and sat up. "I haven't called him yet, have I? Nobody's stopping me."

"True, but I think Kelira would, if he could."

"Well, he'd be in deep shit if Rahul knew about it, wouldn't he?"

"You bet I would," said Kelira from the doorway.

"Hey Kelira," said Magnolia, "what's shakin'?"

Kelira stretched out in the white easy chair next to the couch. "Not much. Hey, switch over to weather for a second, will you?"

Cid changed the channel. The satellite picture showed a huge mass of clouds headed east across the Siberian plain. "Holy fucking chao," she said.

"It's a blizzard," said Kelira. "We better batten down the hatches tonight."

"Hey, put on Channel 90," said Dex from the doorway. He walked across the room, scooped a handful of popcorn from the bowl, and threw himself into the recliner.

"Where's Spider?" asked Kelira.

"Aw, he's got Ms. Wujcik up in his room and he won't let me have her. I don't even think he's fucking her anymore. He's just being a bastard."

Magnolia and Cid laughed.

"Hey, you lezzies can laugh, you've got it made." Dex shook his head. "Kelira knows what I'm talking about. I swear, this job sucks."

"It doesn't suck, that's the problem!" said Magnolia, and she and Cid again dissolved into gales of laughter.

Dex looked to Kelira for support, but he was laughing too. "I thought blue was your favorite color," he said, smirking.

"Oh you're hilarious. It's nice to know my suffering can bring others such joy. Turn on 90, Cid, it's Edmonton against the Red Wings."

"Hey cool, my home team," said Magnolia. "Put it on."

"Hockey?" Cid wrinkled her nose. "Don't you guys get enough violence around here?"

"Hey, nothing wrong with a little scrap to liven up a game now and then," said Dex.

"What's the matter, you don't like hockey?" asked Magnolia. "You ever watch it?"

"No."

"Then how do you know? You're always talking about dynamic systems and strange attractors. Hockey is like that."

"It is?"

"Change the channel."

Cid thumbed the remote to 90. Skaters swirled about on the ice in pursuit of the puck.

"Is that the score? No way!" yelled Dex.

"Detroit rules!" shouted Magnolia, grinning at him.

"Eight to nothing. Wow, the Oilers are getting creamed," said Kelira.

Magnolia leaned towards Cid and pointed at the players, tracing their movements with her finger. See? They swirl around like balls floating in a tilting pan of water. See the way they collect around the puck and break up again? And it's all contained by the arena, like an attractor, right?

"No! Stop them! Knock 'em out!" Dex shouted as Detroit drove the puck into Edmonton's goal zone.

"You're right," said Cid, "they're like fish swimming around in a tank. The motion of frozen water. It's kind of relaxing, actually."

"No! Shit!" Dex pounded the arm of his chair as Detroit scored another goal on Edmonton. "That's only because you don't care about hockey," he said.

Out of the corner of his eye he saw Spider standing in the doorway. "Hey, Spider!" he yelled. "Get in here, guy. Edmonton's wishing we were playing for them right now. You have to see this."

A fight broke out on the ice. Evequoi pulled Hansen's shirt off and was now pounding him on the neck. "Oh man, look at that! Hansen oughta kill that guy. What's wrong with the Oilers, man?"

"Hansen's getting traded, to Prince Edward Island," Spider said from behind Dex's chair.

"Prince Edward, ouch, Alcatraz."

"Yeah, so you can see why the guy doesn't have much fight in him."

"I guess. But the whole team stinks, I mean look, the score is nine to nothing, Detroit."

"Hey," said Magnolia, "Detroit's kicking their ass."

"That's my point."

"Well, they haven't been up to much since Ygarev left for Winnipeg," said Spider. He put his hand on the arm of the chair. "I hear the Saskatoon Moose Heads are set for a comeback."

That was the signal. "Yeah sure, and nudism is flourishing in the Yukon," said Dex. "Well, I can't bear to watch this anymore. I'm going to drown my sorrows in a game of Tornado. You want to join me, Spider?"

"Might as well. Nothing's going to happen here, it's halfway through the third quarter. Looks like the Wings'll get a shutout."

They went to Spider's room. Spider sat on his bed, his legs crossed. "Rahul's dropping the axe tomorrow," he said.

"What's he going to do?" Dex shoved a pile of laundry off the chair by his desk and sat down.

"He wants us to gather everyone in the greenhouse at three o'clock. He's going to talk to the whole staff. Of course for us it's just for show, because he already said we both have jobs with him after this."

"Jobs doing what?"

"He says he's not sure yet. It depends on how the conference call goes. Can you get the camera out of Cid's room?"

"Shouldn't be too hard, they don't lock the door."

"Good, he wants us to plant it in the greenhouse. When he's done talking to everyone, we're supposed to leave. We'll come back up here and call him from the second portable, and he'll tell us what to do."

"How are we supposed to get everyone in the greenhouse? What are we supposed to say?"

"We'll just say he wants to talk to them."

"Oh, and that won't arouse suspicion. Especially when Magnolia is included. We're not even supposed to know she isn't supposed to be here. We need an excuse to get them all in there, something natural, so that it seems Rahul just happened to call while everyone just happened to be there."

"Dream on," said Spider. "They're going to tumble no

matter how many martinis you sip while muttering 'Bond, James Bond,' to yourself. We have to rely on the power of being in Rahul's court. I mean, we could be under orders to kill them for all they know. They'll be too scared to fuck with us."

"Well, Kelira will be," said Dex, "because he's the pussy of the universe. Cid, we don't have to worry about, I mean what's she going to do?"

"Laugh."

"Exactly. But Magnolia now—how's your nose feeling?"

"Fuck her, man. She's going in there if I have to use a can opener. I'm not worried about Magnolia."

Dex shook his head. "You should be, buddy. She is one wild card. We can't predict what she's going to do, but if she knows you're involved, you're gonna need more stitches."

Spider glared at him, his eyes suddenly pits of rage. "You saying I can't take her?"

"No, I—"

"Really? Because it sounds like you think I can't take her."

"I know you can take her, Spider," Dex said quickly, "but don't you think it would be better to avoid the situation altogether?"

Spider shook his head. "Only reason to avoid it would be if I can't take her. I can clean the floor with that bitch, man. That thing with the paint gun, that was a cheap shot, a sucker punch. I shouldn't have let her surprise me, but it won't happen again."

INSIDE OUT

Cid pulled open the bottom right drawer of her desk, grabbed a cup of instant noodles, and pulled the tab without bothering to read the label. The smell of imitation chicken flavor hit her nose as the contents of the cup heated on contact with the air.

Cup in hand she crossed to the LRH-8000 and stared at the display theater, absently forking up a clump of steaming noodles and shoveling them into her mouth. The holograph of her cell sample hung suspended in darkness, a web of membranes dotted with nuclei.

Setting the noodles on a nearby lab table, she tapped at the control keyboard, zooming in on the bright pink cell in the lower left quadrant of the sample to which she had introduced Tumcari's hybrid mitochondria. It and the cells surrounding it were healthy, their functioning appearing normal.

She'd been observing this sample for weeks now, and it

was still healthy. The original T. mitochondria had adapted to her cellular environment without mishap, reproduced, and were now gradually edging out the cell's original mitochondria.

Now all she had to do was figure out a way for them to propagate through the cellular membrane.

She picked up her dinner, walked over to the windows, and looked out into the darkness. A few noncommittal snowflakes drifted downwards from invisible heights. Other than that, nothing greeted her gaze but the unending carpet of accumulated snow towards which they fell.

The windows were old, like the rest of the house. They had no microcircuitry to warm the panes against the bitter winter night outside. The steam from her noodles frosted on the glass and obscured her view.

With a finger Cid drew figures on the glass. A figure eight on its side, a happy face, a heart.

"How's Dr. Frankenstein this evening?"

Cid started and turned to see Magnolia grinning from the doorway. She wore black jeans and a white shirt open at the throat. With that lopsided grin and her eyes gleaming in the light of the fluorescents overhead, she looked like a pirate. She strode across the lab and wrapped Cid in her slim, strong arms. Cid sighed and closed her eyes, cradling her head against Magnolia's soft breasts. For a moment she let herself forget about her work, breathing in the particular smell of her lover, a combination of soap and sweat and something else that was Magnolia's alone.

Looking up into her luminous brown eyes, she said, "Your timing is perfect."

Magnolia smiled but did not look away, as once she would have. "Why is that?"

"I was going to have to throw myself out this window in

another minute," said Cid, laughing. "You came along just in time to save my life."

"Good thing I did, then." Magnolia kissed her quick and wet, and pulled her even closer. Her hand slipped beneath Cid's dingy Yale-Tech sweatshirt and cupped her breast, stroked it. "That would have been a terrible waste."

Later, as they lay together on the tiny cot Cid kept in the lab for naps, Magnolia nudged her softly. "Hey, Cid-child, tell me something."

"Mmm, what?"

"Why were you going to throw yourself out the window, when I came in?"

She laughed. "Oh, I wasn't really. You've made me happier than I've ever been in my life."

"But something's got you down, girl, I can tell."

Cid nodded. "Have you ever been so close to something that you could just reach out and take it, if you only had the right tool to grab it with?"

Thought robbed Magnolia's eyes of their focus. She glanced idly about the room, gradually coming to rest on the LRH at the opposite end of the room. "This project you've been working on . . ."

"Yeah. The hybrid mitochondria thing. Tumcari's mito have survived in my cells for six weeks. For that matter, the Ms. Wujcik sample is still going strong too."

"So what's the problem?"

She shrugged. "Well, I'd like to field-test my hypothesis about Bell's theorem and the cellular functioning of these hybrid mito, but I had to directly implant them in the sample cells. I don't have that kind of finesse outside the petri dish, and besides, so far they haven't propagated beyond the original test cell. I don't think they can do it on their own."

"Field-test?"

"Right. There are a lot of possible ramifications in the nonlocal abilities of these hybrids. The only way to really find out what they do is to experience it firsthand. Since the presence of an observer impacts the results of any experiment, I might as well make the observer the experiment."

"You mean you want to try this stuff out on yourself."

Cid took a deep breath and nodded.

Magnolia shook her head in wonderment. "You're crazy. Screwing around with something like that could kill you."

"Only if it doesn't make me stronger."

"You're nuts!"

Cid smiled and bowed her head in acquiescence. "In the finest tradition of mad scientists since time immemorial."

Angry now, Magnolia stood up and paced the floor. "Where is this . . . stuff?"

"In the LRH—"

Magnolia spun on her heel and headed towards the holoscope.

Cid leapt after her. "Don't touch anything!"

Magnolia glanced at her over her shoulder. "I want to keep on being able to touch *you*, Cid. I can't let you screw around with your, your . . ."

"Cell biology? Look, Mag"—Cid caught up with her and put a restraining hand on her arm—"don't fuck with this equipment, please. It's my responsibility to keep it in good condition. If you just open the refraction chamber and take out a sample now, I might never get this thing working properly again, and if Rahul found out, he'd fire me."

Magnolia stared at her. "So if I want to be with you, I have to just stand by while you fuck yourself up, huh?"

Cid shook her head. "It won't, Mag. Those cells in the sample are doing just fine. The hybrid mito are adaptable."

"Sure, but are you?"

Cid's eyes flashed with anger. She'd never been mad at

Magnolia before. Her face flushed, and she knew it had turned red. "I remember when I took my first course in chaos theory, as an undergrad at Yale-Tech. That course changed my life. Up until then, I was in a program: molecular biology with an emphasis on experimental gene therapy. The only thing I took in liberal arts was a survey course on Goethe. I was prepping for the vanguard of corporate medical research." She shrugged. "I didn't think much about it really. I just accepted it, because I knew it would get me a good-paying job. I didn't think it mattered whether or not I actually liked it. And I knew I was lucky to be there. They had the math requirement up so high that only three percent of the applicants made the cut. Everybody in my family was really proud of me and stuff, but I didn't feel that way at all. I just knew I was supposed to.

"But then I took that course in chaos theory. I remember the day I finally got it, really grasped the implications of concepts like feedback and self-similarity across scales."

Magnolia had moved away from the LRH and was listening to her closely. With a sigh Cid sank into a metal folding chair. "One day the professor showed us a video of fractal animation. For an hour I sat in the dark, mesmerized by these beautiful, infinitely diverse patterns, trying to get my brain around the idea that they *were* patterns, even though they never repeated themselves exactly.

"After class I walked from the darkened lecture hall out into a bright spring afternoon. The sky above was a brilliant blue, dotted with white clouds that were reflected in the pond beside the walk. I stood there, staring at images of water vapor reflected off of the surface of liquid water. And there were swans in the pond, and every once in a while one of them would swim across a cloud, breaking the image into fragments that gradually re-formed in her wake. They broke the symmetry, you see? Sky and pond would have been identical without them, but nothing is ever completely identical. There's always some modification from one frame of the phase space to the next. Reality consists of a nested series of broken symmetries. Pattern is only half of the picture; the other half is disorder, unpredictable and reliable. I felt I was just beginning to grasp how pattern could be omnipresent—interwoven with disorder into the fabric of reality—when my backpack slid off my shoulder, and I bent over to pick it up. My cellular bio folder had fallen out and spilled a series of electron microscope photos from the lab section. They were of aggregates of white blood cells, and they resembled nothing more than clouds in a sunny spring sky." Cid paused and glanced back at Magnolia. "I'm sorry, this probably doesn't make much sense."

"No, go on. I'm listening."

"Well, that was when the world turned inside out for me, because I realized that everything I saw was inside me, mirrored in the structures of my body down to the minutest particle and reflected back outwards, probably to infinity. Around me the trees reached their networks of branches out like the terminals of nerve ganglia, and I knew I could just as well be standing in the forest of my own mind.

"Although I'd been in and out of various women's spirituality circles since I was seventeen, that was the first time I really comprehended my innate connection with all of existence. I knew my Goddess then, for the first time. I'd come home, and I felt that I'd never be alone again.

"But the problem with revelations is that they're transitory. And the everyday reality that has been constructed by human society is based on dichotomies: good and evil, men and women, ourselves and the 'outside' world. It takes a special set of circumstances to force our thinking out of such either/or ruts.

"I never forgot the facts and principles that attended my

revelation, but in the days that followed, I gradually lost the feeling of it. Caught up in the compartmentalizations of language, classes, family, and a host of other social conventions that divide reality into supposedly nonrelated subunits, I became separated once again from the Whole of which we are all a part."

She leaned forward, her hands clasped between her knees. "Now I have a chance to transcend those boundaries through a nonlocalization of my cellular processes, and unlike a transitory feeling based on ideas, this would be a permanent change. It's been a long time since that day, Magnolia, and I want to go home again now, to stay."

Magnolia looked at her steadily. "Do you think this experiment will accomplish that?"

"I do."

She raised her eyebrows and exhaled rapidly. "Well, I guess your mind's made up then."

"It is."

Magnolia frowned. "I just hope you're right, Cid. And if you are, I hope you'll still want to hang around with a puny, nonuniversal entity like myself."

"You're the other side of the coin, Mag. Remember? Reality is the boundary between order and disorder. Something has to break the symmetry. You're a vector, an agent of change. As such, your significance lies in the particulars of who you are. If my awareness becomes . . . universal, then I'll definitely need the perspective of someone tied in with the unpredictability of the moment."

Magnolia laughed and shook her head sadly, heading for the door. "You've got it all figured out, I guess, but I still have a feeling I'm going to regret not trashing your microscope."

"Holoscope," Cid corrected her, but she was already gone, the door shut behind her. Cid switched on her disc deck and returned to the LRH. As she stared at the hybrid mitochondria swimming in her cell sample, the swelling wail of a tenor saxophone enveloped her in a sad embrace. She thought about some of the things Magnolia had said, and the concern she'd expressed for her well-being.

To herself she admitted that Magnolia might be right. She couldn't predict the impact the hybrid mito would have on her physiology once they had spread to all her cells. Now that she'd found someone who cared for her, she was reluctant to risk her life, but not knowing the outcome of the experiment was unthinkable to her. Even if it meant losing Magnolia, she had to find out.

Cid longed for her now, even though she'd just left. Magnolia: her Artemis, her Kali. The beautiful, fierce one whom Kelira had brought to her.

Kelira had brought Magnolia here; not Cid, Kelira. And Cid's connection to him was purely locational. They were in the same place at the same time, nothing more, but it was sufficient to bring Cid and Magnolia within range of each other, and then things just took care of themselves. With an intuitive thrill, Cid realized that she didn't have to get the mitochondria to penetrate the cell walls themselves. She could use a middleman, as it were—one that had already evolved to perform that very task. She could use a viral envelope to transport the mitochondria into her cells and ensure that they'd spread throughout her body.

She laughed and whooped with joy. It would work, she was certain. She practically ran to her desk, seated herself, and started scribbling notes on the parameters of the required virion.

THE MEDITATION OF VEGETABLE MINDS

With nighttime, silence fell upon the greenhouse. Nothing disturbed the stillness but the occasional liquid whisper of the water as Tumcari drifted through it. The birds had all gone to bed, and between the looming shadows of the palms above him Tumcari spotted stars.

Tiny, distant, incomprehensible lights. They were suns, or so Rahul had told him. Their shining was like a song faintly heard. Sometimes he knew the words, or the worlds.

Of all those billions of suns, none was quite like the one that brought light and life to a forgotten creature under glass and left him cold and alone when it set. Nothing was ever repeated exactly the same way twice, and there would never be another one of him.

These thoughts disturbed Tumcari, and so he dived beneath the pond to escape them. In the dark depths of the water his thoughts could not maintain the rational linearity that they pretended to above the surface. Here he was unflinchingly the creature that Rahul and chance had made him. Like his spiraling, serpentine body, his mind curled out into the surrounding water, feeling in its currents the drifting, unformed thoughts of those plants who might one day have been companions, if he had permitted it.

He almost regretted what he'd done. If he had let them grow unhampered, if he had allowed Rahul to use his pond, he might not be alone. But he'd been angry that day. The day he'd severed the taproot with a furious slash of his tail and relegated what existed of those vegetable minds to an eternal, aquatic meditation.

Diving deeper, Tumcari swam to the center of the pond, where the stalk of the plant leaned on its side, unsupported by the taproot that had long since rotted away.

He played games with himself over checking the stem; waiting sometimes for months, and then examining it every day for a week. But always the result was the same. No new roots, but no decay, either. The plant still lived, its stems flowing up around the sides of the stalk to lift green leaves to the surface, to the light.

Rahul wandered the small confines of his templating chamber's observation booth. He'd converted the room into a den. The walls were lined with bookcases, except for the one overlooking the chamber, a panel of glass dark from the dark and empty space behind it.

He drank his whiskey highball and scanned the spines of books he had not read in thirty years. He was putting off the inevitable, he told himself, but still he paced the floor a few more times before seating himself in his easy chair and switching on the vidphone. He dialed Wotroya House.

Ms. Wujcik answered it on the seventh ring. "Hello Dr. Rahul, how are you this evening?"

"Oh not bad, Ms. Wujcik, and yourself?"

"Just fine."

"You still like it there, then, at the mansion."

"Oh yes, thank you."

He smiled at her. "That's nice. Ms. Wujcik, I'd like to speak to Tumcari, is he alone?"

"Yes, Mr. Tumcari is alone right now."

"Good, then take a portable vidphone into the greenhouse so I can talk to him, would you?"

"Oh, I'd be happy to, Dr. Rahul."

The vidphone screen went blank momentarily as he was transferred to the greenhouse, and then he could see the pond, and the trees and flowers, and there, in the water, Tumcari. Rahul adjusted the display to zoom in on his face, floating just above the surface of the pond.

"Hello Tumcari," said Rahul.

Tumcari's eyes widened in mock adoration. "Dad! You remembered my birthday!"

Rahul gritted his teeth. "It's not your birthday."

"It's not? You mean you called just because you miss me?"

"Let's just say I thought of you."

"Oh, you don't know what it means to me, that you haven't forgotten your firstborn."

Rahul smiled. "So how is everything? Are Ms. Wujcik and the rest of the staff taking good care of you?"

"The best they can. Of course, nothing can match the hospitality of a team of researchers or, moreover, your own gentle ministrations. But my situation is much as it was the last time we spoke, what, six months ago?"

"Forgive me, the demands of my business have kept me well occupied. Be assured, I have not forgotten you."

Tumcari's eyes narrowed. "You have not forgotten, and neither have I. I would even venture to say that you have not forgiven me. Therefore, what can I forgive, without your example?"

Rahul sighed. "It was only a figure of speech, Tumcari."

"Come back to Wotroya House, continue your research, doctor."

Rahul shook his head; this was an old argument. "I am continuing my research, but I cannot work at Wotroya House. You made sure of that when you destroyed the *Nymphaea Matera.*"

"But the leaves still live! You could fix the plant, I know you could. But you won't even try, because you're afraid to get in the water with me. You're afraid that if you do, I'll kill you."

"And can you be so sure that you wouldn't?"

Tumcari smiled slowly, widely, and cast his eyes up, gazing at the tops of the trees surrounding the pond. At length he sighed and looked back at Rahul, still smiling, his eyes brimming with some unfathomable emotion. "No."

"No. You see? That's where we stand, nothing has changed. That matter is not for consideration. However, the last time we spoke, you asked me to send another researcher there to study you. If you are still willing, I can honor that request."

The creature was silent a long time. "It's very generous of you, to grant my wish after all these months, but I've changed my mind. No mind but your own could discover anything about me that I would value, and I do not wish to be poked and prodded merely for the sake of keeping up appearances."

"How unusual for you, to refuse human companionship, under any guise."

Tumcari stared at him. "I would think you'd be glad,

doctor, to learn that I am content with the companions you've provided me."

Just as Rahul had expected, Tumcari did not want him to send any additional staff. He already had extra staff. Even the promise of further research did not sway him, but then, he already had that too. "Oh, I am glad. Glad most of all that you seem to have accepted things as they must be."

"No. There you're wrong, doctor. I will never accept things as they are. I am the first and only of my kind. My fate could have been that of the proud founder of a new species, but you have reduced me to this, a curiosity kept under glass. You have no further use for me, it is clear. At least you could give me my liberty."

"How? You cannot walk."

"There are oceans. Put me in one."

"That is out of the question."

"Why? Because I want it?"

"Because I have a responsibility—"

"Responsibility? Don't talk to me of responsibility. You have a responsibility to what you began with me. What was it you said you wanted? An independent, intelligent, artificial life-form? Did you ever consider what you really meant by that? A species, never before seen on this planet, developed through the evolution not of nature, but of your own mind.

"You made me, but I am not parthenogenic, and you have abandoned your responsibility by refusing to make more of me."

"I cannot make more of you; your destruction of the *Nymphaea*—"

"Yes! Yes! My mother, and I killed her. Yes! I know. But she lives, doctor."

"If you will recall, I tried other methods; all failed."

"What you mean is that I failed you. And now you have

abandoned me to pursue other avenues of research. But none of them will ever get you any closer to your dream."

"My dream? You destroyed my dream a long time ago, Tumcari."

"No. No, I didn't. I am alive. I am your dream."

"A disobedient, malformed monster? That's not what I wanted."

"You wanted to create an independent, intelligent life-form. And as for my shape, that too, doctor, is your doing."

THREE IN THE AFTERNOON

The crawl space beneath Wotroya House was three feet high, cold, damp, and dark. Magnolia stripped the worn plastic casing from a ground wire and switched on a halogen penlight. Behind her, Kelira used the microtorch to resolder a junction box. The tiny blue flame sent flickering shadows up the wooden struts all around them.

Late the night before, a blizzard had wrapped itself around the ancient mansion like a hungry lover, howling at the windows and pressing against the doors. It was impossible to see anything outside except for snow swirling against the blackness.

The storm broke several panes on the greenhouse and took out the electricity in the kitchen. First thing this morning, Kelira had the Goon Squad on repair detail. He sent Spider and Dex to work on the greenhouse, a simple matter of replacing a few panes of glass. He picked her to accompany him down here, definitely the more demanding of the two tasks. Magnolia supposed she should be pleased. Her electrical skills were getting some attention. Lying in dust and ice, searching for bad connections and worn wires in an apparently endless tangle of outdated electrical lines, she felt she could do without the honor.

Under the tight beam of her penlight the bared wire gleamed crimson. "Jesus, this is copper!" she said in frustration, "I'm surprised the whole place didn't go up in flames years ago." She rolled over to look at Kelira, his face bathed in the intermittent light of the torch, pupils flashing like strobe lights. "You'd think a big shot like Rahul would be able to afford decent wiring."

Kelira glanced at her, a thin smile twisting his lips. "He just needs this place to keep Tumcari in. Do you think he cares as long as he stays under wraps?"

Magnolia reached into the pocket of her parka and pulled out a roll of polymer tape. Gripping the penlight in her teeth, she wound the pale, faintly luminescent film around the wire in a tight spiral.

A flashlight stabbed the darkness of the crawl space. "Kelira?" It was Spider.

"Over here," called Kelira.

"Can you come take a look at the greenhouse?"

Kelira groaned. "All right, I'll be there in a few minutes, okay?"

"Okay." The beam of the flashlight receded and then disappeared.

Kelira finished with the microtorch, switched it off, and handed it to Magnolia. "I'll be back in a few minutes."

When Kelira got to the greenhouse, Spider and Dex were there, so was Cid, and Ms. Wujcik. A glass table stood in the middle of the patio, the portable vidphone sitting on top of it, facing the pond. Lawn chairs were set up in front of the table, six of them, arranged in an arc with a gap in the middle, presumably to give Tumcari a clear view.

"Who set all this up?" asked Kelira, wiping his dirty hands on his pants.

"Spider and Dex did it this morning," said Tumcari. "It seems we are to be treated to a spectacle. Very thoughtful of the doctor, don't you think, to provide us with entertainment?" Tumcari's eyes were as green as ever. Behind him the repaired panes of the greenhouse stood out from the others, patches of clear plastic, which transmitted the light in a milky haze.

Kelira looked at Spider and Dex. "What's going on?"

Spider's shrug was as eloquent as a waterfall. "We didn't want to worry you, but Rahul's going to call in a few minutes. He wants to talk to everyone."

"What? He told you that? Why didn't he talk to me?"

"You were busy. Don't worry, we've taken care of it."

"What does he want to talk to us about?" Kelira asked him.

"Beats me. Where's Magnolia?" Spider started walking towards the greenhouse doors.

"She's under the house, why?"

Spider turned and looked at him with a satisfaction so sublime as to amount to a state of grace. "He wants to talk to her too."

"He wants to talk to Magnolia?" Kelira's chest tightened. "I'll get her."

Spider smiled. "I don't think so." He stepped to the side to block Kelira's path.

"Get out of my way." What a complete bastard the kid was, anyway. Always striking these fucking macho badass poses. Always rubbing it in Kelira's face for not being as big an asshole as he was.

"Dex," said Spider.

Kelira turned to see Dex advancing on him. Kelira stepped back and to the side, then suddenly pivoted to dodge around Spider.

But Spider turned as he passed and wrapped Kelira in a double armlock, hauling him away from the doors and shoving him into Dex's waiting arms. Dex had never really gotten a handle on joint holds, he just hung on. Still, it was hard to go much of anywhere with a hundred-and-eighty-pound anchor attached to your waist.

"What are you doing?" shouted Kelira as Spider fooled around at the door.

"Locking you in," said Spider, and then he shut the door and was gone.

Dex released him, and Kelira took a deep breath.

"So Rahul wants to talk to Magnolia too," said Cid.

Kelira looked at her and sat down heavily in one of the lawn chairs. "I guess he does."

A high-pitched warble, like the cry of a demented and ominous bird, interrupted the silence. Ms. Wujcik stepped to the phone and switched on the receiver.

Rahul appeared on the view screen, neatly dressed and collected as always. He looked each of them over in turn. "Good afternoon, Kelira, Cid."

"Hi, Rahul," said Cid.

"Dex, how are you today?"

"All right," drawled Dex.

Rahul nodded. "Tumcari, you're looking well."

"What's going on, Rahul?" said Kelira. "Why did Spider lock us in here?"

"I'm afraid current circumstances make such precautions necessary. I didn't mean to alarm you. Dex, I assume Spider has gone to fetch Magnolia?"

"That's right, sir."

"Fine, we may as well get started. Who wants to begin?" Rahul looked pointedly at Kelira.

Nobody spoke. Kelira felt like a bird paralyzed in the gaze of a hungry cobra.

"Very well, then," said Rahul, "I'll start. Six weeks ago I was in New York. I met a young lady there. Her name is Magnolia. I know you know this, Kelira, because I told you myself that very night, when I asked you to send Ms. Wujcik to pick her up in St. Petersburg. Do you remember where Ms. Wujcik was supposed to take her?"

Kelira's voice shook. "Tunis."

"But she didn't go to Tunis, did she?"

"No," whispered Kelira. His eyes lost focus. He was no longer seeing Rahul on the vidscreen, but Magnolia, his not-sister, looking up from a bed of gauze.

"Did you tell Ms. Wujcik to take her to Tunis?" Rahul's voice was gentle now with the promise of forgiveness. Forgiveness that hinged on Kelira's answer.

Kelira glanced at Tumcari as his mind flitted to the technicalities of the answer. He had not, in fact, told Ms. Wujcik to go anywhere. Tumcari had, and if it were not for his assistance, Kelira never would have been able to bring Magnolia to Wotroya. But it had only been assistance. It was his own idea. "No."

"You didn't? What did you tell her?"

Kelira shook his head. "Look, you know already. You know all about it. So why are you playing this game?"

"Games, as you should know, are fun, Kelira."

Dread collected itself in the pit of Kelira's stomach, anchoring him to his chair.

"Come come, now. The best thing for you to do is cooperate, believe me."

Kelira's cheeks burned, and he knew that deep red spots had appeared there, betraying his calm facade. One of his colleagues had squealed on him, and it was unlikely that it was Tumcari, who was loath to cooperate with Rahul on any matter, or Cid; her reasons for wanting to keep Magnolia at Wotroya House had become obvious over the last few weeks. He turned to face Rahul in anger. "How do you know she's here?" he challenged.

"As the administrative acolyte said to the priest, 'Nun of your business.' "

Out of the corner of his eye Kelira caught the smug expression on Dex's face. He wheeled on him. "You have something to do with this, don't you? You and Spider."

Dex gazed at him with wide-eyed innocence. "Who, us? I don't know what would make you think that."

"Spider's had his nose out of joint ever since Magnolia shot it with a paint gun. Ever hear of motive, Dex? You two have it in huge steaming chunks."

"Kelira, I'm surprised," said Rahul. "You seem to be taking this personally. When I realized Magnolia was at Wotroya House, and had been for some time, I assumed it was the machinations of our fine feathered friend, Mr. Tumcari, that had brought her there, but your behavior is about to make me change my theory."

"It wasn't Tumcari," said Kelira. "It was me. I had Ms. Wujcik bring Magnolia here, instead of to Tunis like you asked."

Rahul stretched his eyes wide in feigned alarm. "You're taking full responsibility for this on yourself? There was no one else involved?"

Kelira shook his head and stared at him hard. "No. Not in any way that matters."

"That's not entirely true," said Tumcari. "I was the one who spoke to Ms. Wujcik."

"Ah, I thought so."

"I put him up to it, Rahul. It was my idea."

"Mmm. How heartwarming to see you two stand up for each other like this. But tell me, Kelira. If you did bring Magnolia to Wotroya, and your behavior here seems to support your claim, what did you hope to gain by it?"

Kelira shook his head. He didn't have an answer to that.

"Have you been dissatisfied with your job? Do you feel that I've treated you unfairly in any way?"

"No, it's not that. I didn't do it as something against you, I just . . ." Kelira searched for words. "I saw her on television, just like you did. She reminded me of someone I knew once, that's all."

"I see. Your long-lost sister. You told me about her. But you should have known she wasn't Rose."

"I did. I did know. I just . . . Never mind. It doesn't matter. Here, I'll save you the trouble of firing me. I resign."

"You're not even going to give me the satisfaction of an explanation, are you?"

"Nope," said Kelira. "It's none of your business."

Magnolia trudged wearily upstairs to Cid's room. Kelira never returned from the greenhouse, and she didn't see why she should troubleshoot the whole house by herself. At least now the kitchen was in fairly good shape. Her back ached, and her hands were blistered from unkinking the twisted wires of Wotroya's ancient nervous system.

The room was empty, and she went immediately to the shower. Cid's room now was hers too. They used her old room as a place to store part of Cid's ever-expanding collection of papers, hardware, computer disks, and priceless junk. It hadn't made much of a dent in the clutter around here, as it turned out. Magnolia fished a strip of black-and-white photo negatives off of the showerhead and turned on the water, letting its warmth ease her sore shoulders. Relaxing, she rinsed the dirt of Wotroya from her body, admiring the muscles that four months of training had made sleek and strong.

Someone pounded on the door. "Magnolia, you in there?" She heard Spider's voice over the shower's spray.

Groaning, she dried off and wrapped a towel around her dripping hair, threw on jeans and a T-shirt, and opened the door. "What are you doing here, Spider?"

"Rahul's calling. He wants to talk to everyone in the greenhouse."

"So what, he doesn't even know I—" She stopped herself too late. Spider and Dex were supposed to think she was supposed to be here.

"He knows, baby," said Spider with a sickening smile, "he knows."

Magnolia stared at him. He was way too happy. "You told him, didn't you. Somehow you figured out he didn't know, and you told him."

Spider rolled his eyes. "Save your theories, puss. Right now Rahul wants you down in the greenhouse with everyone else." He reached a hand out to grab her arm.

"Fuck you, asshole!" Magnolia moved to the side and shoved him in the chest. It was a mistake. As soon as she got close enough, he wrapped his arms around her, and instead of bowling him over, her momentum helped him swing her through the doorway. She kneed him in the groin, and he loosened his grip on her. She stepped back and hit him in the jaw.

"Oh dear," said Rahul as Magnolia and Spider came into view, ragged, bloody, and torn. They were breathing heavily from their exertions. Spider had just launched Magnolia into the vidphone's viewing range with a violent shove. She landed on the gravel, but immediately stood and turned to face him.

"Enough!" said Rahul.

Spider turned to look at him and was blindsided by Magnolia, who knocked him to the ground and proceeded to straddle his chest.

Dex and Kelira jumped up and pulled her off of him, dragging her to the chair next to Cid's. She jerked in their grasp, trying to break away, but she must have been getting tired. "Every time I've got him, you make me stop. Why is that, Kelira?"

Rahul's eyes followed Spider as he walked stiffly to the chair next to Ms. Wujcik's and sat down. "That was regrettable, Spider," he said.

Spider only looked at him sullenly. Rahul turned his attention to Magnolia. "Please accept my profoundest apologies, dear. It was never my intention that you be harmed in any way."

"I'm fine. He's gonna feel like a sack of shit for two days. But I'm fine."

"Good. Because I would very much like you to come to Tunis now. The offer I made you in New York still stands."

"I don't know." Magnolia hesitated, glancing at Cid.

"Of course I want Cid to come too," said Rahul, "if she will. My business is expanding, and I have need of a qualified lab supervisor."

Cid's eyes narrowed, but she said nothing.

"She's going to be a lab supervisor. What am I going to do?" asked Magnolia, pushing her disordered hair out of her face.

Rahul smiled. "Just be yourself."

She looked at Cid again, who stared at her, shaking her head ever so slightly.

"I know what you want to do," said Magnolia, facing him again. "You want to use me to make more robots."

Rahul pursed his lips. "Templating you is part of it, but not just to make another strain of robots. These will be different, because, like you, they will be unpredictable."

She was thinking about it. Rahul carefully schooled his features to hide his eagerness.

"No, I don't think so," she said. "It creeps me out too much. I don't want a bunch of duplicates of myself running around. It's like I'd lose all control over what happens to me."

"And you have so much control now, don't you? Shanghaied out there by Kelira. Well, I'll go to twenty, but that's it. I can always find someone else with similar qualities to yours and a much lower price."

"Twenty." Magnolia looked back at Cid again. "Are you going?"

Cid looked back at her, her eyes bright with tears. "No," she said, her voice hardly more than a whisper.

Magnolia smiled. "Then neither am I. Get yourself another guinea pig, Rahul. We're history."

Rahul bit back his anger. "Very well, then," he said in clipped tones. "I think you'll regret it, but it's your decision." He nodded curtly. "I want the three of you packed and ready to leave by tomorrow at this time. Ms. Wujcik will fly you to the airport in Tarko Sale. There you will disembark. You're free to go anywhere you like from that point on, as long as it's not Wotroya House. I suggest you refrain from doing anything foolish. You've all been remarkably lucky so far. Don't forget it." He hung up, and the screen went blank.

For a moment the greenhouse rang with Rahul's final words. They were all still, suspended in that instant. Spider, Dex, and Ms. Wujcik on one side, Magnolia, Cid, and Kelira on the other, and Tumcari between them. Then Cid stood and threw herself into Magnolia's arms.

Her tears, warm and damp, soaked through Magnolia's sweater. Magnolia held her, almost absently, her mind still reeling from what she'd done.

"When he went up to twenty, I thought for sure you'd go," Cid whispered.

Magnolia shook her head. "So did I. I can't believe I didn't."

They were interrupted by the scrape of Dex's feet upon the gravel. He and Spider were leaving and taking Ms. Wujcik with them. She walked between them, her arms resting on their shoulders, and theirs twined about her waist. She was nearly a head taller than Dex and on a par with Spider. In silence the rest watched them go. When the greenhouse doors closed behind them, they turned to each other.

"It was them," said Kelira.

"Oh, obviously," Tumcari replied. "Not that there's anything we can do about it now."

"What's going to happen to you, Tumcari?" asked Cid.

He grimaced. "God knows. Apparently I'm to be on my own for at least a day or so, since Ms. W is accompanying you all to Tarko Sale and then continuing on to Tunis. Perhaps he'll send another robot out here, perhaps that's all he'll use here now, or maybe nobody at all."

Cid broke away from Magnolia's embrace and paced the gravel. "This sucks. I can't believe we have to go *now*. You know I've been looking into your cellular functioning, Tumcari. I'm right on the brink of something really interesting, something with potential. Shit! Why do we have to be out of here by tomorrow, for Goddess's sake?"

"So that we don't have time to pull any monkey business," suggested Kelira.

"Yeah, like murder Spider and Dex," said Magnolia.

Tumcari nodded. "An attractive idea, to be sure, but I'm afraid the consequences would be rather dire. It's well within

Rahul's resources to hire a hit man. That's what that last little bit there was about, in case you missed it. If you don't cooperate, you probably won't have a second chance to leave here."

Kelira, who'd been staring at the water in silence, looked up at them. "This is all my fault," he said.

Tumcari nodded. "Right you are."

Cid sighed. "Kelira, what you did was ill-advised, and pretty weird, but I can't honestly say I'm sorry you did it. As a matter of fact, on the whole, I'm glad."

"Me too," said Magnolia.

"How nice. I hope you two lovebirds will think of me, languishing here alone, while you're off wherever you're off to," said Tumcari bitterly.

An awkward silence pervaded the greenhouse as they stared at him. Magnolia realized that for the small part he'd played in all of this, he'd probably pay the biggest price.

Kelira shifted his weight and cleared his throat. "So, where are we going to go?"

Cid's eyes gleamed, and she looked from Magnolia to Kelira and back to Magnolia again. "Let's go to Amsterdam," she said, grinning in delight. "I've always wanted to, and it's on the continent, so the tickets should be fairly cheap."

So they were going to Amsterdam. Rahul grimaced and turned off the vidphone. It would be another half an hour before Spider and Dex called for their instructions. Rahul left the den and went downstairs to his laboratory.

He wandered among the tanks, adjusting an intake hose here, a temperature gauge there. Magnolia had refused to come to Tunis and be templated. Refused despite the shocking amount of money Rahul threw at her. Once again she had behaved unpredictably. The incident only served to increase her value in his eyes. If he could isolate that contrary aspect of her personality, he just might have the foundation on which an independent new life-form could be built. And this time, he'd do it right.

Something had gone wrong with Tumcari. Somewhere in the very early stages of his creation, Rahul had made a mistake, and the error amplified itself as Tumcari developed. It could have been a very small thing at first, but what was small at the stage of grafting and cloning genes magnified as the scale progressed to cells and cell structures until, at the end, what he had produced was so thoroughly entwined with that error that there was no extricating it. He could no more "fix" Tumcari than he could change the color of the sky. Rahul had gone over the preliminary stages of the project so many times he knew every step by heart, and nowhere had he found a lapse. Tumcari's gene code was exactly what he'd wanted it to be. The error, whatever it was, lay somewhere else.

But Rahul had given up pursuit of it many years ago, when he realized that even if he could duplicate Tumcari, he would not want to. No, the key to realizing his dream of an independent, intelligent artificial life-form was elsewhere. In Magnolia, perhaps.

Rahul gritted his teeth and threw an air filter to the ground. Nothing ever went the way he planned it. All his years of education and research, his dreams. Somehow, something always went wrong, and though he had done well for himself, he was bitter with thwarted design.

He remembered the Goddess in the temple, and he heard her laughing at him. He should have known long ago, very long ago, that he could not sway fate by force.

He needed a plan, then, that was not a plan.

If the things he tried to make happen were bound to fail, then perhaps the best approach was to mimic the symmetry of the situation at hand. Go with the flow, so to speak.

Kelira had said that Magnolia reminded him of his sister Rose. That was, in fact, his only stated reason for stealing her.

Well then, Magnolia had brothers. One in particular that she mentioned by name: Manus, a half-wit cripple.

Rahul's grandmother had always insisted that such people were sacred. "Touched by God," she'd called them. Certainly, Rahul could do with a little divine guidance in this situation.

And then there was Kelira. Kelira who had worked for him for more than ten years, who had always been dependable, reliable. Rahul had always liked Kelira, and he'd come to trust him. His betrayal was an injustice he could not tolerate, but perhaps there too, fate had given him a weapon.

BY MOONLIGHT

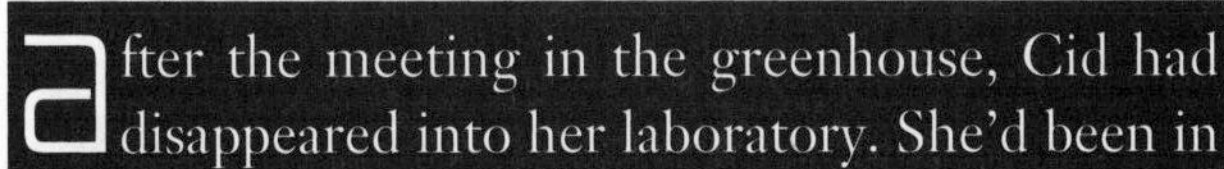

After the meeting in the greenhouse, Cid had disappeared into her laboratory. She'd been in there for hours now. Magnolia had finished her packing and was tired of sitting around with Kelira in the video room. She decided to drop in on her lover.

On the way upstairs she passed Ms. Wujcik coming from the direction of the lab. The tall, blond automaton smiled at her vaguely, her forehead glowing with faint phosphorescence. Magnolia wondered what Cid had done to her, and how she'd pried her away from Spider and Dex to do it.

The hallway leading to Cid's lab was dark. Magnolia walked slowly past the doors of storerooms, their pebbled glass hinting at the shadowy forms of crates and instrument stands. At the end of the hallway was the door to the lab. It was dark too. She paused, resting her hand on the cool brass doorknob. Maybe Cid had gone to bed, she thought, but then she heard the singing. High and sweet, Cid's voice reached her in a faint, wordless thread.

Magnolia opened the door and caught her breath in wonder. The room was dark except for the moon outside the open windows, glittering in hundreds of slender glass rectangles which hung suspended from the ceiling. She stepped inside and closed the door behind her, gaping in wonder at the garden of moonlight above her.

Like the light dancing through glass, Cid moved around the lab, at once fluid and unpredictable. Papers lay scattered all about the room, on the floor, on tables and benches, and every step Cid took landed her on one of those papers, covered with her own crabbed scribblings. Her singing continued, a soft, jubilant wail, wafting about the lab like a vapor Magnolia dared not disturb. Something was happening here, there was something with them in this room. Something that she could not see gathered around them in silence. Magnolia panicked and felt for the door, but she caught sight of Cid's eyes, saw the light of a million moons reflected there, and she had to stay.

Cid's path took her through the center of the room and back out to the edges, weaving around tables and chairs that had been rearranged since Magnolia had seen them last. When she caught sight of her leaning beside the door, Cid's smile broadened to a grin. She spun to a stop in front of her. "You came," she said, reaching her hands upwards to cup Magnolia's face. "I knew you would come."

Magnolia grasped her hands and brought them down. "What are you doing?" she asked, glancing at the transformed lab.

"I'm celebrating. And recording the moment for posterity," she added, pointing to the video camera mounted over the doorway.

"You're hot," said Magnolia, feeling Cid's forehead, which was damp with perspiration.

"It's the fever, a slight side effect from the carrier virus; it'll pass." Her face was in shadow, out of the glitter of the reflected moonlight, but still her eyes glowed with phosphorescent intensity.

Magnolia peered closer in wonder. "Your eyes," she said, "they're changing. The patterns—" The patterns of her irises flowed and swirled around each other, like the tides, like the holograph that hung over their bed.

Cid smiled with a glee that chilled Magnolia to the bone. "My eyes can see the patterns of the chaos of the world." She stretched her arms out from her sides, her lab coat gaping to reveal the soft swell of her belly, the rosy tip of one small breast. She sang, her voice no longer a sweet high echo, but powerful and deep. "Amazing Grace, how sweet the sound, that saved a wretch like me. I once was lost, but now I'm found, was blind but now I see."

Magnolia gasped, "The virus!"

"Yes."

"But you'll turn into a creature like Tumcari!" Magnolia backed away from her, knocking her head on the closed door.

"No, I won't. I won't change much physically at all." Cid moved towards her, trapping her against the door. "I've got Goddess vision, Mag, and soon others will have it too."

"It's contagious!" Magnolia looked frantically from side to side, searching for escape, but it was no use. Cid had her backed up against the door. There were tears in her eyes as she looked back at her lover's radiant face. Cid leaned even closer and kissed her. Magnolia shook her head, dislodging the soft lips. "No! I don't want to catch it!" She pushed Cid away from her and turned to open the door.

"You won't catch it."

Magnolia turned to face her again. Cid leaned against a table, her smile gone for the moment. Magnolia took her hand from the doorknob. "How do you know?"

She shrugged. "I just know. You're a carrier. You can transmit the virus, but it won't affect you."

Magnolia narrowed her eyes. "I've heard that one before," she said with a wry smile.

"Yeah, but I bet it wasn't from a molecular biologist."

Magnolia laughed in spite of herself and moved away from the door. She sat down on a metal folding chair. "So what's it like, Cid, this Goddess vision?"

She sighed and spread her arms wide. "I'm home again, for good. It's not just that I'm aware of the fact that I'm connected to Her, to All that Is. I don't just know it, I feel it. It's hard to explain, but the tides, and the pulse of my blood, they sing in unison and I can hear it! I can hear it! The beautiful music . . . We know each other now, Magnolia. We can communicate. I feel it all: rain in Sumatra, smog in L.A., the earth frozen beneath this house, above us the moon slowly turning in her periodic dance. And you, I can feel your heart beating, rather loudly, just now. The sound your breath makes as it fills your lungs is like the wind in a cornfield in Montana. And your eyes, they're the color of a particular mineral embedded in the crust of an undiscovered planet, thousands of light years away."

Magnolia stared at her in awe and fear. "You're mad," she whispered.

"Perhaps," she said, "but I will not be the only one."

For the first time in his life, Tumcari was not alone.

He surfaced and broke the mirrored calm of the water into a million fragments, softly glimmering with the pale, distant light of the stars. A single undulating trail of red danced across the water, reflected from a light nearly hidden among the dark leaves of the nighted jungle, the recording indicator of a miniaturized camera.

In the daylight it would be too faint to be seen. He wondered how long he'd been under the patient, bloodshot gaze of this observant cyclops. A day, probably. He had a pretty good idea of who had put it there. The only people he knew of who'd been among the plants recently. It was unlikely that anyone could have snuck past him. He slept but little.

Many a time he would have delighted in the opportunity to speak to Rahul without interruption or argument, but tonight it did not interest him. He had better conversations going on already.

It began about an hour ago, as he was swimming around the *Nymphaea Matera* in long, slow circles. He did not hear it or feel it in the strictest sense, but he became aware that upstairs in her laboratory, Cid was becoming one of him.

He was aware of her now, not of her thoughts or what she was doing, but he could feel her body, talking to itself, talking to him. In her cells tiny swimmers sang as they plied their eukaryotic oceans, and inside him a chorus of millions answered back.

Rahul would send her away, but it didn't matter. Distance could not separate them, and at any rate, she would make more, and they would be back. Oh, they would be back.

a RIVER IS a CaR

The little hut was without heat except for what his body could provide. Manus shivered in the good deerskin-and-fleece coat Mule Pritchard had lent him, and shifted on the narrow boards of the bench. The toes of his remaining foot were numb. Far more so than those he had lost but still felt.

He leaned forward to poke at the film of ice crusted over the hole. The ice broke with a beautiful splintering sound, and he scraped around the sides, riming his gloved hands with ice.

He sat back and plunged one hand into the bucket at his side. The rubber glove lined with an old sock that he wore protected him from the wetness of the water, but not its chill. His fingers stiffened, and he had difficulty grasping the struggling minnow. Its silver body wriggled in his clumsy grasp like a desperate slice of lightning. He speared it with his fishhook, but still it struggled on, as if it didn't know that it would never go anywhere again without a tether of metal through its gut.

"Go and find something in the river," he whispered to the little fish, and then he lowered it through the black hole in the ice, into the dark winter waters of the river.

Manus stared at the hole until he stopped seeing it. The itch and tingle that existed where his other leg did not increased. With a sigh Manus closed his eyes to hear what his leg had to tell him today.

There wasn't very much smell to the partition in wintertime. Mostly the electric smell of cold air, and sometimes the warm, cooped-up smells of cooking or liquor or kerosene, which wandered out from indoors. This time of year people stayed inside as much as possible, hiding from the vacant air.

Through the thin vapor of odors wound the smell of carbon dioxide. A car was winding its way through the partition like a minnow on a line.

In the partition a car was a red flag, a humiliating reminder of lost prosperity. Most of the roads had long since crumbled into jagged, pockmarked tracks. It took guts, firepower, four-wheel drive, and an overwhelming desire to impress to drive a car here.

It had been done; the gang that killed his sister Doralee had ridden in on an Audi HumVee, but they knew where they were going, went there, and booked back out again. By the smell of it, this car was trolling, slowly making its way south and east, deeper into the partition, towards Manus.

The city spread itself out around him, white with snow and immobile as a corpse. Even the river hid its movement beneath the ice, as if to avoid attracting attention. You had to poke a hole in the ice and stab a fish if you wanted to feel the river moving.

Manus could feel it moving in the quiver and twitch of the line in his hands; the minnow was swimming still.

The river led out of the city, and somewhere, out there, was his sister. His leg often led him down along the river, following its currents, searching for clues as to where she might be. Today, in the invisible rolling motion of the river, his leg spoke to him. It said, "Sometimes a car can be a river."

Manus had caught two bass when the rickety door of the shack opened, letting in a large quantity of pale winter sunlight. Mule Pritchard stood silhouetted in the doorway, well over six feet tall and spindly, with long arms and legs. "I figure you been fishing long enough," he said, stepping forward to pick up the bait bucket and the string of bass.

Together they made their way up the path to Mule's rusting double trailer.

Manus had been staying with Mule and Granny Daisy for several months. Doralee's death was like a stone dropped into the unquiet waters of their family. The members spread out in ripples from the impact of the bullet that killed her. Magnolia disappeared, Drew went off on a bender and never came back, Albert found his own digs, Cherry went to live with a man downriver and took Augustina with her. Only the youngest three, Moriarty, Roswell, and Corona remained with their mother.

It was Moriarty who met them halfway down the path. "Manus!" he yelled, breaking into a run as he spotted them. "There's a car at Mom's! It's an Absolut ATV90, and you should see the guy who was driving it. He's got on a suit, and there's these two huge guys with Tektronic subcannons backing him up. He wants to—"

"Hush now, boy," said Mule, "no need for the neighborhood to know more than they already do." He glanced at Manus. "Why don't you come on inside now, huh?"

Manus smiled and followed them up to the trailer. He deposited the fish in the sink, sat down by the space heater, and pulled off his gloves.

Mule poured two mugs of coffee and handed him one. "Moriarty's got it right about that car, Manus. Pretty strange, that, in and of itself, but the thing is—"

"Car's going to take me out of Detroit," said Manus, looking up from the swirling steam of his mug.

Mule stared at him. The trailer was silent except for the muted sounds of Granny snoring in the bedroom. She'd be sore when she woke up and found out she'd missed all the action.

"How'd you—? Aw never mind, I know," said Mule, "your leg told you that car had something to do with you, didn't it? Well you listen here, Manus, that guy's a real high roller. I expect he could bring another twenty fellas with sub-cannons in here and waste us all if he wanted, and for some reason or other he wants to talk to you. He's down at your mother's now, waiting.

"You can do one of two things, Manus, and I hope you understand. You can go out now, down to the river, take my boat, and float on out of here, or you can go talk to him. But there's something he wants from you, and if you go near him, you can be sure he'll get it."

Manus could see that Mule was upset. The man with the car scared him because he didn't understand. "The car and the river are the same thing."

Mule just shook his head. "Goddamn. Rich bastard comes down here, messing with a half-wit cripple doesn't know his ass from a hole in the ground." He slapped the table, hard.

Manus jumped at the noise and grabbed his crutch. Standing up, he nodded at Moriarty, who scrambled to open the door for him. "Bye Mule," he said, gazing at him over his shoulder.

Semolina's house was a hub of activity. A crowd of onlookers stood a respectful distance from the gleaming black car; a thing that looked like it might shoot you itself if you got too close. But just to be on the safe side, a tall, heavyset, bald man in a dark overcoat leaned against the door of the house, cradling a subcannon larger than his arm and keeping a watchful eye on the crowd.

As Manus and Moriarty approached the house a little cluster of spectators broke off and scurried towards them.

"Oh Manus, you should see the man that's come to talk to you," said Callie Winston. "He's wearing a silk suit, and Donitra Davis says he's from New York."

"It's true," chimed Hal Alfonso. "The car has New York plates."

"Don't talk to him, Manus. He probably wants to peddle your ass," said a deep voice. Manus couldn't make out the speaker in the rising press of the crowd.

"Yeah, he dresses like a pimp."

"All right, all right, back off you all." Albert's tenor staccato cut through the rising babble and quelled it. "Let my brother through, he's got important business inside."

The crowd parted, and Manus stepped through into the clutches of Albert, who briskly assisted him to the house. Of course Albert would be here, drawn inexorably by the smell of money.

Inside, the stranger was seated at the slab of plywood on cinder blocks that served as a table in the large, single room of Semolina's squat. Behind him stood a guy that was the same guy as the one outside. It was the same gun, too. If he used it in here, the roof would probably cave in.

The stranger was a small man, and old, with just a little bit of white hair around the sides of his head, trimmed short. His eyes and his skin were the same color, a brown like acorns in the fall. That color and the man's coat, his hands and everything else about him told Manus that this was the last day he would ever be poor.

Semolina was also there, sitting with her hands in front

of her. She looked up as they entered, and stared at Manus in silence for long moments before returning her gaze to the clasping and unclasping of her hands.

Albert pulled back a chair for Manus. "I want you to meet Mr. Rahul, Manus."

"Doctor," said the stranger.

"Oh, doctor. Sorry," said Albert.

The doctor stranger was looking at Manus like he wanted to fit him right into his eyes, but Manus could tell he didn't fit. He giggled and opened his eyes wide to get the doctor all in his, instead.

"—has some things he wants to discuss with you, but first I want you to know that he and I have been negotiating, and I think we've reached an agreement that will be of great benefit to you."

Albert had seated himself and was now leaning towards Manus with his arm on the table. His face was coated with the mock sincerity of a TV lawyer, and he nudged the dripping thing close to Manus as he spoke. "You see, Mr. Rahul wants you to go with him, to a place where he can take better care of you than anyone here can. You'd get medical attention and"—Albert glanced at Rahul, who nodded—"a new leg."

"I don't need a new leg," said Manus. "I like the one I've got."

"No, Manus, an artificial leg, to replace the one you lost."

"But an artificial leg wouldn't talk to me." He looked at the doctor. "My leg talks to me."

The doctor nodded. "I see."

"Manus." Albert just wouldn't stop talking. "Mr. Rahul is prepared to be very generous—"

Manus watched the wood grain flow from his side of the table to the doctor's and back again.

"—could make a big difference, not just for you but"—

Albert grasped Manus's arm and turned his head to look at Semolina—"for others."

Manus followed his gaze to his mother, who no longer looked at him. He doubted very much if anything would ever make a difference to her again. He eyed Albert with only mild disgust, the rest of it having collected on his tongue. "Don't worry, Albert, I'll go with him, and you'll get your money. Stop talking now and go away."

Manus heard Albert's mask of sincerity hit the floor with a muffled splat.

"You idiot," Albert shouted in his face, "you can't tell me—" But his protest was cut short as the doctor's bodyguard lifted him under the arms and carried him out of the squat.

"Madam," said the doctor to Semolina, "would you excuse us, please? There are some things Manus and I should discuss privately."

Semolina looked at him for possibly the first time. Her face suddenly transformed with rage. "You want to take my boy from me? I've already lost a son and two daughters. Your money doesn't mean anything to me."

"Please, my dear lady," said the doctor, "I simply wish to speak with the young man. Any decision as to his future whereabouts is his to make."

She must have had the knife in her lap all along. Suddenly she lunged at the doctor with her arm thrust out, the blade in her hand glinting as it plunged towards his face.

The bodyguard was just returning from ejecting Albert; he leapt across the room, but it was too late. Semolina's blade drew a thin red line from Rahul's right eye to the edge of his lip.

The bodyguard grabbed Semolina and took the knife away from her. She struggled with him, crying, her hair falling in her face, but the bodyguard twisted her arms behind her back, and she stopped moving.

Rahul was dabbing at his wound with a handkerchief; little spots of blood marred its brilliant whiteness. "It's all right, Henri, just a scratch. Remove her, please, and see that she stays away until we depart."

As the door shut behind them Rahul's attention returned to Manus. "I must say, you have a singularly bad-tempered family. The women, in particular, have this propensity for knives. . . . Actually, it's about your family that I wished to speak with you, Manus. Your sister Magnolia."

"You will take me to her," said Manus.

Rahul paused and then smiled. "I hope to have that honor. You're quite an extraordinary young man, aren't you? How did you know what I was going to suggest?"

"A river is a car. The river and the car both go the way Magnolia went. My leg knows this."

"Your . . . leg. The one that was—"

Manus smiled and nodded. "It's gone somewhere. Sometimes it feels like it's still here"—he waved his hand below his stump—"but it's not. I'm just walking in two places at once. My leg is in places that I can't be. It tells me things about the world."

an eye and a leg

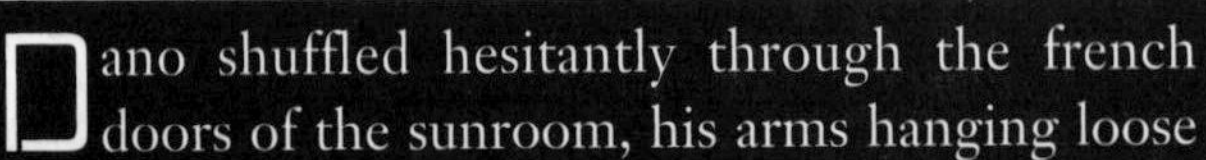

Dano shuffled hesitantly through the french doors of the sunroom, his arms hanging loose at his sides. On his face faint lines were discernible, the seams of his skin graft. "Clyde said you were asking Edgerton about me."

"Please sit down," said Rahul. "I'd like to take a look at your face."

Dano sat in a damask-covered wing chair. His clothes, the same ones he'd been in when he came to Rahul for treatment, were filthy, and so was he. As Rahul walked around the tea table, past the fragrant barrier of a vase of roses, he could smell him. He should have told Henri to bathe him before their interview, but no matter. His new strategy suggested that he use the tools at hand, and that did not allow for squeamishness.

Despite his unsanitary condition, Dano's grafts were healing well. Rahul leaned over him, gently prodding at his patchwork skin.

"Mmm. You've got a little infection here." His finger traced a section of the seam that was red and felt warm to his touch. "Have you been using the ointment I gave you?"

"I lost it," admitted Dano.

"Oh, well, no matter, I'll give you some more. But you'd better use it; that could become serious. Tell me"—Rahul returned once more to the love seat—"how are you doing with your new eye?"

Dano smiled eagerly. "It's wonderful, Doctor. Sees better than my old one, I swear. I saw Blanks on Bourguiba Avenue with it the other day. He must have been six blocks away, at least. Saved my life. But sometimes I have to put my hand up over the other one, because I get dizzy."

"When that happens, try focusing both your eyes on something fairly close," suggested Rahul.

"Oh, all right." Dano shrugged.

"You know, Dano, I've noticed there seem to be a lot of people, here and there, who are a danger to you."

"Well mostly here, Doctor. I've been in Tunis for too long, I guess."

"Would you like to go someplace else?"

"Oh sure, but . . ." Dano held his hands palms up beside his pockets.

"I see. Well, perhaps something could be arranged that would be beneficial to both of us, but first let me ask you something. Those television appearances of yours, usually you kill those girls, don't you?"

Dano tilted his head. "Ah, sometimes. Usually I'd just cut them up a bit, is all."

"Mmm. Never bothered you?"

Dano shook his head thoughtfully and gazed out the

window. Rahul could see the green eye looking far, far away. "Not really. It's not like I knew any of them or anything. I mean, I wouldn't have done it to Rose, not before this, anyway." He gestured vaguely at the right side of his face. "Now," he laughed, "I can't think of anything I'd like better."

"Yes, well. Do you have any experience with guns?"

"Naw, guns are no good, man. Everything happens too fast, viewers don't like it."

Rahul closed his eyes and shook his head. "Not on television."

"Not on television? You mean like for real?"

"Yes, for real." Rahul sensed he was losing ground irretrievably, sliding down a cliff in the mud slide of Dano's mind. But it was entertaining. People were so much fun.

"I had a gun once; bought it in New York. But I never had a chance to use it."

"But do you think you could shoot someone with one?"

"I guess so. I mean, my aim would be pretty good, wouldn't it?"

"Yes."

Dano's mouth widened in a smile. "You want me to off someone for you, is that it? Sure! You've been good to me, Doctor Rahul. I'd be happy to repay the favor—" Dano hesitated. "Wait a minute, is this somebody I know?"

"No." Rahul picked up a picture of Kelira and showed it to him. "This is the man."

"Huh." Dano peered at the photograph. "He looks kind of like Rose."

"He's her brother."

"Oh yeah? Then by all means, let me put him out of his misery, eh?"

Rahul smiled and lifted another pair of photographs from the table. "These young ladies will be with him. Only hit the man, do you understand?"

"Hey, it's that bitch from New York! Let me do her too, okay?"

Rahul shook his head. "Like you said, Dano, guns are no good. She's coming back here, to be filmed for a project of my own."

Dano laughed. "I'd think twice about that; she's a lousy actress. But . . . Do you have an actor yet?"

"If you do this job, hit the man and no one else, there could be a starring role in it for you," lied Rahul.

Dano grinned. "Yeah, you're right, that's way better than just shooting her. You know, Doc, you're a real stand-up guy. Really all right."

"That's kind of you."

"So when is all this going to go down?"

"You'll leave for Amsterdam in a few days. In the meantime, it seems to me, you could use a meal and a warm bed, perhaps a bath, no?"

"Sure. I'm a little down on my luck right now, actually. Edgerton probably told you that we decided to go our separate ways."

"He mentioned something like that, yes."

"We just felt it would be best for both of us if we pursued our own endeavors. You know, creative differences."

"Yes, of course. I'll have Henri ready a room for you, but first there's someone I'd like you to meet."

Althea showed Manus to a room made of windows, filled with flowers drinking in the light. Rahul sat on the little couch that was covered with blue and pink roses. Roses that didn't need the sun at all.

A man he'd never seen before sat in a big blue chair that, if it had ever wanted anything, wanted to swallow him in its upholstered depths. His face didn't belong to him anymore,

Manus could see that right away, so he knew not to believe anything the man's face said, because it would not be him talking.

"How are you feeling today, Manus?" asked Rahul.

Manus shrugged. "Fine." Having another leg made walking a lot easier, but it hadn't changed anything else very much. He'd been afraid that his old leg would stop talking to him, but it didn't, and today it told him he was going to see his sister very soon.

Rahul lifted a teapot littered with rosebuds, close relatives of the ones on the couch. "Manus, I'd like you to meet Dano. He's going to help us get your sister back."

Manus glanced at the man dubiously. "Hello."

"Hey, how's it going?"

Rahul passed Manus a tray of pastries. He grabbed the biggest, flakiest one of the bunch and bit into it, scattering crumbs across his shirt and his face. It was filled with apples, and the taste of apples was filled with the day Magnolia and Cherry and he had walked far, far, and far through the city, until they came, in the afternoon, to a place seemingly uninhabited. A large, one-story building—"a school," said Magnolia—with apple trees in its front yard. Manus still had both his legs with him that day, so even though he only knew what other people know, he could climb. He climbed to the top of the tree, higher even than Magnolia dared to go, and picked an apple there and ate it, in the sight of the sun and the sky and the birds that flew above.

"—has to be timed carefully. They all have to be together when it happens." Rahul was saying. "Wait until Manus greets them. Then hit the man and get out of there. I'll provide you with a plane ticket to Tarko Sale and transportation from there to a house where you can stay until things settle down."

"But then I'm going to come back here, for the movie,

right? You just have to let me take another crack at that bitch."

"Don't worry, I won't forget you," said Rahul. He looked at Manus. "Your job is to bring your sister and her friend back here. They will no doubt be shocked over the sudden death of their compatriot. You will be their comfort and their guide, do you understand?"

Manus nodded. He wouldn't have any trouble getting Magnolia to come to Tunis, his leg assured him of that.

BORN AND GONE TO AMSTERDAM

Like New York, Amsterdam was a consumer's paradise; only here the drugs and black-market items were sold openly at stalls and in shops, instead of in musty back rooms and dark alleys.

Magnolia ambled down Kloveniersburgval with Cid on her arm. On their left the canal moved sluggishly; a grey, murky waterway plied by barges and speedboats, its banks fringed with houseboats. As they neared Nieuwmarkt these residences gave way to floating shops peddling everything from flowers to high-tech electronics.

Along the sidewalk, dealers spread cloths on the ground or erected makeshift stalls to display their goods. The general cacophony of the crowd was intensified by the wild, atonal sounds of fusion buskers, their bodies wired to amplify and distort every sound they made, from the steady backbeat of their hearts to the dizzying scales of their digestive tracts.

Though they were well south of the red-light district,

they saw prostitutes wending their way here and there throughout the crowd, handing out promotional holofiches and religious icons. A tall, red-haired boy sporting cell-animated tattoos and a bifurcated penis smiled at them and handed Magnolia a cheap red-plastic rendition of the Buddha reaching enlightenment by autofellatio.

Along the canal Magnolia spotted a houseboat with clothes for sale. She pulled Cid from the crowd and stepped across the short gangway to the deck. Racks of leather jackets stood in rows beneath a green-and-white-striped awning. "Mm. What do you think?" she asked Cid, trying on a black bomber with slash pockets.

"Oh, it's you," said Cid, her eyes sparkling.

Magnolia turned to the proprietor, a husky, middle-aged man with stylishly sculptured whisker stubble. "How much?"

"Eighty-five," he replied in a thick accent.

"What? For vat leather? You're nuts," she said, taking it off.

"Isn't vat leather. It's real. Feel it."

Magnolia hesitated, fingering the jacket. Its texture was smooth and supple, and there was a thickness and weight to the hide that you didn't get with synthetics. She glanced at Cid, who raised an eyebrow. Leather was banned on the open market. Of course, beef was available on the black market all the time. They had to do something with the hides. "I'll give you sixty for it," she said to the dealer.

He shook his head. "Seventy-five, cash only, please."

Magnolia examined the jacket closely. It was lined, the zipper worked, no holes in the pockets or wear on the cuffs. Reluctantly she nodded. When would she even have the opportunity to buy such a thing again? "Okay," she said, and opened her wallet.

"Allow me," Cid interrupted, and reached into the black-and-silver-beaded handbag that hung from her shoulder. She produced a roll of bills, counted off seventy-five in Eurodollars, and handed them to the dealer.

"Where did you get that purse?" asked Magnolia, noticing it for the first time.

"It's a family heirloom; my great aunt on my mother's side was into the vintage revival. She found it secondhand, had it repaired, and passed it on to my mom. Mom gave it to me when I graduated high school. It's the only purse I've ever carried, and now I'm glad, because just touching it, I can feel the spirits of my female ancestors whispering in my veins."

The merchant handed Magnolia her jacket. She wrapped her arm around Cid as they stepped off the boat. "Thanks," she said.

"Anything for you, honey, besides, it really looks hot. Why don't you put it on now, huh?"

Magnolia stopped amid the clotting throng of passersby and slipped her arms into the sleeves of the jacket. It fell on her with a cool, reassuring weight, like a second skin. From her breast pocket she pulled a pair of round mirrored sunglasses and slid them on. She strutted around in a circle, the strong and flexible hide moving with her. She stopped and, cocking her hips, pointed a menacing finger at Cid. "And whose little chickie are you?" she snarled through a curled lip.

"Oh baby," gushed Cid, sliding up beside her and wrapping an arm around her hips, "we've got to get you boots and a whip."

Magnolia lost it, her icy, butch cool dissolving into a giggling cackle. "Shit, what do you want to do now, crazy eyes?"

Cid pointed to a shop on the other side of the canal. Above the white-painted and meticulously clean door hung a large disc decorated in blue and gold with a broad, smiling face. "Let's go to the Blue Moon Cafe," she said.

They took a bridge across the canal and doubled back.

The Blue Moon sported a gleaming shop front of crisp white-framed windowpanes, and blue flower boxes overflowing with dwarf cannabis and begonias.

Inside, the walls were naked brick. The high, vaulted ceiling echoed the sounds of conversation in an ever-rising feedback loop. It must be about two-thirty, thought Cid. Judging from the amplitude, they were still a couple of hours before saturation.

They made their way through clusters of tables and chairs to a couple of empty seats in the far corner. Cid slid into a chair and slung her purse over the back. An ancient staghorn fern hung over the table, its green antlerlike fronds splayed in advanced bifurcation. A young woman with long, brown hair falling freely down to her waist approached and handed them menus.

Cid glanced at the selections and let out a low whistle. She'd been to several hash shops already, but this place was definitely five-star. She leaned across the table, grinning at Magnolia. "Isn't this great?"

Magnolia looked up at her in bewilderment. She'd been staring at the menu with the fixed, concentrated gaze Cid herself got trying to decipher a differential equation. "Yeah," she said absently.

"I mean, I feel like I've died and gone to heaven."

Magnolia smiled in spite of herself. "But you don't believe in heaven."

"Oh, that's right." She shrugged. "Well, I've gone to Amsterdam, anyway. So what are you going to have?" she asked.

Magnolia's reply was automatic. "I don't know, what are you going to have?"

Cid considered this, should she go with old standbys or take the chance on something she'd never tried before? She decided on a combination of the exalted and prosaic. "I'm going to have the blond hash, a chocolate eclair, and a cup of coffee."

"That sounds good," said Magnolia. "I'll have that too."

Cid smiled. Except when they were in a ham-and-eggs joint, Magnolia consistently ordered the same thing she did. And they'd been in Amsterdam for over a week now. "You know, you could order something else; they've got black hash and brown, not to mention a wide variety of sativas and indicas."

"I know," she said defensively.

Cid hesitated, then shook her head slightly. "No you don't."

Magnolia stared at her, and Cid knew she'd made a mistake. "What are you saying, Cid?"

She sighed. "Just that you don't have to pretend that you can read. I know you can't."

Magnolia's gaze hardened, her eyes sparkling with unshed tears. She stood, slammed her menu down on the table with a resounding smack, and fled the cafe.

"Mag! Wait!" cried Cid, and she ran after her.

Magnolia left the Nieuwmarkt area and headed east to their tiny apartment in Jodenburt. There'd been a waiting list for it, but Cid had bribed the housing board so they could move in right away. It was one room with a kitchen alcove and a bathroom. Already Cid had begun decorating it, festooning the walls with colored paper flowers.

Magnolia flopped onto the unmade bed and closed her eyes. Shit, she thought, how could she have expected to keep her illiteracy a secret, especially now, when Cid seemed to know so many things she'd never been told.

A soft ping sounded from the door, indicating that someone had just deactivated the lock. The door inched open slowly, and Cid stuck her head in. "Magnolia?" she called softly.

"Yeah," she answered her, opening her eyes and staring at the ceiling.

Cid lay down beside her on the bed. "I'm sorry," she said, stroking the side of Magnolia's face with a finger. "I didn't mean to embarrass you."

Magnolia shrugged and rolled away to face the wall. "It doesn't matter," she muttered, staring fiercely at the cracked paint.

"Yes, it does." Cid's hands rested on Magnolia's shoulders. "Otherwise you wouldn't have run out of the cafe. You're upset. I understand."

"Do you?" Suddenly Magnolia was angry again. She sat up, facing Cid. "Do you really?"

Cid looked as if she'd struck her. "I guess not," she conceded sadly.

"I didn't want you to know, you fool. You're so smart. You know about things I've never even heard of, all that biology, and the Goddess stuff. And now, with the virus—I can tell sometimes that you're somewhere else, experiencing something I'll never understand."

"Yeah, all that chaotic wisdom pouring in from the dynamic systems of the universe, and still I don't know enough to keep my mouth shut."

"But I don't know anything at all, Cid. Just a little practical electronics and a working knowledge of the drug trade. I mean, pretty soon we're going to have to get jobs, and it would be nice if we could get straight jobs. I'm tired of running around. I want to settle here with you, but I can't even fill out a fucking job application! And you're sitting there with your graduate degree in whatever the hell it is, telling me you understand."

Cid nodded tensely. "So where did you go to school?"

Magnolia laughed. "I didn't go to school."

"Yes, you did. You went to the River Rouge Partition

school. So reading wasn't in the curriculum, big surprise. You learned a lot of things there that I'll probably never pick up, and best of all, my love, you got out. If you could survive there, you don't have anything to worry about anywhere else. It's no wonder Rahul wanted to study you. You're the strongest person I've ever met."

"But—"

"But nothing, Mag. If you want to learn how to read, you can. I'll help you. But don't give me any more of this shit about you not knowing anything. You know as much as I do, it's just about different stuff, and we're not in the laboratory anymore."

Antonin shifted his schoolbag on his shoulder and made his way through the crowd at the counter of the Blue Moon. The tiny wad of Mylar bills in his fist was clutched to dampness. His mother had told him he could use the change from her coffee for a treat for himself. She was working late at the Bun and Fun around the corner, so she'd sent him here with a little extra cash to get him out of her hair.

Craning his neck between two adults, he peered at the pastries in the case. There were eclairs and tortes and tarts and, in the center of the case, squatting like an enchanted toad, a triple-glazed chocolate cream puff, the cherry on its top a single red eye, winking at him.

He straightened up and found himself at the counter. The cashier smiled at him. "Carry out?"

"Yeah. A pound of fine-ground Arabian, and that." He pointed at the cream puff.

"Okay." She paused, glancing sidelong at the line of customers. "We ran out of Arabian coffee and Jamaican Mind Fuck," she explained. "I'll tell you what, why don't you have a seat, and as soon as we have your order, I'll bring it to you, okay?"

Antonin slid into a corner table, pulling his schoolbag onto his lap. His legs stuck out from the seat just far enough to kick the table's pedestal. Idly he rocked it while gazing up at the plant above him. It hung from a suspended piece of driftwood and seemed made of green segments shaped like antlers. It was as if a spidery green alien were hovering above, waiting to drop on him.

He shifted edgily in his seat. Something long and thin was digging into his back. He turned and saw the strap of a beaded handbag. He unhooked it and, sliding his schoolbag onto the floor between his feet, held the purse in his lap.

It was black and silver, glittering all over with fine spirals. He opened the metal clasp. Though delicate, it was a roomy bag. He reached a hand inside and pulled out a crumpled piece of cardboard. He unfolded it to see a dark-haired young white woman, grinning in the snow, her black hair and eyes in stark contrast to her surroundings. It was a photograph, he realized, a black-and-white one. He slipped it carefully back inside and bent over, stashing the purse in his schoolbag.

When his order came, he paid for it and then hurried to the small *hofje* off of Koestraat where he was supposed to meet his mother after she got off work. Hopefully she'd have to work the hour out, which would give him some time to examine his treasure.

Antonin settled himself on a bench in the tiny courtyard, away from the thickening tide of pedestrians and traffic on the street. Behind him a small fountain tinkled merrily, its spouting water diffracted into liquid amber by the fading afternoon sunlight. The only others here were an old man scattering pellets for the pigeons, and a woman crooning to the unseen babe in the holowalker parked at her side.

Carefully Antonin drew the purse out of his schoolbag and opened it. It held more than the photograph, that was sure. His hand fumbled against several objects; a small jar, a hard, rectangular slab of plastic, and a small lump of fabric that revealed itself to be the wallet of the purse's owner. Antonin opened it, tearing at the archaic Velcro fastening. There was some money, quite a good bit, actually, although Antonin was at the moment more interested in its other contents. There was a driver's license for the state of Ohio, sporting a flashing hologram of a small, thin, blond-haired woman grinning rather maniacally into the camera; "Cidiera Avonda Marcelese" was the name listed. She was born on July 3, 1992. The license had expired two years ago.

Antonin returned the license to the wallet and replaced it in the bag. Next he drew out the rectangle. It was a videodisc, as he'd suspected. He looked to see if it was labeled, but all that was written on the matte plastic case were the words Watch Me, scrawled in orange grease pencil.

The jar was of thick glass, encased in some sort of plastic skin. With his thumbnail Antonin broke the seal and tore it off. He opened the jar and peered inside. There was some sort of salve inside, like the Tiger Balm his mother still tried to rub on his chest if he complained of a cold or coughed too much. Antonin sniffed at it, but there was none of the mediciney tang of Tiger Balm to it; in fact it was apparently odorless. Antonin stared at the bottle. Through the clear glass the salve shined with pale opalescence, like a badly washed-out hologram. He stuck his finger into the jar and brought out a dab of it. It was faintly warm, smooth, and cool all at once. A little of it seeped into his fingertip and made it tingle. Delicately Antonin spread a bit on his forearm. It left a faint trail of phosphorescence on his skin that disappeared after a few minutes. He smiled and began to paint circles and spirals up and down his arms.

SURVEILLANCE SAFARI

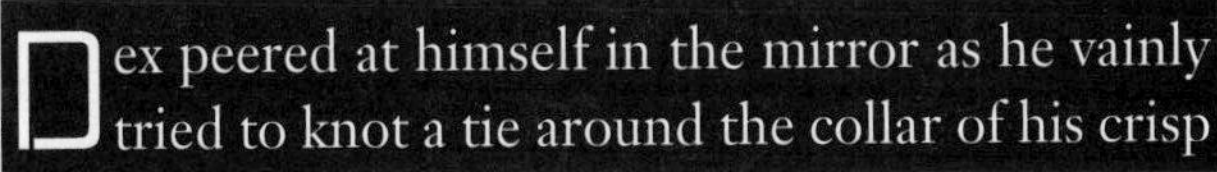

Dex peered at himself in the mirror as he vainly tried to knot a tie around the collar of his crisp new fifty-dollar shirt. His hair gleamed in slicked-back streaks except for a few of the shorter wisps, which sprang free, framing his broad forehead with what he considered endearing disarray. "I can't believe you're not going out tonight," he said to Spider. "We've been in Amsterdam for a week now, and you've yet to take advantage of the biggest red-light district west of Bangkok. What's the matter with you, man? You turning limp on pussy, or what?"

Spider, reclining on his bed, continued to stare at the ceiling. He'd been staring at the ceiling for about two hours now, ever since they'd gotten back from dinner. It was starting to drive Dex nuts. "Naw, but why should I go out and pay for it, when I can spend a quiet evening here alone with Ms. Wujcik?" He gestured to where she sat at a table, busily drawing on the back of a paper place mat.

Dex tugged at his tie in frustration. "Shit guy, you said you were tired of fucking her, remember?"

"Did I? Oh well, she's not very interesting as a person, it's true, but just the same, I don't think she should be alone tonight. I mean, that scene in the dining room was most anomalous."

Dex laughed. "Yeah, all that poor waiter wanted to know was what kind of salad dressing she wanted, and all of a sudden she's explaining to him how to repair the engine of a Yamaha microjet. I thought the guy was going to shit right there. Good thing you told her to draw a picture for him. It should keep her busy for quite a while, I'd think."

"Yeah, she's doing a complete technical schema of the engine. Incredible detail, considering it's all by hand." He shook his head. "She's been pretty bizarre since we left Wotroya, though. I wonder if being away from Tumcari has unsettled her."

"Ahh, since when do you give a shit about anybody but yourself, anyway, huh? I'm telling you, man, ever since you had that fever a few days ago, you haven't been the same. You've lost your edge."

Spider didn't answer him. He just laughed, staring at the ceiling, his eyes moving around as if tracking unseen patterns on its blank white surface. Dex frowned sourly at him and removed his tie, admitting defeat. What idiot brought those back into fashion, anyway, he wondered? They resembled nothing more than a finely sewn noose.

Dex stepped over to the radio track display hulking on the dresser. The screen displayed a map of Amsterdam, three little lights indicating the whereabouts of Kelira, Magnolia, and Cid. "That was a good idea," he said, "planting the radio transmitters in their shoes."

"Yeah, unless they get new shoes," replied Spider.

Until the three of them were together, Spider and Dex

were stuck waiting. Rahul demanded that the hit on Kelira take place only when the other two were present. As the days passed, it seemed more and more unlikely that such an intersection would ever take place. Kelira and the other two had gone their separate ways, and the tap on their phone lines had yet to document any communication between them. "Keep an eye on this thing while I'm gone, okay? Don't fall asleep."

Spider didn't answer.

"Hey," said Dex, moving over to the bed and shaking him. "Did you hear me? Don't fall asleep."

Spider looked up at him. Something funky was going on with Spider's eyes. His irises seemed to shift and pulse as his gaze focused on Dex.

"Did you take something?" Dex asked, alarmed. "Have you been sampling the city's other specialty, huh?"

"No. Don't worry, I'll keep an eye on it. Nothing's going to happen, anyway."

"Well if it does, contact me immediately, okay?"

"Okay," Spider said, and he returned to his meditations.

Dex hesitated, wondering if he should leave the operation in Spider's hands, even for an evening. Still, if the radio pulses got close enough together, an alarm would go off on the minicom he carried. It had been days since they'd arrived, and he was sick of sitting around in this room, breaking only for meals in the hotel lobby. Fuck it, he decided, and went out.

FAMILY MATTERS

It didn't take long for Kelira to zero in on Nieuwmarkt. In fact he'd only been in the city two days before his footsteps inexorably brought him farther and farther from the north-central canal area where he rented a cheap motel room to the red-light district on the eastern edge of central Amsterdam.

And tonight he wandered once again through the neon-lit corridors of flesh, looking for Rose. He paused at a window. The girl inside flourished a video headset and beckoned. She was blond—really blond. Her face a rigid mockery of Scandinavian beauty, the planes of her cheekbones augmented detectably. Not a chance, he thought, and walked on.

Deep bass thrumming from the amplified sound system of a live show spilled out onto the street, its insistence setting the rhythm for his steps. Ghazi Haus waited on the next corner. It was one of the busiest sex clubs in Nieuwmarkt and his reluctant destination.

At the entrance a whore was being ejected. Her nipples flashed with neon implants and a coruscating tattoo on her belly read Buy Independent. She struggled briefly in the bouncer's arms, her long red wig swaying across her shoulders, and then gave up. "Your girls are all ugly and your boys are diseased," she called out loudly over her shoulder as she stepped off the curb.

Kelira entered a dusky, cavernous room designed as a temple courtyard, its walls and columns upholstered in red and gold velvet. The high ceiling supported a network of lights and holoprojectors. He'd arrived between show times; a holoplay depicting the rape of a temple priestess by an armored centurion repeated itself monotonously, the screams and moans of the actors blending into a low-level throb beneath the chatter of the crowd.

The bar was lined with prostitutes. Men and women in flowing robes, their costumes serving to distinguish them from patrons and the few guarded interlopers who had evaded the bouncers at the gate. Kelira strolled past them, paying heed only to the women. A young Javanese, her hair styled in intricate braids behind a golden coronet, smiled at him and proffered a garland of hibiscus. He took it, well aware of the blankness behind the admiration in her eyes.

She took his arm and steered him to a table. A waitress, observant of their transaction, appeared at their side, and Kelira ordered damiana brandy for them both.

The whore had her arm around his waist now. She leaned over and whispered in his ear, "You want a hand job, blow job, or fucking? Sorry, no anal; for that you have to get one of the boys."

He smiled. It probably wasn't strictly true, but in a place like this it was considered good manners to allow prostitutes some preference, there being so many to choose from. He did not answer her until their drinks arrived. After she had swallowed, he said, "I don't want sex with you, but I'll pay you all the same."

She raised her eyebrows. "It's fifty dollars for half an hour, plus drinks. If you want a room, one hundred."

He took out his wallet and handed her a fifty-dollar bill, then he unfolded Rose's picture and showed it to her. "I'm looking for her. She's my sister."

The whore glanced at the picture, then eyed him sidelong. "That's an old picture," she observed. "She's probably not more than fourteen there. How old is she now?"

"Twenty-nine," he answered automatically.

She laughed, her lips parting to show a sparkling array of false teeth, a tiny Amoco logo etched in gold on each one. She was doing well here, he thought; those teeth were some of the best on the market. "Twenty-nine? Goddess, in this business, she could look like anything now." She noted his crestfallen expression and relented. "Okay, john, you're paying, what's her name?"

"Rose Karganilla, from Djakarta. My name is Kelira."

"You can call me Mylea. I haven't seen her. I know a woman named Rose, but she's not the right age. I'm sorry. You know, looking for her in Amsterdam is like looking for a drop of water in the ocean. Be careful. Many would be only too happy to be your Rose for you, you know."

He nodded, staring into the murky depths of his glass.

"Look," she said, "if I see her, I'll tell her you're asking for her. Then it's up to her if she wants to see you or not, right? Anyway, I doubt I will. Here." She handed him his fifty. "I don't want to take your money for nothing," she said, and left.

Kelira finished his brandy and made his way to the door. A slender young man detached himself from a pillar and stepped alongside him. "I heard you're looking for someone, mister."

Kelira stopped, and eyed him. He was dressed as a Greek transvestite, with long golden curls, red lips, and blue eye shadow. "Yeah. You know something?"

The whore smiled. "No, but if you really want to find her, the best way is from inside the life. You'll never get anywhere as a john, you know."

Kelira laughed to cover the sudden dread his words evoked. "Thanks," he said, slapping him on the shoulder, "thanks for the tip."

He left Ghazi Haus and made his way across town to his motel. He didn't feel like looking any more tonight, and he didn't want to think about the transvestite's suggestion. On the way he stopped at the liquor store for more brandy.

When Rose found Antonin in the *hofje*, he was flushed with fever. She took him home and tucked him into bed immediately. He didn't protest, even when she made him drink miso and rubbed his neck and chest with Tiger Balm. In fact, he didn't even ask for the marvelous cream puff he'd purchased at the Blue Moon. Rose eyed it now, lifting the lid of the white plastic carton gingerly, as if it were a wild bird that might simply fly out of the box directly into her mouth. She sighed, closed the lid, and placed the carton in the refrigerator. Her son had an excellent memory. When he recovered, he'd ask for his pastry, and he'd never forgive her if she'd eaten it.

Softly she crept to the door of his room and listened. She could just make out his soft, regular breathing. He was asleep. Rose took her coat from the hook by the door and went out, walking briskly towards the liquor store on the corner. If she had to live with a pastry like that in her fridge, the least she could do was buy herself a fucking candy bar.

The bell on the door jingled as she entered. Behind the

counter a crude mechanical waldo decorated with a Tokyo Raiders cap and T-shirt counted change for a young man purchasing a bottle of damiana brandy. The actual proprietor, she knew, was sequestered behind the wall, controlling the waldo and keeping an eye on things through video screens.

Rose sauntered to the candy rack, eyeing Supernovas and CocoChasms. From the counter she heard her name called softly, "Rose?" and then again in a jubilant shout, "Rose!" Suddenly she was accosted by the man buying the brandy. Grinning broadly, he wrapped her in his arms and squeezed. "Rose! I can't believe it, it's you!" he exclaimed, releasing her.

She backed away, eyeing the stranger warily. He did not appear to be armed. With that idiot grin on his face he wasn't even menacing, and now she saw that there were tears on his face. She knew she could expect no help from the proprietor, who could probably be coaxed from his hiding place only by the threat of arson. She shook her head in bewilderment and ran for the door.

"Wait, please!" he shouted, chasing after her. "It's me, it's Kelira!"

She paid no heed to him, running swiftly down the street towards a busy intersection. She was less than a block away when he caught up to her. He grabbed her arm, jerking her to a halt. "Stop. Please, don't run, I've been looking for you for such a long time. I'm your brother, Kelira."

She hesitated, eyeing him closely. He had high cheekbones, which tapered down in a long curve of jawline. His large eyes glowed at her from beneath a sheltering fringe of glossy black hair. He had a trace of razor stubble at his chin and lips, which was irrelevant in the recognition process. The last time she'd seen her brother, he was twelve years old and delirious with fever. "Let go of me," she said, and he did.

"So you say you're my brother. How do I know you're not some friend of Dano's, trying to trick me? Let me tell you something, if you are—I won't be so easy to take." She put her hand in the pocket of her jacket and grabbed her lipstick case, pushing it forward like the muzzle of a gun. "You want to play, you might get hurt, bro."

His face remained passive, but his eyes glittered with suppressed amusement. "What is that, a roll of Safety Mints?" He shook his head. "If you want to be CEO of the Universe, Rose, you gotta get the right equipment."

She drew breath sharply and stared all the harder at his face, willing the years of their separation to drop away. His face could be anybody's face by now, and fifteen years of living had brought depth and gentleness to the adolescent tenor she recalled, but there was something indelible and unmistakable in the combination of his face, his voice, the way he stood, the way he moved. Some immutable kernel of Keliraness remained after all these years, informing his every action. It was his personality that she recognized.

She sighed and leaned against the wall of a spice market, gazing at the traffic flowing by in steady streams. "Kelira." She didn't know what else to say. It was the last thing she expected, running into him like this. She had rarely thought of him in the years they were apart. He was a stranger still, even though he was her brother.

Kelira laid a hand lightly on her shoulder. "I looked for you, Rose. Ever since you were taken away, I've been trying to find you. I wanted to help you." His dark eyes stared at her so intensely that she thought she'd be sucked into their fathomless depths. "I still do. I want to make it up, if I can—"

"You can't." She said it harshly; it was a warning.

He hung his head. "I know. I know you're right, but—" He took a deep breath. "It was because of me. They sold you so I could get that damn medicine. I didn't want that."

"Are you sorry you're alive?"

"No, but—"

"Then shut up, Kelira." She grabbed his arm roughly, making him look at her. "It had to be that way, and now it's over, so just shut up and leave it alone. And know this too, brother"—she pointed a finger in his face—"I don't need to be rescued. I don't want to be rescued. I've already had all the rescuing I can stand.

"I'm out of the life now, and I did it by myself. I don't need you, understand?"

He was pale, his eyes glittering with tears, but he swallowed and nodded his head. "Yeah, okay. But if there's anything I can do for you, I hope you'll let me know."

Across the street the lights of a fancy restaurant beckoned, and Rose remembered she was hungry. "You can buy me dinner," she said.

They sat in an island of soft light, the murmur of the other patrons sighing softly like waves around them. Rose watched Kelira as he shoveled salmon in white wine and mushroom sauce into his mouth. If she'd still questioned his identity, his table manners would have obliterated all doubt.

Kelira took a thoughtful gulp of wine. "How's your veel?" he asked politely.

"Oh, it's wonderful. Really nice consistency." She toyed with her baby yams, pushing them around a puddle of ginger sauce with her fork. She laughed. "You remember how we used to play, as kids?"

He grinned. "Oh yeah. We could be anything we wanted, as long as we forgot that we were ankle-deep in mud on the streets of Djakarta."

"I always wanted to be CEO of the Universe."

"With a glass office and a magic pen."

"And a briefcase that allowed me to fly." From across the littered wasteland of the table, cluttered with glasses and dishes and wine, Rose gazed at her brother. He had grown up well, she thought. His once childish features had solidified into a pleasing combination of delicacy and strength. And he looked at her like . . . Well, like she'd always wished somebody would.

A string quartet at the edge of the wood parquet dance floor stirred into a soft sweet tune, a Japanese waltz that had been popular ten years ago. Kelira stood and extended his hand to her. "Madam Executive, would you care to dance?"

"I'd be delighted."

For the first time in her life Rose felt safe in a man's arms. It made her feel free, like she had when they were children playing make-believe. Nothing had been off-limits then, and whatever she'd said she was, Kelira had believed her.

Rose sighed and rested her head against her brother's, his silken hair soft against her cheek. He was a good dancer, his shoulders comfortingly solid beneath the cotton shirt he wore. Closing her eyes, Rose imagined that the fabric she felt belonged to a black tuxedo jacket, and she was dressed in something slinky, white, and glittering, her hair done up with strings of pearls and diamonds. Together they moved through the crowd on the dance floor with predatory sophistication, truly a pair to be reckoned with.

"Kelira," she murmured, "I still want to be CEO."

His hand flexed against the small of her back, and he pulled her closer, his breath warming her ear. "You can," he said.

MORNING WARNING

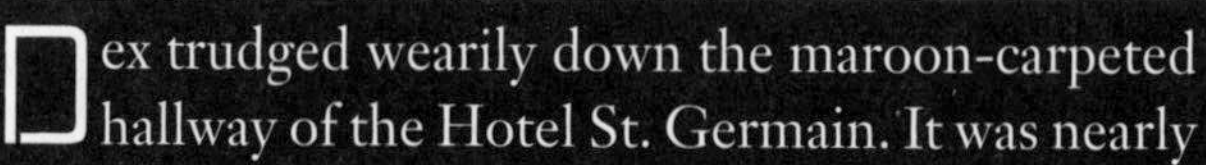

Dex trudged wearily down the maroon-carpeted hallway of the Hotel St. Germain. It was nearly ten o'clock in the morning, and all he wanted to do was climb into bed and go to sleep. Already his brain grumbled with a distant warning of the smashing hangover to come. He wanted to be good and unconscious when it hit.

At last his room number, 203, appeared on a door, and Dex leaned heavily against the wall beside it. A musical condom fell out of his wallet as he fumbled for the key card, its microcircuitry activated by the motion. A tinny rendition of "When the Saints Go Marching In" echoed down the hallway, muffled only slightly by the condom's plastic wrapper. Grumbling, Dex bent over to pick it up, and as he did so the door to the room opened.

"Oh, it's you," said Spider, standing in the doorway and staring at him blearily. His hair stood up from his head at odd angles, as if he'd been sleeping on it.

"Of course it's me," said Dex, "what did you expect? I hope you haven't been sleeping."

Spider hesitated, then stepped back. "Get inside," he said.

The room was nearly dark, the dawn sunlight muffled behind the drapes on the windows. The air was heavy with the musty smells of beer and showers and dirty clothes.

Spider closed the door and turned on the hall light. He stood in the archway, backlit; a tall silhouette with spiky hair. "Ms. Wujcik's gone," he said.

"What? Where'd she go?"

Spider shrugged. "I don't know. She's in the air."

Anger flushed Dex's face. "You fell asleep, didn't you?"

"Of course," replied Spider. "What did you expect? That I was just going to stay awake all night while you partied?"

"You could have taken some speed. We've got plenty of it in my suitcase."

Spider shook his head and sat down on the rumpled covers of his bed. "I didn't want to."

Dex nodded his head, his jaw clenched. "You didn't want to. Meanwhile, our ride out of here has disappeared." He glanced at the radio signal display screen, which indicated that their quarry was still dispersed, and moved over to the phone tap. A red light flashed monotonously on and off, the signal that they had picked something up on one of the lines. "We got a call!" Dex exclaimed. "I can't believe this; Ms. Wujcik walks, and we get a call, and *you* sleep through everything." He glanced nervously at Spider, expecting a reprisal.

He needn't have worried; Spider just sat on the bed, ignoring him. "I think she's going back to Wotroya," he said.

"How do you know? Did she tell you?"

Spider shook his head. "No, I was asleep. But I'm certain that's where she's gone."

"Why would she do that?"

"I don't know, to be with Tumcari, maybe. She missed him."

"But Rahul gave her to us, and besides, she's not supposed to miss anyone, she's a robot." Dex pressed the play button on the phone tap, and Cid's voice emerged from the speaker, groggy with sleep. "Hello?"

Dex glanced at the data display; the call had been made at twelve minutes past nine that morning.

"Cid? It's Kelira. Can you two meet me today? I have a surprise for you."

Cid groaned. "It's nine o'clock, Kelira, don't you have any respect for the dead?"

"I'm sorry. I waited as long as I could stand it. Something's happened, but I don't want to tell you about it over the phone. Can you guys meet me at the Vondelpark Mall, say, around eleven o'clock?"

"Eleven? Make it eleven-thirty, okay?"

"Great! Meet me by the swimming pool in the atrium courtyard. Cool, I can't wait."

"Bye, Kelira."

"Bye, see you soon." The tape went dead as Kelira hung up.

"This is it," said Dex. "This is our chance." He glanced at Spider. "Get dressed. I'm calling Dano and Manus and telling them to get down there. We've got to haul ass if we're all going to be in position in time."

"But what about Ms. Wujcik?"

"Forget about Ms. Wujcik; we'll take a commercial flight to Tunis if we have to. C'mon." Dex picked up a shirt and pair of pants from the chair by the table and threw them at him. "Get moving."

THE RHYTHM DIVINE

Cid and Magnolia came in on the uphill side of the mall in Vondelpark, into the wide cavelike mezzanine above the atrium courtyard. It was decorated in black. Dark columns stood around the floor like embarrassed giants, hoping no one would notice them.

"I heard there were over a hundred dance boutiques up here two years ago," said Magnolia. "People would spill out the doors and dance here. Look"—she pointed at the ceiling—"see those projectors?"

Holoprojectors nestled forgotten in alcoves amid the ceiling tiles, their lenses coated with dust. The boutiques were all closed now, their doors sealed with steel shutters. All the mezzanine offered now was a few scattered kiosks peddling bioreactive cosmetics and pneumatic wristwatches.

Magnolia had Cid's hand, and Cid trailed after her towards the balcony. The atrium courtyard was a stark contrast from the darkness of the mezzanine. Even on an overcast day like this, the light from its glass-paneled dome was brilliant, and the white-tiled floor swarmed with shoppers.

"Look," said Magnolia, pointing to the swimming pool that dominated the courtyard below. "It's the bug."

It was. The Mandelbrot bug. At the sight of it the coalescence of things she'd been feeling all morning suddenly took shape. She looked down into the chaos-bound waters of the pool, at the people swimming inside it, then leaned far over the rail, and spit.

Magnolia laughed. "I think you hit that guy with the water wings," she said.

Cid was becoming aware of something she had not known before. The shape of a world without her. All the little coincidences she'd noticed all day. The way the color of that woman's eyes at the coffee shop matched the coins she paid her. The traffic on Tiergard, coming to a halt at their intersection the same instant the balloon vendor across the street lost his grip on his strings, and sixteen balloons floated up into the air, free. Sixteen was the number of trees they passed walking down Valerius Street. Tall sycamores like sturdy fountains, their branches, and the branches on their branches, lifting possibilities into the air.

Of course, she'd been aware of Spider for days now. He must have caught the virus from Ms. Wujcik. He was outside the mall now, but she didn't mention it to Magnolia. There was someone else too, inside the mall. Someone she didn't know.

It was all coming together here, in that recurring pit of chances into which, on the escalator, she descended.

In the courtyard they were surrounded by a whirlwind of commerce. A frenzy of shops lined the atrium, mood music and scent stimuli pouring from their doors in a riot of enticements.

Magnolia paused at the window of a shop selling designer handguns. She noted with pride that her gun, the Walther-Kodak, was prominently displayed among the Sanyos, Mitsubishis, and Brittanias. "Hey Cid, check it out," she said, pointing, but Cid, who'd been beside her only a moment ago, had disappeared into the swirling crowd. "Cid!" she shouted, her voice drowned in the cacophony of the mall.

"When you have a score to settle, do it with style," a female voice intoned from a speaker above the display window. Magnolia moved away from the gun shop, scanning the crowd. Kelira detached himself from a group surrounding a holograph makeover booth and started towards her, accompanied by a woman and a boy of about six or so.

"Kelira, have you seen Cid?" she asked as they came up to her.

Kelira shook his head. "No, wasn't she with you?"

"She was until a second ago. I don't know where she went." Magnolia glanced around the courtyard again fruitlessly.

"She went to the bathroom," said the boy.

"She did? You saw her?" Magnolia bent down to look at him.

He shook his head from side to side, his eyes whirling.

"He doesn't know that," said the woman, drawing him closer. "We never went near the rest rooms. He just says things, sometimes."

"She went into the bathroom and took off her clothes," said the boy.

"Antonin!" said the woman sharply. "Talk like that again and I'll smack your face." She looked up at Magnolia. "I'm sorry. I don't know what's gotten into him."

"Magnolia, I want you to meet my sister Rose. And this is her son, Antonin," Kelira said, beaming.

Magnolia nodded to Rose. "Kelira's been trying to find you for a long time. I'm glad he finally did."

"Thank you."

"I saw you in the snow," said Antonin.

"What?"

"Magnolia," said Kelira, staring at something behind her.

"Magnolia," said another voice, strangely familiar. She turned and saw her brother Manus standing behind her, on two legs.

His soft round face was like a memory from childhood, aged with beard stubble. Magnolia remembered birds wheeling in a grey sky, and the shouts and cries of the children running towards her, and behind them, Manus, keeping up as best he could with his crutch.

"Manus?" She had escaped them, her brothers and sisters, and now it seemed to her she'd been running ever since, but Manus had finally managed to catch up to her. The last time she'd seen him he'd been hobbling towards her in Detroit, and she'd thought of him doing that all this time that she'd been in New York and Siberia and Amsterdam, making his way with his crutch, across oceans to find her. Only he didn't have a crutch anymore. He didn't need one, apparently.

Magnolia looked from him to Kelira. "What's he doing here?"

Kelira raised his shoulders and shook his head in bewilderment. "How should I know? Who is he?"

"He's my brother."

"Your brother? Oh yeah, I can see it. That's weird. Did you know he was in Amsterdam?"

"No! What the fuck is going on here, Kelira? If this is another one of your little games, you can forget it. Fooled me once, know what I mean?"

"Don't talk to him like that! Who do you think you are?" said Rose, stepping in front of Kelira.

"Stay out of this," said Magnolia, putting an arm out to move her aside.

"Look!" shouted the boy, pointing. "It's the spiral lady!"

It was Cid. She was naked, standing on the glass wall that surrounded the swimming pool.

Antonin's shout was taken up by others, and for a moment the din in the mall was louder than ever. But then she started to move, and the voices fell silent.

Cid stood in the cleft of the Mandelbrot pool, felt the mall go quiet, and heard the song in her cells. She began to dance outward along the crenelated path of the wall, her body following the rhythm of the song moving through her.

Somewhere, on one of the balconies above, someone began clapping in time with her dance, and it was taken up by the rest of the crowd. As the rhythm intensified she was no longer conscious of dancing at all. She was swimming in a sea of faces, buoyed by the pulse of the world.

She saw the moment as an equation graphed into phase space, all the lives of the people around her represented as lines spiraling about one another, weaving themselves together and apart. It was an attractor, and she was in it, her path a soaring arc into singularity.

Magnolia stood transfixed, her eyes riveted on Cid just like everyone else's. She looked so small up there, and beautiful, reflections from the glass wall painting her body with fractals of light, and her blond hair gleamed as she twisted and whirled. Everyone was clapping, everyone except for Magnolia. Along with the ecstasy of the sight before her sat a tight little knot of fear.

What the hell was she doing, dancing up there? She was crazy, but, oh the sight of her . . . Magnolia remembered what Cid said about the Goddess. This was it, what she was seeing, a Goddess. Cid, her Cid, was a Goddess. Oblivious to the tears suddenly streaming down her face, Magnolia squeezed closer to the pool, her hands outstretched before her, hoping that somehow she could touch that shining essence, feel it, know it for her own. "Cid!" she shouted, "Cid, I'm here!"

And Cid looked. Their eyes met, and Magnolia had no idea what was going to happen next, and she didn't care, because Cid's eyes were telling her things she'd waited her whole life to hear. There was no past, and no future, in that instant that they saw each other. Suddenly, and for the first time, Magnolia knew who she was. She knew Cid too, in her infinite entirety, and she realized that in every way that really mattered, they were one and the same.

When the shot came, the first thing Magnolia thought as Cid lunged from the wall was that she was going to fly. She was going to swoop down and grab Magnolia and they'd fly away together to the land of the Goddesses.

But then Magnolia felt something warm like a raindrop strike her cheek. She looked up, but it couldn't be raining in here. She brushed it away with her finger and, looking back at the wall, saw that Cid was gone.

Somebody screamed, and the spell was broken. People started running in every direction. Magnolia swam among the schools of frightened bodies to the one that belonged to Cid, lying facedown on the white tile, blood pouring from her demolished head.

A few strands of hair trailed from the ruin of her skull, clotted with blood and pieces of bone. "Cid!" she screamed, dropping to her knees and knotting her fingers in the twisted strands.

She felt strong hands on her shoulders, pulling her back, but Magnolia struggled against them. "No, leave me alone!" she cried, turning to see her brother Manus standing over her.

The last time they'd been together was when Doralee was shot, just like this, and now he was here again, like a bad rerun. And then Kelira appeared by his side. "Magnolia, Magnolia, I'm so sorry. Now, come on, we've got to get out of here."

"Why?" Magnolia rounded on him, lifting her bloody hands. "Why do we have to leave? Why did we have to come here in the first place, Kelira? You set this up, didn't you? You knew what was going to happen."

"Oh yeah, I knew she was going to jump up there and act like a maniac. I think we all saw that coming."

Rose came up to them, carrying Antonin in her arms. "Kelira, we have to get out of here. The shooter could still be around somewhere."

"You know who it was?" said Magnolia.

"No, but I—I have my son with me. Kelira, let's go!"

"I don't think so," said Magnolia, advancing on her. "You know who did this!"

Rose set Antonin down and faced her. "I don't know anything about it. You're crazy with grief. If you can't come with us, you should wait for the paramedics."

"Paramedics? She's dead!"

Rose nodded. "They will come."

She turned to leave, but Magnolia grabbed her by the shoulder and swung her back around. Rose shoved her back, and Magnolia launched herself at her, wrapping her hands around her throat and squeezing.

Rose struggled, bringing a hand up to claw at Magnolia's face as she stomped on her instep with her foot. Pain rocketed up Magnolia's leg, and she lost her balance. Still clinging to Rose's neck, she tilted to the side, bringing them both down onto the hard tiled floor of the mall.

Rose twisted around onto her hands and knees, and Magnolia wrapped her arm around her neck in a choke hold. "Why did they kill her? Was it the virus?" she gritted between her teeth as she put on the pressure.

Suddenly Kelira was there, pulling her head back by the hair just in time for her to see his fist coming at her. Her face exploded with pain, and her nose snapped. Magnolia stumbled backwards and would have fallen, except she bumped into someone who placed a steadying hand on her shoulder. "Hey! Hey! Come back here!" she shouted, still reeling. Wiping the tears from her eyes, she watched as Kelira and his family disappeared into the scattering crowd.

COCKEYED AND DRIVING CRAZY

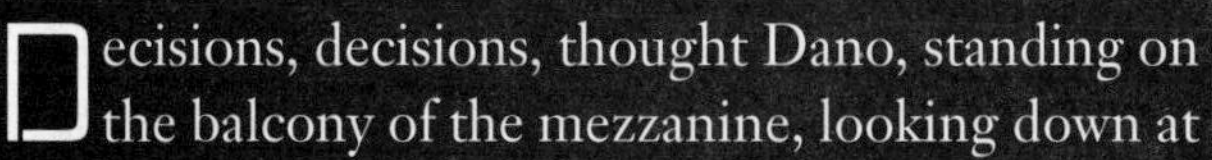

Decisions, decisions, thought Dano, standing on the balcony of the mezzanine, looking down at the little scene by the pool below. There was Kelira, the guy he was supposed to hit, and standing with him were Rose and Antonin. They had just been joined by the girl who stabbed him in New York, Magnolia.

He hadn't expected Rose to be here. Rahul should have told him about that. Dano wondered if he could get all three of them, and who he should start with.

He raised his rifle to the eye Rahul had given him, trying to line Kelira up in the sight, but he kept straying to Rose. The crosshairs complemented her, accentuating the symmetry of her face. Dano aimed the rifle at Magnolia, but it didn't do the same thing for her. Besides, Rahul had as much as promised Dano he would do her on TV if he left her alone now.

They were all staring at something now, and Dano

concentrated, trying to focus on Kelira. Business, before pleasure. The hairs of the sight divided Kelira's nose and drew a line through his eyes, and Dano squeezed the trigger.

He searched for Rose next, but his line of sight was blocked by someone running past, and when it had cleared, she wasn't there anymore.

He scanned the panicking crowd, but everyone was running around in all directions. A stream of people poured up the escalator to the mezzanine, and he slid the rifle inside his coat and walked away.

He went around the outside of the mall to the plaza in front of the main entrance. Three people stood together near a gleaming abstract sculpture: Rose and the boy, and Kelira, the man he was supposed to have shot.

He almost pulled his rifle out of his coat again right there, but down on the street he saw the flashing lights of police cars. Dano walked swiftly towards his little group of targets, his eye now focused on Antonin.

As he approached, Rose ran at him, but he knocked her down and went on. He wouldn't waste his time with her now, not when he could do her so much worse with this.

Antonin stood alone as Kelira dashed to Rose's aid. The boy stared at him, unresisting as Dano scooped him up in his arms and ran.

Dex fled with the rest of the mall crowd, letting their panic carry him out to the lawns and sidewalks of the park. Once he was away from the throng he took off across the grass to Van Eeghenstraat, where a dark brown sedan idled by the curb. He yanked open the door and climbed inside. "Move it," he said to Spider. "Get this tank to the airport. We've got to get to Tunis."

Spider was pale, staring at him. "Cid . . . Did you see?"

"No shit, that idiot Dano shot her instead. Did you leave the car?"

"No, I was here."

"Then how do you know?"

"I felt . . . I felt her go. . . ." Spider fell silent, staring at nothing.

Dex was about to lose his patience and hit him when Spider looked back up. "We have to go to Wotroya House."

"Fuck that. We're going to Tunis, just like Rahul told us to. If we go to Wotroya now that Dano screwed up the hit, he's going to think we were in on it. That it was intentional. Now get going, we don't want to end up talking to the police."

Spider shifted the car into drive and pulled into traffic. "Ms. Wujcik is changing," he said, still looking at Dex. "She won't know what to do. We have to help her."

"She walked out on us, fuck her, man. Watch out!" A bright green Warner Convergence blared its horn angrily at them and changed lanes. "Watch where you're going, okay?"

Spider wasn't listening to him. He was staring out the window as he sped the car through an intersection, taking a left turn against the light.

"Jesus!" Dex clutched the dashboard convulsively as cars swerved to avoid them. "Keep your eyes on the road, fucker!"

"Don't worry," said Spider, looking at him, his eyes whirling. "I know where we're going."

Dex stared at Spider. In all the years of their association, there had only been one way, Spider's way. And Dex wouldn't have dreamed of talking to him the way he did now. Spider knew a lot of ways to hurt a guy, but he hadn't even threatened Dex, and Dex had been pretty rude lately. With every unanswered insult, his respect for Spider decreased. Now, he thought, it's time for a change. Dex pulled the small, chrome-colored Sharp hydroelectric stunner out of his jacket pocket and gave Spider a mild jolt with it. "It can be a lot stronger," he told him. "It can kill you. Now I suggest you keep your eyes on the road, old pal, and drive us to the airport. We've got a flight to Tunis to catch."

Rose shook off Kelira's assistance and ran after the man who had pushed her. He had grabbed Antonin and was running down the broad walkway to the street. Kelira followed after them, down to Van Eeghenstraat, where the man hailed a cab and got in, pushing the boy ahead of him.

As the cab pulled away, Kelira raised his hand to hail another cab, but Rose appeared at the curb astride a velocipede. "Get on."

"How'd you get this?" Kelira climbed onto the cycle behind her.

"I stole it," said Rose, and with a few pumps of the pedals they were sailing down the street. The cab was nearly a block ahead of them and picking up speed. They might have lost it, except that at the next intersection it had to brake suddenly when a dark brown sedan turned left against the light.

They followed the cab away from Vondelpark, to the outskirts of the city. "I think they're headed to the airport," panted Rose.

"Probably. Who was that guy, anyway?"

"Antonin's father."

"Oh, well at least he won't hurt the boy."

Rose glanced at him briefly over her shoulder, her face grim and sweating. "You don't know him."

"Do you want me to pedal for a while?" asked Kelira.

She shook her head. "We're going to have to ditch this thing soon anyway; we can't take it on the highway."

They stood on the embankment of the highway, watching as the cab disappeared into the distance.

"Look," said Rose, pointing as it shrank to a speck. "I

think they're veering to the right, towards the interchange for the airport."

The airport concourse was noisy, awash with pounding feet, rolling luggage carts, and frantic voices. Antonin stumbled along, his arm in Dano's viselike grip. He looked around at the people passing by. His mother would have followed them, he was sure, but he couldn't find her, and now Dano was dragging him towards an escalator. "Where are we going?" he asked his father, craning his neck to look at him.

"Never mind. And if you say anything to the stewardesses, or anyone on the plane, I'll smack you silly, you got that?"

Antonin wanted to bite him, like he had done that night at the falafel stand, but terrible things had happened because of that. He nodded his head. "I won't say anything. We're going the same place as the spiral lady, aren't we? Rose is going to be scared."

"She should have taken better care of you. Don't worry, boy, I'll take good care of you now."

"Can't you drive faster?" said Rose to the cabdriver.

"I'm going as fast as I can," she said, "and if you ask me that one more time, I'm letting you out."

"Please," said Kelira. "It's very urgent. Her son's been kidnapped."

"Then you should call the police."

"We don't have time for that," said Rose. "Just drive."

"Did a man in a beige raincoat, with a small boy, about six years old, buy a ticket from you in the last hour?"

The clerk shook her head. "That's a pretty general description. Besides, even if I had seen them, I'm not allowed to give out information about passengers."

"The boy is Indonesian, with dark brown hair and eyes." Kelira nudged a fifty-dollar bill across the counter.

"Please sir. I haven't seen them, and if you don't go, I'll call security." He had exhausted every ticket counter at the EurAir Terminal, and most of his ready cash. Kelira returned to the main concourse, where he found Rose, waiting for him beside a hot-pretzel stand. She looked haggard and pale. "Nobody saw him at the Nike terminal. Did you find out anything?" she asked him.

"No dice."

"Where would he take him?"

"I don't know, maybe we should call the police."

"They won't be much help, but I guess we might as well. You go call them, I'm going to look around some more."

On the way to the pay phones Kelira saw a small sign above a corridor branching off the concourse. SiberiAir Terminal, it said, with an arrow pointing down the corridor. Might as well try it, he thought, and took off running down the moving walkway.

The SiberiAir terminal consisted of a single room, furnished with folding chairs, and one ticket clerk behind a metal desk. There was no one else there except for two elderly women holding grocery bags filled with chocolate, and a custodian emptying ashtrays.

The clerk came out of his boredom-induced trance when Kelira described Antonin and his father. He stared at Kelira a moment and then started to shake his head.

Kelira fished out the fifty-dollar bill again and tucked it between his fingers, laying his hand casually on the counter as he repeated his description of Antonin.

The clerk's eyes bounced from the fifty to the custodian

and back to Kelira. The fifty disappeared in the clerk's hand as he leaned over. "The man had a ticket, but he bought one for the kid. They left on the plane to Tarko Sale five minutes ago."

"They're gone already?" Kelira's heart sank.

The clerk nodded his head. "But don't worry, you're in luck, there's another flight out there tomorrow."

COFFEE AND FILM

Magnolia was vaguely aware of Manus's hand on her arm as he dragged her towards the great glass doors of the mall. Magnolia looked behind her. The sight of Cid lying motionless on the floor, her head wreathed in blood, burned itself into her mind. Whatever else her life brought her, whatever new sights her eyes found, would be cast against that background.

They left Vondelpark and walked for several blocks down a narrow street choked with hash shops and sex boutiques. Her knees felt like rubber, and the pavement of the sidewalk seemed to rise of its own will, meeting her feet before she was ready. Magnolia leaned against her brother, taking from his soft bulk the only comfort available to her. He had two legs, somehow, but she couldn't think about that. It didn't seem important. She willed her mind to disappear in the sensations of her body; the cool, silky-rough texture of Manus's worn canvas overcoat, the pain of her broken nose and sore ribs, the stickiness of drying blood on her face and hands.

Manus pulled her into an alley and pushed her up against the hard stone wall. She tried to push him away, but her uncoordinated arms fought uselessly against him. He put his large, plump hands on either side of her aching nose and twisted. Magnolia screamed as the bone snapped back into place. It was a hoarse, humiliating sound, and the sudden pain brought fresh tears to her eyes.

She gazed up at the strip of grey and resolute sky above the alley. A first few drops of rain fell, increasing rapidly to a downpour. With the edge of his sleeve Manus wiped the blood off her face as she sobbed, insensible to his ministrations. There was no explaining it, any of it: him here, in Amsterdam of all places, and today, and Cid, Cid was dead.

"C'mon, c'mon," Manus said softly, plucking at her sleeve. He was soaking wet. So was she, but that didn't matter. Magnolia swallowed with great difficulty, choking off her sobs and pushing away the thoughts she could not bear.

For long moments they hovered on the edges of her awareness; memories and visions that threatened to dissolve her, turn her into water washed away by the rain. She probed her swollen nose, pressing just at the spot where it had broken. Not hard enough to unset it, just hard enough to be intensely painful, hard enough to drive the other pain away. They had to get out of the rain. Manus hadn't survived the River Rouge Partition, one-legged and half-witted, to die of pneumonia in Amsterdam. Magnolia took his arm, and together they hurried down the street, seeking shelter in the dingy familiarity of a cheap diner.

Neat Eats, the place declared in black lettering above the door. The paint around the windows was peeling, and the curtains were faded from years of sunlight, but it was dry inside, and the jingling of the bell that hung on the door was the only notice their arrival received.

Magnolia headed straight for the rest room. It was a tiny white cubicle which also housed a mop, a pail, a broom, and stacks of boxed plastic straws. She fumbled with the flimsy bolt lock for agonizing seconds before she was forced to abandon privacy, lean over the toilet, and vomit.

Her stomach emptied, she stumbled to the sink and rinsed out her mouth, avoiding her haggard, beaten reflection in the mirror. The room smelled faintly of antiseptic, overlaid now with the sickly sweet odor of stomach acid. Magnolia flushed the toilet and left before she could experience dry heaves.

Manus waited at a booth at the back of the diner with two steaming mugs of coffee on the table. Magnolia sat down across from him, facing the door. The worn vinyl of the seat clung uncomfortably to her wet jeans, and her sopping hair sent chilly rivulets of water down her back.

On the wall behind the counter hung a picture-frame television and a portrait of Pope Joan II. An old movie played on TV, one she'd seen years before, during that summer that she'd been queen. It was about a rookie cop involved with a homicidal maniac. Just now the main character was in her kitchen, talking with her best friend. Magnolia remembered what came next. She poured cream in her coffee, forcing herself to watch as the two women left the apartment and descended a staircase. The killer was there, and he grabbed the cop from behind. He intended to kill her best friend before her eyes. For agonizing seconds she struggled with him, trying to throw off his aim or warn her friend, but despite her best efforts, he fired accurately. Magnolia bit her lips hard as the woman crumpled and the cop, horrified, was dealt a vicious blow to the head. She looked away as the scene switched to her reviving and learning that her best friend was dead.

Her hands shook as she lifted the coffee cup to her sore

lips. She closed her eyes, remembering how the movie ended: she killed him.

But she had no idea who killed Cid. She looked at Manus, who stared at his cup, absorbed by the swirling patterns of milk in coffee. He was her only lead. "Manus," she said, and he ignored her. "Manus." She jiggled his arm.

He looked up at her slowly, as if he had forgotten she was there. More likely, he had forgotten *he* was there.

"What are you doing in Amsterdam? Why were you at the mall this afternoon?"

He smiled shyly, slyly, and whispered to himself for a while. Whatever the results of this private consultation, he must have decided it was okay to give her a straight answer. "Rahul sent me to find you," he said.

"Does this have something to do with the—the shooting?"

"Yes." He nodded. "Rahul told me to bring you to him after the shooting, but this wasn't what he meant. Still, my leg says we should go there anyway."

Magnolia felt cold, inside and out. Stiffly she nodded. "Sounds right to me."

FOR REAL

The limo they'd hired at the airport carried Spider and Dex smoothly down the tree-lined street and through the wrought-iron gates. Rahul's house stood on a hill in the wealthy section of Tunis. It had a roof of interlocking red tiles, and the walls were pale beige stone.

"Go on, get out," said Dex when the car came to a stop in front of the main entrance.

Spider looked at him. He had that dumb stunner in his hand again, like he was going to do something with it. Spider shook his head wearily. "See, this is why I've always been the top dog. You suck at it."

"Just move." He jabbed the stunner towards Spider, and Spider moved.

"All right, jeez, you're such a Nazi," he said, climbing out of the car.

Dex walked behind him with the stunner all the way to Rahul's office.

Rahul was sitting behind his desk when they went in. The place was all done up with brown leather chairs and burgundy carpeting. You could really tell who'd done the decorating at Wotroya, from this. Spider walked over to the desk and sprawled in one of the chairs. "Hey, doc, how's it going?"

Rahul leaned forward and steepled his fingers, resting his chin on their tips. "You tell me. What happened in Amsterdam?"

Dex had seated himself in the other chair. He took this opportunity to jump forward in his seat and yap, "It didn't come off the way it was supposed to."

Rahul's eyes flickered to Dex. "What happened?"

"Cid got shot, Kelira got away," Spider said, just to rob Dex of his moment.

Rahul's eyes remained lidded. "Anything else?" He'd managed to disappoint them both.

Spider took a deep breath and looked at Dex. "She was dancing on top of a wall when it happened," said Dex. "I guess Dano didn't notice her, and she got in the way."

Rahul straightened up. "Why was she dancing?"

"I don't know, man," said Dex, "it was nuts. The whole place was watching and clapping in time. She was naked. And then there was a shot. I saw her go down with my own eyes."

Rahul looked back at Spider. "It took you a little longer to get here than I'd expected. Were there any other . . . complications?"

"Ms. Wujcik walked on us," said Spider.

"While you were sleeping," said Dex.

Spider dipped his head and spread his hands. "While I was sleeping."

"We nearly missed the rendezvous altogether, Dr. Rahul, because he went to sleep while he was on post, and then afterwards he didn't want to come here."

"Really? Where did you want to go, Spider?"

"He wanted to go to Wotroya House," said Dex, "but I made him come back here, instead."

"Quite commendable of you, Dex." Rahul's eyes betrayed the gratitude in his voice. "I wonder, could you leave us? I'd like a private word with Spider."

Dex looked blank. "Sure. Um, I'll wait outside."

"Thank you."

When the door shut, Rahul turned to Spider again. "Why did you want to go to Wotroya?"

"Because I'm pretty sure that's where Ms. Wujcik went. She missed Tumcari a lot."

"And when she left, you missed her?"

"Yeah, I guess so, I'm worried about her, is all, doctor. She was acting pretty strangely."

"Well, don't worry, Spider, I can get you another one."

"But I don't want another one."

Rahul stared at him. "But they're all the same."

Spider shook his head. "I don't think so, not anymore."

A slow smile spread across Rahul's lips. "You're in love with her, aren't you?"

"What? In love? No, I just—though a guy could do a lot worse, you know. Pretty girl, sweet, quiet, no attitude. She's nice. But no, man." Spider laughed. "I'm not in love with her or anything."

"Okay. What happened to Magnolia?"

Spider shrugged. "Dex says he saw Manus with her, but he didn't stick around after the hit."

"I see. I don't suppose either of you tried to find Kelira again, did you?"

"Nope, we just came back here, like you said for us to do."

"But against your wishes."

"Well, I—"

"Spider"—Rahul leaned forward on his elbows—"you may have your chance to go to Wotroya after all. Dano was instructed to hide there after the hit. I want you to find him and take care of him."

"Take care of him?" Spider sat up straight. "That's getting to be a bit automatic with you, isn't it? You wanted Dano to 'take care' of Kelira. You're a real caring guy, aren't you?"

"What I care about is none of your concern."

"No." Spider laughed. "You just asked me to whack a guy I was working with a day ago."

"What, did you two become close?"

"I don't know, Dr. Rahul." Spider gripped the arms of the chair. "It just seems like working for you gets pretty dangerous."

"Well, you're already working for me, aren't you?"

Spider leaned his head back and stared at the textured stucco ceiling. It looked like a topographical model of the moon. "No, no. I don't think so, not anymore," he said, looking back at Rahul. "I just can't."

"Oh, you can't?" Rahul folded his hands on the desk. "How very sad for you."

"Yeah, be that way. But you wanted to kill Kelira, and now Cid's dead. She was cool, man, a dyke and everything, but still cool. And now you want to kill Dano, just to punish him for screwing up. I don't know how you think that's going to help you."

"You misconstrue the reason for my request. Not that it's any of your business, but I have excellent reasons for wanting to tie off Dano's little loose end. I was working on something experimental with him, but obviously it didn't work out. I learned my lesson long ago, about leaving failed projects behind. They tend to haunt you."

"You really get off on it, don't you?" said Spider. "This whole mastermind-directing-people-from-afar jazz. And now with you telling people to go off and kill other people for you.

It's the ultimate power trip. You get to do all these things, yet you don't actually have to do any of them. Like television, only with you it's for real."

Rahul smiled at him warmly. "Oh, television can be real sometimes, Spider."

They took a taxi from the airport in Tunis. Here, even though it was the middle of winter, the weather was mild. Still, Magnolia felt cold. Ignoring the lump of her gun pressing into the small of her back, she wrapped her arms around her ribs and huddled closer to Manus. He was still sweating, his skin warm with fever. She'd noticed it on the airplane too. He must have caught a cold in the rain, she thought.

The sun beat down on the gravel driveway, the sparkling white stones crunching beneath their feet as they got out of the taxi. Magnolia paid the driver and turned around. A very large man stood before the front door, dressed in white pants and a tunic. He was nearly seven feet tall, and he must have weighed upwards of three hundred pounds. His face and body were broad and soft, but his eyes gazed at her, unsympathetic, unmoving.

She should have shot him right then but she hesitated, thinking it might be better to wait and let her attack on Rahul come as a surprise. As it was, she had no chance for that, because she had no sooner stepped away from the cab than Manus grabbed her arm, twisting it behind her as the giant searched her and took her gun.

Manus released her and she whirled on him. "You bastard," she said, punching him in the stomach. It knocked the wind out of him, but she had no chance to follow up on it, because the guard had her arm in a lock again, and he escorted her swiftly through the front door.

They passed through a corridor lined with old photographs in dusty frames and shelves full of forgotten artifacts, small bones and seashells, jars cloudy with half-decayed contents. They came out into a central court, a fountain burbling at its center. The fountain's base was ringed with tile mosaics of dolphins cavorting in stylized waves. Manus opened a set of glass doors, and the guard led her down another hallway, less cluttered than the first, to another door, wooden and unrevealing of what lay beyond it.

Again Manus opened the door for them, but it was only Magnolia who went through, gently but firmly propelled by her guard. The door closed again, and Magnolia heard the click of a bolt. She was in a square room with a high ceiling, unadorned white walls and grey indoor/outdoor carpeting at her feet. The ceiling was crisscrossed with metal girders supporting lights and video cameras. They whirred and rotated to fix their gazes upon her. One wall was all glass; thick, transparent, and impenetrable. On the other side of that window Rahul sat in a deep red armchair, flanked by brass urns erupting with feathery green foliage. From a small table at his right he picked up a brandy snifter and raised it to her. "Magnolia, how good of you to come."

She glared at him and wished for her gun.

"You'll forgive me for your spartan surroundings. I had reason to believe you would be in one of your more foul moods."

Rage immobilized her. "You set it up, didn't you?" she said, her voice a bare whisper in her effort to contain her fury. "You had her killed, because of the virus."

"What virus?"

"You know what I'm talking about."

Rahul shook his head. "I'm afraid not. I was aware that she was conducting research on Tumcari's cellular structure, that's all."

Magnolia knitted her brow in confusion. "She was up there dancing. It was because of the virus."

"Tell me more about this virus."

Magnolia looked at him. Why would he have killed Cid, if not because of the virus? "I don't know much," she said. "It was supposed to give you Goddess vision."

"Goddess vision," said Rahul. "Really?"

Magnolia stepped closer to the glass. "Manus told me you sent him to find me, that he was supposed to bring me back here after the hit. It was your hit."

"Yes, but it was supposed to be on Kelira."

Her self-control broke, and hot tears streamed down Magnolia's face. "It's still your fault," she said, pounding on the glass, smearing it with her tears. "If it weren't for you, she'd be alive. She'd be alive," she sobbed.

"And if it weren't for me, you never would have met her, either. You see, Magnolia, you will learn in time that the world gives with one hand and takes away with the other.

"You're quite right that I set in motion the events that led to Cid's death. You are quite right in blaming me. But why stop there? Ask yourself why Kelira arranged to meet you in the mall in the first place. And what about your sweet brother Manus? By now it must be obvious that he's working with me. Just what kind of role did he have in the shooting, you might wonder? And then there's the question of how my assassin knew where you were. Your precise space-time location. Quite a trick, eh? Of course it could have been Tumcari who let me know that you were headed to Amsterdam. I've had an extensive series of monologues from him in the last couple of days. But that wouldn't quite explain how I knew you were at that particular mall at that particular time, would it?" He gazed thoughtfully at her for a moment, a smug smile twisting his lips. "Perhaps you were observed by someone else who was already cooperating with me, someone who wanted to pay you back for his wounded dignity. If so, the score seems to have been settled. Judging by those bruises around your eyes, I'd say you've had your nose broken recently."

He took a long sip of brandy and set it down on the table. "So you see, my dear, it's everyone. Everyone you know. We're all part of it, aren't we? Except for you, of course. No, you couldn't have anything to do with Cid's death, could you? You loved her. So much that you'd turn down an awful lot of money just to remain virtuous in her eyes. But you see, Magnolia, virtue is as virtue does. And she could be alive now, if you hadn't aspired to be as she was."

He drained his glass and stood. "Well, if you'll excuse me, I have some other matters to attend to. But I wouldn't want you to be lonely, so I've arranged for some company for you. Enjoy."

The door opened and there stood Henri, holding Spider by the arm. Spider had not come willingly. His hair stood up on end on one side of his head, and sweat trickled around the scar on his nose. He stood mainly, it seemed, because Henri supported him with an arm around his back, which also prevented him from escaping. Henri pushed him into the room and shut the door on them.

Spider stood framed in the white square of the door, his black hair stark against the white background. He wavered on his feet, and for a moment Magnolia thought he'd fall to his knees, but then he straightened and looked at her. "Magnolia."

"Hi, Spider. You look like shit," she said, and twirled, her leg vaulting up into a roundhouse kick. It struck a little low, but still landed square in his chest, knocking him back into the door. He crumpled to the floor and sat there, looking up at her. "Please, don't. I—"

"Don't what? Don't do this?" she said, stomping her foot down on his outstretched hand.

He screamed, and with the other hand, grabbed her foot as it retreated. He yanked, and Magnolia lost her balance and rolled to the floor. He was on her immediately, grabbing for her wrists, trying to pin them to the floor.

She twisted her hands free of his grasp and then clawed at his face. One lacquered red fingernail drew a line of blood from his cheek. He backed off, taking a defensive position in one corner.

She advanced and threw a punch to his jaw. He blocked her with his right forearm, and his left fist smashed into her jaw, knocking her head sideways. Though he was breathing hard, he no longer seemed on the point of collapse. "You never were as good as me, remember?"

Magnolia blocked his next punch and kicked him in the groin. He went down and rolled to the side, swinging his legs behind hers. The motion was too fast for her to follow, and the next thing she knew she was on her ass, and Spider was up. She lifted her arm to pound him in the nuts again, but he grabbed her hand, bent it against her wrist, and twisted her arm around her back. She struggled to get to her feet but only managed to land herself on her stomach. She rolled over and, with her free hand, grabbed his hair and pulled.

Rather than let her pull his hair out, Spider rolled forward as she yanked. He lay beside her now, his face next to hers. She looked into his eyes. They were crazed, the irises whirling in a fashion she'd only seen once before. His breath felt warm and moist against her cheek. She lunged at him, mouth open. Her teeth clamped down on his nose and she tasted blood. She kicked, the toes of her boots hammering at his shins.

Spider slammed his knee into her groin and slapped her hard across the face. Magnolia tucked her thumbs under her index fingers, made fists, and drove them at his eyes, but Spider caught her hands, forced them down to her sides, and shifted his knee up so that it pressed painfully into her abdomen. "Stop it, bitch," he whispered, "we both have to get out of here, don't we?"

She spit at him. Her pale saliva struck his eye and he turned his face to wipe it against his shoulder. She struggled to break free, but then he leaned more of his weight on her stomach, and she couldn't breathe.

"Listen," he said in an undertone, "don't be stupid. Do you think that even if you finished me off, he'd let you out of here? Can you overpower Henri by yourself? Come on. I know we haven't been friends in the past but—"

"You were in Amsterdam, you followed us to the mall. You led Rahul's assassin right to us. You bastard, you killed Cid!" she screamed.

His eyes were wide, like two blue, turbulent oceans. "He was supposed to get Kelira, I swear. It was a mistake. It was supposed to be Kelira!" He drew a long, shuddering breath. "I'm sorry. I'm sorry I was such a shit to you before. I never realized." He gazed at her with such intensity she thought she'd drown in his eyes. The look in them was a new one for Spider. For the first time, it seemed, he really saw her. "You need to breathe?" he asked. "Here." And the pressure eased up on her abdomen, allowing her to draw a deep breath. "But don't fight me now, because the clamp can always come down again, right?"

She lay still, catching her breath.

He leaned even closer, and for a terrifying moment Magnolia thought he was going to kiss her, but he brought his mouth down beside her ear instead. "Rahul's still watching us on a remote monitor somewhere, so listen carefully. In a minute you'll break free, we'll fight a little more, and then we'll pretend that you knock me out. When Henri comes to get me, we'll jump him and get out of here. Ready?"

She nodded a fraction of an inch, and then Spider reared

back, releasing one of her hands as he telegraphed a powerhouse punch to her face. At the same time his knee lifted off of her, and she rolled. She turned and leapt at him just as he was getting to his feet. They tumbled across the room in each other's arms, Spider only pretending to grab hold of her. But she wasn't pretending. She slammed his head into the floor and backhanded him across the face with her fist. Spider rolled his head to the side, as if he'd lost consciousness, but he hadn't. He was right. She needed him to get out of here, but she pasted him in the mouth one more time anyway.

He lay still, blood trickling from the corner of his mouth. His breathing was shallow and regular.

Magnolia sat back on her haunches and leaned against the wall. Perhaps Rahul thought he'd revive, or that she'd take this opportunity to kill him, because it was at least fifteen minutes before Henri came back.

They waited until he was bending over Spider before they moved, Spider suddenly springing to life and burying his fist in Henri's groin. For her part Magnolia leapt on his back and wrapped her arms around his thick neck, choking him. Then she remembered that he'd taken her gun. He might still have it. She loosened one arm from around his neck and groped for his pocket. Her fingers grazed the handgrip of the Walther-K, and she grasped it just as Henri began twisting furiously in an attempt to dislodge her from his back. She hung on tight and brought the gun up to the side of his head. He paused when he felt the plastic muzzle against his temple, and then she fired.

The air exploded with the sound. He fell backwards, burying her beneath him. She was still struggling to get free when Spider rolled Henri's body off her and offered her a hand up. She shook her head, getting to her feet on her own. Her ears rang.

Henri's blood was not red. In fact it was almost transparent, with just a faint hint of phosphorescent green to it. The streaks and puddles that surrounded them reminded Magnolia of the pool of fluid that had come from that water plant Tumcari had shown her months ago.

"Good job finding that gun," said Spider. "Let's get out of here."

She'd almost forgotten about Spider. Magnolia turned to face him, a smile playing across her lips. "You've got to be kidding."

Spider's face was blank; his eyes, staring at her, flickered for one instant to the gun in her hand. "What?"

She shook her head. "You're not going anywhere, Spider. And this isn't just any gun. It's my gun. I got it from the first man I killed, and I should have used it on you a long time ago."

Tears sprang to his eyes. "Magnolia, I'm sorry. It wasn't supposed to be Cid. Really."

"That's what Rahul said, but it doesn't matter, does it? Because none of this would have happened if you hadn't opened your dirty trap in the first place. You were mad at me for shooting you with a paint gun"—she waved the Walther-K at him—"and now it's time for the real thing."

Spider fell to his knees. "Please, Magnolia, it was an accident!" he screamed. "Nobody wanted to kill her! Don't—" But his plea was cut short by the bark of her gun. Two shots to his chest. He fell onto his side, coughing blood and babbling something. Frantically he motioned at her with his arm, beckoning her closer. She knew she shouldn't go, but he was staring at her with those whirling eyes, Cid's eyes, and she couldn't leave without hearing what he had to say.

She crept closer to him, her gun trained on him. He tried to take her free hand, but she wouldn't let him. His eyes were unfocused, seeing something that was there only for him. "The sky and the sea"—he laughed, and blood poured down his chin in a dark tide—"it's all the same." And then he looked at her again, when she thought he'd never look at anything again. His voice was no more than a whisper, and she had to fight to hear him over the ringing of her ears. "Go to Wotroya. . . . She's at Wotroya," he gasped. And then his eyes stopped whirling, and so did he.

NIGHT OF THE PROSTHESES

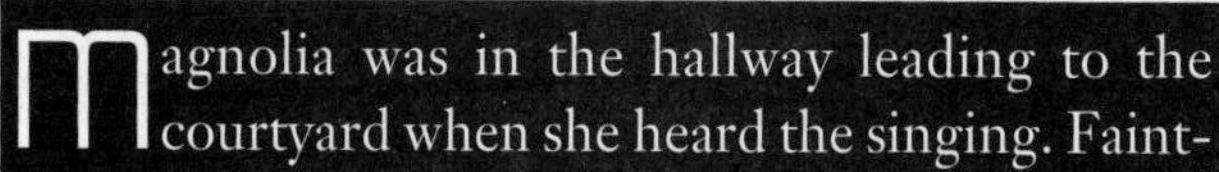

Magnolia was in the hallway leading to the courtyard when she heard the singing. Faintly, faintly, coming from a doorway up ahead like the thread of a dream, a soft tuneless voice. With the Walther-K still in her hand Magnolia crept forward and opened the door.

It was Rahul's kitchen, vast and spacious. Huge soup kettles and gleaming saucepans hung from a ceiling rack in the center of the room. Beneath them, an island in a sea of enamel tile, stood a stove, buffered on three sides by a polygrained countertop. The room itself was lined with counters and cupboards in seemingly endless variation.

There was no one here, but the singing continued, a little louder now, coming from behind a door next to two massive, stainless-steel refrigerators. She opened the door and looked inside. Brown-carpeted stairs led down into the basement.

She could hear the singing quite clearly now, a wordless

warble in a voice that she recognized. Slowly she descended the staircase, emerging into a twilight world of blue fluorescents. The air was warm and soft, the light easy on her dilated eyes. Aquariums gurgled softly all around the large, open space.

Manus stood beside one—a large, shallow rectangle—singing and splashing in the water. Something inside the tank splashed back. "Manus," said Magnolia, coming up beside him. She leaned over his shoulder and then recoiled as she caught sight of what he was playing with. "Jesus, Manus!"

He turned and smiled at her, indicating the mobile appendages that floated in the water. "These are my legs," he said.

Manus's legs drifted lazily within the confines of their glass box, and Magnolia stared at them, bewildered past horror or disbelief. There were five of them, all left legs, of course; all chunky and strong, just like the one Manus grew himself. They weren't disembodied, per se. They grew on a vine.

At the top of the thigh each leg was encased in a pale, fleshlike cap that tapered off to a stem and joined the rest of the plant at the bottom of the tank. Feathery, frondlike leaves floated on the surface of the water, undulating with the currents caused by flexing ankles and toes.

Magnolia gazed into her brother's soft brown eyes. She should hate him. She tried to hate him. He was a part of the plot that had led to Cid's death. But he was also the only thing she had left now. Rahul had used him against her; maybe someday she'd find out how much he really understood about what he'd done.

She glanced around the basement. There were many other tanks; filled, undoubtedly, with things she'd be more comfortable not knowing about. But the smell of salt water and the gentle hum of air filters soothed her. This place was clean and carefully tended. The temperature, the lighting, all meticulously adjusted to nurture some strange new life.

Beneath fluorescent lamps the aquariums glowed with fantastic colors, inviting her eyes to behold their contents. Magnolia walked among them, entranced by the proliferation of forms. Clusters of eyeballs darted about one tank, propelling themselves with translucent, filmy tails. In another bloomed a spidery hand, crimson flowers bursting from its fingertips. Everywhere she looked, creatures flourished in an intense profusion of shape and pattern. She thought they might be beautiful.

In the middle of the basement, surrounded by coils of tubing, stood three octagonal tanks about ten feet in diameter and at least ten feet tall. Each tank held the same type of plant at a different point in its development. Beside the tanks stood metal scaffolds.

Magnolia had seen a plant like this before, but not from this angle, and only in one of the phases represented here. She climbed a scaffold and gazed down at the pale green membranes that she'd once mistaken for lily pads.

This plant seemed to be in the fallow period of its reproductive cycle. The others were in various stages of fruition. Magnolia climbed down to the basement floor once again, examining the inhabitants of the other two tanks more closely.

The plants themselves were thick stemmed, with roots that held tenaciously to the wire grid at the bottom of the tanks. The light color of the membranes/lily pads deepened as the stalk joined with others in a multilayered central trunk. The pads were, apparently, far more than just filtration systems, as Tumcari had told her. On one of the plants they were submerged, curled up like flower buds. Some of the more mature ones were just beginning to open, revealing the crenelated brain of the "seed" inside and the tiny, embryonic body that floated shell pink and obscenely vulnerable from its center.

The third plant was nearly at fruition. Here the flower had opened completely, forming a gelatinous halo about the heads of fully formed humanoid bodies. The brains were now encased in protective skulls, which were still transparent in some of the younger robots. The others were indistinguishable from drowned human beings; their faces peaceful in meditative repose.

"Beautiful, aren't they?"

At the sound of his voice Magnolia spun around, extending her arm to aim her gun, unable to prevent herself from imagining some monster about to suck her brain out even though she knew it was Rahul. He leaned against the scaffold, smiling at her alarm, his hands in the pockets of his burgundy velvet robe.

Beside him stood Dex with a submachine gun in his hands; he smiled too, pointing the gun at her. "I can get Manus too," he said.

Slowly she raised her gun arm.

"I'm glad you've had a chance to see these"—Rahul waved at the tanks—"although you've already witnessed the best of my handiwork along these lines."

"The legs?"

Rahul shook his head and frowned. "No, no. Prostheses are a small but profitable sideline. These robots are much more of an accomplishment, but even they are a far cry from my original intentions."

Manus wandered away from her side, and Magnolia tensed, watching Dex. His gaze strayed, and Magnolia's hand tightened around her gun, but before she could decide what to do, he was back on her again, his eyes as hard as the muzzle of his gun.

"I wanted to produce artificial intelligence," said Rahul, his eyes focused somewhere between Magnolia's head and long ago. "I followed the efforts of the computer people, and I thought I had learned from their failures. I suppose you could say that I succeeded on my first try, with Tumcari, but the International Bureau of Research grant board deemed the project a failure. 'No practical applications,' they said."

He laughed bitterly, his eyes sharp with fresh anger, and focused once again on Magnolia. "In other words, they couldn't make any money off him."

Behind Rahul and Dex, Manus was climbing a scaffold. Magnolia's eyes widened as he leaned over and spit into the tank. As he proceeded to the next one she returned her gaze to Rahul and checked Dex out in her peripheral vision. But neither of them seemed to notice, or care.

For long moments Rahul gazed at nothing in particular, and Magnolia found herself wondering how old he was. Seventy, maybe eighty, she thought. Definitely the oldest man she'd ever seen. Manus had finished defiling the robot tanks and came back to stand at her side.

"I've never gotten any closer to my true goal than I did with him, and now I don't think I ever will." Rahul shrugged and leaned his head towards the tank in which mature robot bodies drifted, occasionally bumping up against one another. "Instead I produce highly marketable human simulacra without minds of their own. Characterless zombies of infinite malleability. They're quite popular, especially the females.

"I'm expecting to harvest these within the week. They all have buyers already—in fact, there's a waiting list. I'll be sending them along to their destinations with a suitcase and a change of clothes." He laughed again, not so bitterly this time. "One of the really nice things about dealing with this kind of merchandise is the ease of shipping. There aren't many commodities that you can tell to go buy an airplane ticket for Belize."

Magnolia felt strangely outraged. On whose behalf, she couldn't be sure. "You're a pimp," she charged.

Rahul nodded his head in agreement. "Yes, but I'm a state-of-the-art pimp. Now, would you be so good, my dear, as to put your gun down, carefully on the floor in front of you, and step away from it?"

"Are you going to kill me?" she asked.

"No, not at all. You have many more adventures ahead of you. You wanted to avenge yourself on Cid's killer, did you not?"

"Yes, but that would mean killing you."

"I'm afraid I can't allow that. Please do as I ask; that gun Dex is holding has a rather broad spray, and your brother is quite close to you."

Magnolia swallowed and bent over, placing her gun on the floor. She stood up again and backed away.

"Don't worry, it will be returned to you as soon as you leave," said Rahul. "Althea will fly you to Wotroya House. There you will find the one responsible for Cid's death."

THE FURTHER ADVENTURES OF ANTONIN

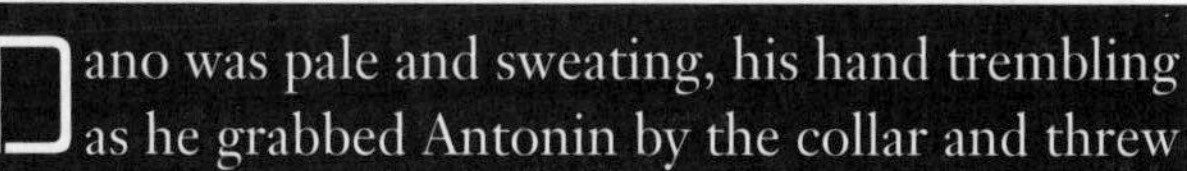

Dano was pale and sweating, his hand trembling as he grabbed Antonin by the collar and threw him out of the helicopter into the snow. For a moment Antonin lay on his back, cradled in icy softness, looking up at the darkening, bloodstained sky and waiting for his father to fly away and leave him. But instead, Dano climbed out of the helicopter with difficulty and began staggering towards the big mansion with sad window eyes.

Antonin stood up, picked up his schoolbag, and followed his father to the house. He didn't much want to be with him, but it was too cold to stay outside.

Dano put a card in the lock and went inside, leaving the door standing open. Antonin stepped through and shut it behind him.

There were shadows living in the house. They collected around doorways and in the corners, staring at them as Dano wandered about the main hall. He seemed to have forgotten about Antonin and soon disappeared through an archway into darkness.

Antonin spent a little while staring at the shadows, but they made no move to harm him. At length he crossed a wide red carpet and went up a broad, curving staircase to the second floor. A balcony ran along three sides, overlooking the hall below. Antonin walked along it, past closed doors to one that was open. He went inside.

The room was empty except for a bed, a dresser, and a chair. Antonin lay down on the bed and thought of his mother, so far away, wondering where he was. After a little while he cried, and after that he fell asleep.

He dreamed of a purse thrown backwards from the future, to be caught by the one who had dropped it. As it flew through time it lost its shining silver beads, and they flew into eternity, forever spinning in the void.

Antonin opened his eyes to darkness. A woman stood beside the bed, her figure hazy in the glittering blackness, barely present, like something left over from a dream. It was her attention to him that awakened him, and that was why he saw her now, because she saw him. She was made up of spirals and swirls of all colors, the patterns the darkness makes for your eyes when there's nothing else to see. If he rolled over and turned on the light right now, she might disappear, because she was a member of the darkness in the room.

He wasn't afraid, just sluggish, as if his body had become too heavy to move. He could not take his eyes away from the face of the woman standing there, and the longer he looked at her the more solid she became. Her patterns seemed to spread out from her, moving towards him through the darkness to sink in through his skin and infect him. Some day, he thought, he would look just like she did, nothing but beautiful patterns, changing all the time. Absently he rubbed the inside of his elbow and discovered that he could move, after all.

The spiral woman whispered something through the long silence of the room. "Du liebes Kind, komm, geh mit mir. Gar schöne Spiele spiel ich mit dir."

It was a lullaby, and for the first time since his father had taken him, Antonin felt safe.

When he awoke again, it was morning, and the spiral lady was gone. He went to the door and peered outside, but saw no sign of his father or anyone else.

Antonin crept to the next door and listened at it. He heard nothing and tried the knob. It turned smoothly in his hand, and the door eased open with a creak. The room inside was basically the same as the other one, but it had obviously been occupied recently. The bed was unmade; blankets and sheets lay in a tangled heap at its foot. The table by the window was piled with monitors and keyboards.

Antonin waded across the junk-strewn floor and flipped a switch experimentally. The center screen came to life in a whirlwind of shapes and colors. Spirals within spirals, turning around each other in endless variation. Antonin glanced away for a moment, looking for the source of the program. A disk drive hummed merrily beneath a sheet of printout. At the bottom left-hand corner of the screen was a message: "For holo press 9."

He pressed the nine on the keyboard. The graphic leapt out of the video screen and into the room like a live thing. This wasn't just any holograph, either, not like the fuzzy-edged ones they sold in party stores and shopping malls. Whoever made it had gone to great pains to give it all the pixels it needed for a sharp image, and the colors were true, not washed out by the glare of laser reflection.

In three dimensions the shape was even more complex

than it had been on the screen. Tendrils shot out and reformed themselves, cloud banks boiled outwards in incremental waves, and colors strobed through the spectrum at varying speeds. Despite its chaotic nature, however, the holo was not random; it had a pattern. An intricate one, reiterated at all levels under all sorts of varying conditions. Antonin sank down into the chair beside the desk, absorbed by what he was seeing. Of course he'd seen fractals before, but this one, just now, reminded him of something he'd seen recently. In a dream. A dream he'd had last night, about a woman whose body was covered with patterns like this, patterns that had infected him as well. He still had her purse, he recalled, hidden in the bottom of his schoolbag.

He went back to the other room to get it, but when he got back and fished out the videotape, he found that despite the abundance of electronics in the room, there was no VCR.

He went out into the hallway and down the stairs. The varnished wood of the banister gleamed like a serpent in the light from the windows. Off the main hall downstairs was a white-walled, white-carpeted room. White blinds covered the windows at the front of the house. The opposite wall was lined with shelves, filled, floor to ceiling, with videotapes. In the center hung a picture-frame television with a built-in VCR.

"Ah, there you are there socks in my head?" said a voice behind him. He turned around to see a tall blond-haired woman standing in the doorway, clinging to the wall to steady herself. "Socks and drugs are illegal without permission. Poor mission, poor Mr. Tumcari wants to meet you." She focused her gaze upon him with difficulty.

Antonin stared at her in silence. She was the woman from his dream, only now he could see her, and the patterns in her skin were only visible if he concentrated on them.

"Fall low and be. Follow me." She lurched into the front hall, beckoning erratically. Antonin followed her as she staggered down a dark-paneled, red-carpeted hallway, which ended in a set of double doors. She shoved the doors open, and they were greeted by a gush of warm, moist air.

It was a greenhouse of some kind. Vegetation grew everywhere in a vibrant green riot. Vines wound themselves around palm trees and twisted across an overgrown gravel pathway. Antonin glanced up in time to see a bird flit from one treetop to another, its song joining that of others in a jubilant cacophony. He came to a pool: still, smooth waters reflecting the light from the glass panels above. Ripples spread slowly outwards from the center of the pond, and a man surfaced. Antonin sat down on the bank. The man swam towards him and then stopped, floating effortlessly a few feet away. He had green eyes and blond hair, and he smiled in a blinding flash of white teeth. "I'm Tumcari," the man said. His voice was rich and deep, as if it came from the bottom of a cave. "Tell me, who are you?"

Antonin hesitated, but there didn't seem to be any point in lying. "My name is Antonin."

"Antonin. You are welcome here, you and the man with you—"

"He's my father."

"Your father, I see. I am delighted to have you as guests in my house, but tell me, to what do I owe the pleasure of your visit, Antonin?"

"My father brought me here. He took me away from my mother. I didn't know this was where we were going until we got here." He looked over his shoulder at the spiral lady, now sitting in a lawn chair, her head bent forward. "I had a dream."

Tumcari leaned backwards in the water and sighed.

When he gazed at Antonin again, his eyes had become clouded with some memory or thought. “You had a dream. I know all about dreams.” He reached towards him, his arms wet and corded with muscle. “Come, my boy, come with me and tell me of your dreams.”

SOMETHING FOR THE PAIN

Tarko Sale was a half-deserted little outpost on the edge of the Siberian tundra. Kelira held Rose's arm as they disembarked the little orange-and-purple snow goose. She shivered in the cold Arctic air.

"Here," he said, reaching into his duffel bag and pulling out a navy blue microthin parka. "That jacket isn't adequate. Give it to me and put this on instead."

She did as he asked, wordlessly, her face pale and drawn as it had been for the nine or more hours it had taken them to get here. Kelira layered her jacket over his canvas windbreaker, hunching his shoulders against the cold.

The airport lobby consisted of several dingy stackable plastic chairs, an old-fashioned microwave, and an old vending machine that dispensed sandwiches and mummified fruit.

"You know, you should eat something," he said. "I had some cheese and crackers in the airplane, but you didn't touch a thing."

She shook her head without quite looking at him. "I'm not hungry; besides, we still have to get to Wotroya House."

Just outside the airport was a little office with a big sign in the window. RENT ADVENTURE! it read, and beneath it, in smaller print:

> EXPERIENCE THE JOYS OF ISOLATION! CAMP IN REMOTE AREAS MILES FROM HUMAN CIVILIZATION! SAVOR THE BEAUTY OF UNTOUCHED WILDERNESS! HELICOPTER CHARTER RATES START AT ONLY FIFTY-FIVE DOLLARS!

Kelira tapped her on the arm. "Look! We can rent a helicopter."

Their pilot was a hefty middle-aged woman with glossy black braids going to grey. She wore a bulky old-fashioned flight jacket with the insignia of the Dragonfly Corps on the shoulder, and at her hip hung a heavy-duty Smith & Wesson automatic. Kelira showed her where they wanted to go on the large wall map in the office.

"You know, that's funny," she said, sizing up the two of them with shrewd eyes. "I just took someone else out there yesterday."

Tumcari floated with the child on his back. He was a good boy, not afraid to go under the water, but he couldn't stay down there for very long. He'd have to make some sort of arrangement if he was going to show him the stalk at the bottom of the pool. For now he was content to have Antonin ride around on his back, as if he were a tame dolphin at a children's park.

When Rahul dismissed the staff, Tumcari had assumed he'd be left alone to meditate on his sins. But then Ms. Wujcik had returned.

She was clearly malfunctioning, to the point where even her motor skills were deteriorating, and her speech had become garbled, the cross-referencing out of sync, as if her whole cognitive system were under the influence of some powerful, destabilizing force. She was losing order, and order was the only structure she had.

And now there was this boy and his father. Tumcari could not imagine that they were new staff from Rahul; he could not imagine who they were.

Antonin slid from his back, pushing off Tumcari's side with his feet. He swam a few strokes and turned around to face him, laughing. He was learning to swim quite rapidly. At the moment he was struggling to remain afloat upright; under the water his feet and hands fluttered frantically. Tumcari reached a hand under the boy's armpit, steadying him. "Don't be afraid to bob up and down; that's how it's done."

The child swallowed a little water and coughed, but he maintained his composure. "Let your arms sweep slower, that's it." Tumcari continued, "Now, remember the kick I taught you? Do that once for every sweep of your arms. It'll bring you well above the surface, and your arms will keep you balanced in the water, see?" The boy nodded his head, but before he had the chance to put this advice to work, they were both startled by the sound of footsteps approaching down the greenhouse path.

"Who do you think that is?" said Tumcari.

"My father?" Antonin looked at him with worried eyes.

"Quite likely. Are you afraid of him?"

Antonin nodded.

Tumcari boosted him out of the water and onto the bank. "Then hide in those bushes." He pointed to the thickest part of the overgrown jungle that surrounded the pond. "Quickly now."

Antonin picked up his blue-and-red schoolbag and disappeared into the foliage. Tumcari turned to see a man with a rifle in his hands walking unsteadily around the curve in the path. The right side of his face was covered with partially healed skin grafts, and the skin around his left eye was badly inflamed.

Tumcari swam closer to the bank, peering at the man's eyes. The good one, the one on the right, was green. He wondered if the other was an implanted prosthesis that was being rejected. As the man glanced rapidly about the greenhouse Tumcari's suspicion was confirmed; through the mucus that veiled the left eye he caught the faintest glimmer of blue. It wasn't even the same color as the real one.

"I'm over here," said Tumcari helpfully. The man started and stared at him. Clearly it hadn't occurred to him that there might be someone in the pond.

"G-get out of the water," he said, pointing the rifle at him. "Put your hands up and get out of the water." His voice was shaking, his hand was shaking. Tumcari was more afraid of the gun going off accidentally than of him actually hitting anything he aimed at.

Obligingly he raised his arms. "I can't get out of the water, sorry."

"Get out of the water!"

"I can't. Look." He dived, making sure that all twenty feet of his tail surfaced as he arced through the water. When he emerged once again from the depths, the man had lowered his rifle. He stared at Tumcari in blank amazement.

Gradually he regathered the scattered threads of his consciousness. At length he said, "What are you?"

"An accident." Tumcari nodded towards him. "You look like you've had a rather nasty one."

He nodded and stared into the jungle surrounding the

pond, glancing back at Tumcari from time to time, as if he expected to be grabbed by a tentacle and dragged to a watery and ignominious death. "Yeah, I got burned," he said, lifting a trembling hand to his good eye. "Rose, she burned me. I've been taking something for the pain, but I ran out a while ago. It really hurts. I need heroin. I can't stand this pain. My eye—" Again he cupped his good eye, staring around with the infected blue one. "My eye is gone, man. She melted it." He was getting agitated. He started waving the gun around again. "I've got to find something for my face. It's burning. Please, I won't hurt you, just tell me where you've got your junk."

"Hmm. There might be some whiskey in the kitchen," said Tumcari. "I don't think I can help you out with heroin, but in one of the bedrooms upstairs there might be some marijuana. You can help yourself."

"Okay, okay. I'll be back. Don't try to call for help, or I'll kill you. Just stay in your pond, man, and you'll be all right, but don't try to call anybody. Don't do anything." He backed up the walkway and faded from view.

Tumcari listened as the greenhouse doors opened and slowly fell shut again. He waited several minutes. Dano did not return. "Antonin," he whispered, leaning over the bank of the pond. "Antonin." But he got no reply.

The door of the greenhouse shut softly behind him. Antonin looked down the hall and saw his father just disappearing into the living room. He crept down the corridor, trying to silence the pounding of his heart. The noise, he felt sure, would give him away any minute now. He leaned against the paneling, hidden by the shadows, and calmed his breathing.

Dano staggered, holding one hand out to steady

himself on the banister. Slowly he began to climb the stairs.

Antonin hung back until Dano was past the first curve, and then he followed. Dano was so preoccupied with reaching the next step that it was unlikely that he would be spotted, nestled in the curve of the railing. Above him the sweep of the spiraling staircase hid him from view.

When he reached the second floor, his father was nowhere in sight. The doors of the bedrooms were shut and silent, speaking their own unmoving denial. Antonin continued upwards, to the third floor. Here the landing was graced with three tall, arched windows, and through them the afternoon light was fading. In the gathering shadows Antonin heard his father crying.

He followed the sound up yet again, although by now the stairs were narrow, dark, and close. He came out into a long corridor, harshly tiled and painted an industrial green. Doors with translucent glass windows faced him on each side. At the very end of the hall one door hung open, and from the narrow crack seeped the desolate sounds of misery.

Antonin barely dared to breathe as he nudged open the door and slipped inside. It was cold in here, and dim in the pale grey light from windows standing open to the evening air. Dano crouched with his back to the door in the middle of a large tiled floor scattered with papers. Around him stood black-topped worktables heaped with obscure equipment. In a far corner of the room, near the windows, stood a cot, and beside it a desk with a computer monitor, keyboard, and stacks of software.

Antonin suddenly realized that this was a laboratory of some kind. Shallow plastic dishes and glass vials littered the spaces between microscopes and incubators and other things that they don't show in the movies. Glancing up, he saw that the ceiling was hung with hundreds of glass slides, suspended from strings. A few had slipped from the masking tape that had held them aloft and lay shattered among the litter on the floor.

Dano lifted his head and looked behind him, right at Antonin, who backed up, inadvertently shutting the door with a soft click. "Antonin," he whispered in wonder. The left side of his face was swollen and pink, particularly around the eye, which glimmered faintly blue. His right eye was wide open, staring at Antonin in startled green.

Antonin swallowed and stared at him in fear and pity. It was hard to recognize him now as the hated person who had brought him here, who had struck his mother that night at the falafel stand, and who had bullied and frightened her on all those other nights and days. "What's wrong with you?" he asked.

"My face hurts," he said. "Please, Antonin, will you help me?"

Silently he nodded his head.

"I need something for the pain. I can't stand it. Please, help me find something for the pain. I haven't had a fix in days. I thought I'd find it up here, but there's nothing here, and I can't take those stairs again."

Antonin looked around, relieved to take his eyes off his father's ruined, pleading face. Absently he walked over to the desk and pulled open the drawers. In the long, shallow drawer in the center, among a confusion of pens, pencils, eyedrops, and aspirins, he found the remains of a partially smoked joint. He picked it up and offered it to Dano, who was still crouching on the floor.

He shook his head. "No, I need something stronger than that, heroin or barbiturates."

Antonin tossed the joint back in the desk. He took the purse of the spiral woman out of his schoolbag and opened it. He reached inside and took out the jar of salve. "Here," he said, "try this."

"What is it?" With trembling fingers Dano took the jar from his hand.

"It's a salve."

"For burns?" His father gazed at him with desperate hope.

Antonin shrugged. "I don't know, it might help."

Dano fumbled open the jar and smeared the salve over his inflamed face, using nearly the entire jar. He leaned back against the leg of a table and sighed, his face glistening with iridescence. His shaking began to subside. "The doctor gave me a new eye, after your mother burned my old one. It works great, but my face itches all the time now."

So it had been his scream that night, for sure. Antonin had no reply.

"You see what she did to me?" he asked Antonin. Only his green eye was looking at him, staring from its pool of phosphorescence. "Your mother did this to me. And it's your fault," Dano continued, "because you tried to run away."

Antonin backed up slowly towards the door.

Dano's breath came out in a long whistling sigh. "Whatever this shit is"—he fingered the little jar—"it sure is making me feel better."

For an hour or more, Antonin tried to get to the door without being noticed, but his father's green eye watched him constantly. Still, he inched backwards so slowly he began to wonder if the eye noticed he was moving. When he was within reach of the door, he heard the faint reverberations of voices downstairs. He turned and reached for the doorknob.

Gunshots echoed up from downstairs in a staccato rhythm. Suddenly Antonin was pulled backwards, hard, his father's arm wrapped tightly around his chest and throat.

The rifle that had lain dormant, slung across Dano's back, was in his other hand.

"Rose!" Antonin screamed, his voice hidden by another burst of shooting. The hard muzzle of the rifle was like a cold ring set against his temple, and he fell silent and absolutely still, like an animal frozen in the headlights of a car, too afraid to move.

GUN SPITE

It was a long flight, taking Magnolia and Manus into the morning and through the day as they crossed the path of the sun. They arrived at Wotroya House in the afternoon of the same day that they left Rahul's, even though it had taken them fifteen hours to get there.

Magnolia had Althea land the jet about a half a mile from the house, behind a heavy stand of pines. She stuck her Walther-Kodak in the waistband of her jeans and jumped out the door, landing in crunchy, ice-frosted snow. Manus followed her. She looked at him wearily. She'd been completely unsuccessful in convincing him to stay with Rahul. "Come on then, if you're coming."

The back door was already open. Magnolia slipped quietly inside and briefly surveyed the kitchen. There was nothing more alarming than dirty dishes stacked on the counter, still there from when they'd left. It seemed impossible that they could still sit there, crusted with food, when everything else had changed so completely.

She nudged a door open gently and covered the hallway with her gun. Nothing moved. The corridor was empty and silent. "Wait here," she whispered to Manus, and for once he listened to her.

Magnolia sidled down the hallway with her back to the wall, stopping at the door to the video room. Faintly she heard whispering on the other side. "We should check the greenhouse." It was Kelira's voice, and the sound of it made her hands clench. She stepped back and kicked the door open.

Rose and Kelira stood in the middle of the room, frozen for a moment in the crash of the swinging door. Neither of them seemed to be armed. They stared at her stupidly, mouths hanging open.

"Kelira!" Magnolia crowed, "What a pleasure it is to see you again! And your charming sister Rose is with you too. Have I ever told you two exactly what you mean to me?" She raised her gun and fired on them. Rose dived behind the couch, unharmed. Kelira hadn't been quite that quick. He took a bullet in the upper leg and fell to the floor.

Magnolia strode to where he lay bleeding on the carpet. She readjusted her grip on the handle and aimed carefully at his face. "Surprise!" she said.

Kelira gazed up at her in confusion and pain. He shook his head. "Don't," was all he could manage at first. He clutched his leg with both hands in a vain attempt to stop the flow of his blood. "Please."

"You set us up, you pig. 'Meet me at the mall, I have a surprise,' right!"

"Please, Magnolia, I didn't know—"

"Oh, yeah." She laughed, high and shrill, delivering a sharp kick to his ribs. "Don't give me that shit."

Kelira groaned and rolled over. "I'm sorry," he sobbed.

Magnolia grinned and advanced on him again. "So am I."

There was an explosion of noise from behind the couch, and Magnolia's right shoulder blossomed with pain. Apparently she'd been wrong about them both being unarmed. The force of the shot threw her to the ground, and she rolled. Steadying her arm against the floor with the weight of her body, she fired at Rose, who disappeared behind the couch again. The gunshot was echoed by the crash of shattering glass as the bullet broke the window she'd been standing before a moment ago.

Magnolia struggled to her feet, staggering in a low crouch for the cover of an easy chair. She clutched her right shoulder, holding her upper arm tight against her chest. Leaning against the wall behind her, she peered around the edge of the chair.

On her hands and knees Rose crawled from behind the couch towards her brother. Her gun, a pink Sunbeam automatic, was still clutched in her right hand. Magnolia fired, but the pain in her shoulder made her aim unsteady, and she missed again. Rose scurried behind the couch once more, like a startled cockroach.

"Why are you doing this?" cried Kelira, his voice nearly drowned out as Rose took a potshot in Magnolia's direction. The bullet hit the wall above her head, raining little fragments of plaster and white paint down on her hair.

"Because you killed Cid, you shithead!" she shouted. To her right the wall sprouted another pockmark. Magnolia dived to the left, firing at Rose and hitting the arm of the couch instead.

"What?" Kelira's face was pale, sweating with the effort of dragging himself towards her. "You were right with us when it happened."

"You didn't pull the trigger, but you arranged for us to

be there so someone else could. Rahul sent me here, he said I'd find the one responsible here."

Magnolia ducked as Rose fired from around the end of the couch. Her arm was shaking badly, aching with a hot, steady throb. She slid behind the chair once again, resting against the wall. "You know, Rose, I'm not having much luck hitting you, but Kelira's right in my line of fire. He's already taken one in the leg. If I have to keep shooting at you, he's bound to get another."

"Let me go to him," said Rose.

"No!" shouted Kelira. "Stay where you are, it's a trick." There was silence for the space of two heartbeats, and then Kelira's voice again, screaming hoarsely, "Duck!"

Magnolia threw herself to the floor just as the back of the easy chair erupted with bullets. So she had full auto too. Shit. Magnolia slid to the other side of the chair and scrambled towards the door to the hallway, firing at the couch as she went. She reached shelter behind the door as Rose peppered the walls she'd just passed.

It had been a mistake, she realized at once. This wasn't one of the solid wood doors that graced the house. It was hollow. Rose's bullets would pass right through, and from this angle Magnolia couldn't get a shot at her.

Kelira was still crawling towards her. He had to know she'd shoot him, but he kept coming anyway. With a sudden, sickening wrench, she realized he was putting himself in Rose's line of fire.

"Get out of the way, Kelira," hissed Rose, but he ignored her.

"I didn't know anything about a hit, I swear to God," he said to Magnolia. "Who told you that I did, Rahul?"

Magnolia stared at him. She'd almost forgotten what they were talking about. He was so close now she couldn't miss him if she tried. But she could also see that he wasn't lying.

And no one had told her he was responsible for Cid's death. Rahul had suggested it, along with a batch of other possibilities. When she found them here, she'd chosen to believe it, because it gave her something to do, when there was nothing she could do that would make Cid live again. To her surprise, she found she wasn't willing to kill him for the sake of distracting herself. "What you did, leaving me in the mall like that. That was cold," she said.

He closed his eyes—in relief or pain, she couldn't tell. "I know. I'm sorry." He laid his head down on his outstretched arms. "Rose, don't shoot her, please. I don't want either of you to die."

"Tell her to throw her gun out," she replied harshly.

Magnolia shook her head. "Won't do that," she said stubbornly. "You better stop your brother's bleeding, Rose. He can't afford to lose much more."

The door blocked her view of most of the room, but Rose appeared, covering her with her gun. Rose glanced quickly at the Walther-K, lying idle in Magnolia's lap, and picked her brother up by the shoulders, dragging him away to relative safety.

Magnolia leaned her head against the wall and closed her eyes, suddenly wishing Manus would appear and take care of her again. "What are you two doing here, anyway?" she asked, for want of anything better to say.

"Looking for my son," said Rose, and the sound of her voice made Magnolia think of Cid, who she'd miss like that forever. It was easier to do something about her arm than follow that line of thought. Clenching her teeth, she pulled her jacket off, managing not to cry as she pried her right shoulder free. She ripped the right sleeve off her shirt and used it to bind her arm. Holding the cloth tight with her teeth, she wrapped it around the bullet wound and across her chest, tying it off beneath her left arm. This rig, though time-consuming, also immobilized her right shoulder to some extent.

From behind the couch she could hear Kelira directing Rose's first-aid efforts. "Wrap that strip around tight. I think the bullet's still inside, but there's nothing we can do about it right now. Just try to stop the bleeding."

He'd need a real doctor, she realized with dismay. She closed her eyes again. She'd fall asleep, she thought, if her arm didn't hurt so much. In the front hall she heard footsteps. Manus at last, she thought, and she almost called out to him, but something in the stumbling shamble of that gait stopped her.

From the doorway came a voice that was not her brother's but was vaguely familiar all the same. "So this time you're sticking around to patch your victim up, huh Rose? How considerate of you. Y'know, guy, if I were you, I'd crawl away from her as fast as I could. She's poison, not to mention a lousy lay."

Magnolia peered through the crack between the door and the wall. It wasn't one person, it was two. A man, holding on to a small child. An unwilling small child, judging from the flickering of little legs that was the only detail her limited view provided.

"Antonin!" gasped Rose. Something significant was going on, on the other side of that blank white door.

Rose stared at Dano with horrified eyes. He held her son pinned against his chest with one arm, while he held the muzzle of a rifle to the boy's temple with the other. Antonin gazed at her blankly, not moving, barely breathing, it seemed. A bead of perspiration slowly trickled down the side of his face.

Dano himself was a monstrosity. His left eye was blue and

watery with mucus, surrounded by skin pink and puffy with infection. His other eye was clear and green, staring at her with an almost inhuman hatred. The right side of his face was blotchy with partly healed skin grafts where she'd burned him.

Rose was well aware of the gun in her hand; a weapon she couldn't use. "Let him go, Dano." Her voice was no more than a whisper.

"I don't think so," he answered her in a singsong voice, rocking from side to side, forcing Antonin to sway with him. "I think you're going to drop that little washer/dryer number right in the middle of the floor, oh, say about halfway between us." He looked at her expectantly, his green eye dancing with glee.

Slowly Rose did as she was told. Dano took the barrel of his rifle from her son's forehead and aimed it at her. "Good. Now, Antonin, you're a bright boy. My pride and joy, in fact. Do you think you could pick that up, and shoot me with it, before I drilled your mother?"

Antonin shook his head, just barely not crying. "No." His voice was very small, choked with held-back tears.

"Ah, a very bright boy. Now, I want you to pick up your mother's gun and bring it back here to me, and if you don't do as you are told, you'll be halfway to being an orphan." He loosened his arm around Antonin's shoulders, then grabbed him again just as the boy was at arm's length from him. Antonin staggered and gasped, the whites around his dark eyes gleaming. "Don't do anything heroic, Rose," Dano said, glaring at her. "I have no use for him except to control you, remember that." He released him again, and Antonin picked up the Sunbeam, turned around, and handed it to Dano.

"Very good." Dano stuck the gun in his breast pocket with one hand, keeping the rifle trained on Rose the whole time. "Now, as your reward, you can go stand next to your mother."

Antonin came to her, silently, crying. Rose knelt and wrapped her arms around him. "It's all right," she whispered, "it's all right. I've got you now." Desperately she tried to think of something to do. There was no way to confront him physically. The best she could do was buy time. "How did you get here?" she asked, looking up at him. It was the first thing that had popped into her head.

"Rahul told me to come here after the hit in Amsterdam, to await further instructions. Of course, he's probably not too happy with me now, since I killed the wrong person. Anyway, I had the ticket, so I figured I might as well use it.

"Nothing's gone right for me since I met that bitch in New York who almost killed me. And then there's you. Burning me, after all I've done for you. Oh, I wanted to waste you so bad, but I didn't know where you were. Then you show up at the hit. Standing right next to the guy I'm supposed to take out."

Rose held Antonin's face to her chest, carefully keeping her own eyes on Dano. He was so absorbed in his story, he'd missed the flicker of her glance as she noticed the door to the hallway slowly shutting.

He laughed. "I mean, I couldn't decide who to do. You, or him over there, who I was getting paid to whack. Rahul, he gave me this new eye after you burned my old one. He told me it was better than a normal eye. He told me to aim with it, so I did. I saw you, right in my sights, and then him, and somehow I missed both of you. I guess I must have hit someone, though, the way everybody freaked out.

"But I won't make that mistake again. I'll use what's mine this time, and since your brother ain't going anywhere in a hurry, I'll take care of pleasure first, before business." He smiled and raised the rifle to sight down it with his left eye.

Rose dropped to the ground, pushing Antonin under her and covering him with her body. There was a shot, and she turned her head just in time to see Dano lunge forward, a bloody hole in the middle of his forehead. He fell to the floor, reaching out towards her with one trembling hand. For a moment she was transfixed by that grasping hand. She stared at it, unable to move until it went limp and lay on the floor with the rest of him, lifeless.

Magnolia sat behind the door to the hallway, staring blankly at the prone body. She still held the gun in her hands, which were now shaking. Her face was very, very pale, her eyes enormous and dark. At length she looked up, glancing about the blood-streaked room, looking from Kelira, lying behind the couch in silent prayer, to Rose, who got to her knees, still clutching Antonin. Rose opened her mouth to say—she didn't know what, Thank you, maybe—but Magnolia spoke first. "I thought I'd already killed that bastard," she said.

CREATURE OF CHOKE

The place was a mess. That's the problem with white, thought Magnolia. It would be easier just to paint everything rust brown than try to clean up all this blood. She dropped the Walther-Kodak on the floor beside her. She didn't want to look at it, or feel its grip in her hand. In a faint, far corner of her mind, she wondered if she was going to throw up.

The little boy, Antonin, squirmed out of his mother's grip and approached her, stepping carefully around Dano's corpse. "I have a picture of you, in this purse," he said, hauling Cid's beaded handbag out of a canvas backpack that hung from his shoulder.

"Where did you get that?" Magnolia asked, almost not caring what the answer was.

"I found it, in a cafe in Amsterdam."

"Of course." Magnolia nodded wearily. "Mind if I take a look in there?" she asked.

"Go ahead." The boy handed her the purse.

Magnolia held the glittering thing in her hands, wondering if things would be any different if Cid hadn't left it behind, or if she hadn't stormed out of that cafe in Amsterdam in the first place. She unfastened the clasp and looked inside. There was a jar of something or other, Cid's wallet, which she couldn't bear to examine just now, and a videodisc.

She took out the video and examined it. Something was scrawled in orange grease pencil on its plastic surface. "What does it say?" she asked Antonin.

"It says 'Watch Me'."

Magnolia held the disc up to show Rose and Kelira. "Shall we?"

Kelira still lay behind the couch. He was pale, but his breathing was steady, and he looked at her with alert eyes. He nodded. "Move the couch, so I can see, and bring me a cushion for my head."

"I'll do it." said Rose, glancing at Magnolia's bandaged arm. Grunting, she shoved the couch out of Kelira's line of vision. "I'll get the body out of here too." Biting her lips, she rolled Dano's body over and grabbed it under the arms, dragging it into the hallway and beyond.

In silence Magnolia helped Kelira settle his head on one of the cushions from the couch. He was looking at her. Looking at her like he would try to say something comforting, or touch her, maybe. She moved away before he had a chance to act, seating herself in the perforated easy chair.

Rose returned with snow on her shoes and settled herself on the floor next to her brother. Antonin solemnly pressed the play button on the CD deck and crawled into her lap. The darkened room was illuminated by the glow of Cid's image on the screen.

She was in the laboratory upstairs, dancing and singing a soft wordless tune. She wore nothing but a lab coat, which gaped open as she spun around the room. The sight of her sweet, naked body hit Magnolia like a shock wave, forcing her to close her eyes. But it was no good. She could still hear Cid's voice, growing in power and depth of pitch until the singing stopped and she said, "You came. I knew you would come."

Magnolia, her arms crossed tight around her rib cage, opened her eyes to see the back of her own head, and Cid's radiant face looking up at her.

From the front hallway came a gurgling, choking noise. Magnolia turned to see Ms. Wujcik, tottering on Manus's arm. He guided her through the doorway with a blissful expression on his face, like some doped-up father of the bride. The robot struggled with speech. "Coke!" she shouted suddenly, her arm pointed rigidly at the screen. "Ate your own folk!" she continued, taking an erratic step away from Manus. "Feature of soak!"

"Jesus Christ," Rose said. "Can't we turn her off or something?" She paused the video.

"Nope," said Kelira, smiling ironically. "She's completely automatic."

"Fate score a toke!" Ms. Wujcik staggered onward until she stood directly in front of the screen, gesticulating wildly. "Picture of joke!" Her whole body shook with tremors, as if her nerves were receiving too many signals to process them correctly. Her head jerked around, and she stared at Magnolia in a wild blue jitter. "Sate your own hope!" she insisted, her voice fluctuating.

"Nature of smoke?" said Magnolia faintly.

"What?" asked Rose. "Do you know what she's trying to say?"

"I think so," Magnolia said slowly. The hair at the back of her neck stood on end, and she had the peculiar feeling that the world was about to split wide open, sending her flying down a bottomless black chasm. "Something Cid said to me once, about the nature of smoke." Her voice broke, and she stopped, taking a deep breath. "Cid used to say a lot of weird things." She managed a shrug, hoping to keep the unknown at bay with the feeble threat of doubt.

Ms. Wujcik had turned to face the screen again. She put her hands on it and then pressed her face against Cid's static image. With her eyes closed she began to keen. A sound the exact pitch of Magnolia's grief.

Magnolia knew that if she sat there a moment longer, that sound would dissolve her. She shot up off the couch and grabbed Ms. Wujcik by the arm. "Shut up!" she screamed, shoving her away from the screen. Hot tears poured down her face in a sudden deluge, and despite them, she felt like she was on fire. She stalked towards Ms. Wujcik. A fucking robot, Cid had called her. Not even a real human being at all.

Ms. Wujcik stumbled backwards and almost fell, regaining her balance at the last minute. "Nature of smoke," she mumbled. "Given the nature of smoke. Which, given the nature of smoke, is infinite."

She must have been listening that day, thought Magnolia. The bitch must have been eavesdropping on them in Cid's room. "You fucking spy!" she sobbed, pushing her again.

Ms. Wujcik fell. As she looked up at Magnolia the light of recognition dawned in her eyes, and she got to her feet and ran.

"You goddamn cunt!" Magnolia ran after her. "I'm going to catch you, you nosy slut!"

Ms. Wujcik raced through the entrance hall and towards the greenhouse. She seemed to have overcome her palsy, moving with the swift grace of an organism in survival response. She hit the double doors of the greenhouse at full tilt, her arms stretched out before her to break the impact. They were both through the doors before they swung shut.

Ms. Wujcik headed down the gravel path, straight towards the pond. It didn't seem as if she intended to stop. As the path broadened out into that clearing where they had gathered so many times before, Magnolia lunged. As she sailed through the air towards the robot, time seemed to slow down. Her eyes followed every movement Ms. Wujcik made as she dived into the pond. Her arm swung through the emptiness where her feet had been not a moment before. There was a splash, and then suddenly the ground reared up and smacked her, knocking the air out of her lungs.

The sudden impact sent her shoulder into a whole new galaxy of pain. She lay there for a moment, gasping for breath, a last few tears slipping down her cheeks. With an effort she brushed the gravel off her face and looked up, straight into the phosphorescent green of Tumcari's eyes.

HER FRACTAL SOUL

Numbly Magnolia climbed the stairs to the second floor. She was exhausted, worn out with grief and futile anger. Dano was dead, for good this time, but it didn't make her feel any better, and it didn't make Cid any less dead, either.

Just like Rahul had said, Cid's death was an accident. She could blame everybody, or nobody, or herself, or Cid, but it didn't matter. It wouldn't change anything. Magnolia had tried to warn Cid that chaos would kill her, when she herself hadn't even known what she meant.

The house was nearly deserted. Tumcari had managed to talk Althea into flying Kelira, Rose, and Antonin to the hospital in Omsk. "We'll be gone a few days, but we're coming back," Rose told her, although Magnolia couldn't imagine why.

In the hallway she paused outside the room she'd shared

with Cid. She'd planned to use her old room tonight, but Cid's things were the closest she could get to her dead lover now. Slowly she opened the door and stepped inside.

Above the bed the hologram hovered, just like the first time she'd come to this room. It was a sinuous, glowing, live thing, and Magnolia stood frozen in the doorway, staring at it.

It was so beautiful. She'd never really realized how beautiful it was, because she'd never understood *what* it was. Trembling, Magnolia shut the door behind her and lay down on the bed, gazing up, losing herself in the swirling colors, the regenerative shapes. All the things she'd avoided—the thoughts and feelings she'd refused herself since Amsterdam, every precious moment that she'd tried to forget—it was all there for her, in Cid's fractal soul.

When she woke, it was already late in the morning. Sunshine streamed in the windows, fading the holograph above her to a ghostly pallor. Magnolia dug a gym bag out of the closet and began to gather the few things she wanted to take with her.

She shut off the hologram program and ejected the disc, slipping it into her bag next to her clean underwear. She rummaged around in the desk until she found Cid's Goddess Herstory software. She realized it was stupid to take it—she couldn't read the text, after all—but she thought she might like to learn someday, if she had the chance.

Manus appeared in the doorway. "Good," she said to him, "get ready, we're leaving."

Manus shook his head, the way he did when it was going to be impossible to get him to do anything but what he wanted to do. "Tumcari wants to talk to you," he said.

She sighed. She'd just as soon not have to see Tumcari again, but it was easier to do it than to argue with Manus about it. “Okay,” she said, “I’ll go down there right now. Get your jacket and meet me at the front door. The helicopter’s coming in half an hour.”

The greenhouse was filled with sunlight and birdsong. Magnolia breathed deeply of the warm, moist air. She’d miss this place.

Tumcari was waiting for her at the water’s edge. Beyond him, among the water lilies, floated Ms. Wujcik. She was on her back, with her eyes closed, and Magnolia couldn’t tell if she was asleep or dead.

“Ah, Magnolia. I’m so glad you came,” said Tumcari, smiling broadly, showing those big white teeth of his.

Magnolia shifted her weight and readjusted the strap of the gym bag on her left shoulder. “I was about to leave, but Manus said you wanted to talk to me. I’d appreciate it if you made it quick, I’m in a hurry.”

“Oh, you can’t leave,” he said with a dismissive wave of his hand. “Not now.”

“What do you mean?”

Tumcari looked at her, his eyes bright with suppressed excitement. “Get in the water,” he said.

“Are you crazy?”

“No, really. I want to show you something. Take off your shoes,” he said, glancing behind him.

“Yeah, right.” Magnolia laughed. “Look, Tumcari, I’ve already seen your tail, and I’m well aware of how easily you can cut me to ribbons with it. So you don’t have to ‘show’ me anything, okay?”

He shook his head. “No. This you’ll want to see, I promise.”

“You promise?” she said with surprised skepticism.

“Yes, and am I not a monster?” he asked, his green eyes staring into hers, bright with madness and self-knowledge.

"And aren't the promises of monsters always kept, despite the treachery of their creators?"

Magnolia stared at him and sighed. What, after all, did she have to lose?

She sat down on the gravel and pulled off her shoes and socks. She dumped her jacket next to the gym bag and stepped gingerly into the pond. The water was warm. Her shirt clung to her arms when she lifted them above the water, then billowed out like soft folds of white seaweed when she submerged them. "Well, what did you want to show me?" she asked Tumcari.

"It's Ms. Wujcik, sort of. Apparently Cid's virus is also communicable to linear organisms such as robots."

In several short strokes she had arrived at the lily pads. "They weren't all like this last night," said Tumcari. "They've clustered around her since then. The pond seems to have helped her, but she needs you now."

"Why does she need me?" she asked in annoyance.

"Because you love her, Magnolia. Look."

Ms. Wujcik had opened her eyes, only they weren't solely the eyes of Ms. Wujcik anymore. They were the same color and shape that Ms. Wujcik's eyes had been, but the look in them was not a look that Ms. Wujcik ever could have had. It was a particular brand of wicked gleam that Magnolia saw now. One that she recognized.

"The virus—," she said, moving closer to the robot-woman.

"Yes. My guess is that Cid infected her deliberately, as part of her experiment. Hard to say whether or not she anticipated this particular outcome. Still, she must have known that the virus would have a profound impact on a creature without the anomaly of personality."

"But how—"

"Nature abhors a vacuum. Ms. Wujcik, once she was no longer functioning linearly, lacked a personality to tie together the inevitable contradictions of her actions. Apparently she constructed one out of the only material she had, the imprint of identity left behind in the virus by its creator."

"The experimenter always influences the experiment, she said that." Magnolia stared at the prone, floating body, not daring to move. The slightest tremble, she thought, would dissolve everything. "Cid," she whispered, afraid to say it aloud, but the sound slid out across the water just the same.

"Mongolia—" The Cid-thing coughed, struggled for breath, and tried again. "Magnolia." She sighed, reaching her arms out towards her, smiling crookedly. Her face was still Ms. Wujcik's face, but with Cid there too, adding something that had been missing before.

Magnolia took her into her arms, burying her face in the crook of Cid's neck, where her tears could mingle with the sweet pond water. Everywhere she touched her, she could feel the virus coursing, working the transformation Cid herself had caused, if not planned. She had given birth to herself somehow, with chaos.

Magnolia lifted her eyes to look at that impossible face, and Cid laughed, hugging her tighter. "Can you believe it?" she said. "I've died and gone to Polish Siberia."